HOW ABOUT A SIN TONIGHT?

AF513538

BY THE SAME AUTHOR

A Thing beyond Forever

That Kiss in the Rain

Ex . . . A Twisted Love Story

Black Suits You

Cheaters

Stranger Trilogy

Marry Me, Stranger

All Yours, Stranger

Forget Me Not, Stranger

HOW ABOUT A SIN TONIGHT?

NOVONEEL CHAKRABORTY

EBURY PRESS

An imprint of Penguin Random House

EBURY PRESS

USA | Canada | UK | Ireland | Australia
New Zealand | India | South Africa | China | Singapore

Ebury Press is part of the Penguin Random House group of companies whose addresses can be found at global.penguinrandomhouse.com

Published by Penguin Random House India Pvt. Ltd
4th Floor, Capital Tower 1, MG Road,
Gurugram 122 002, Haryana, India

Penguin
Random House
India

First published by Random House India 2012
Rejacketed edition published 2016

Copyright © Novoneel Chakraborty 2012

All rights reserved

14 13 12 11 10 9 8 7

This is a work of fiction. Names, characters, places and incidents are either the product of the author's imagination or are used fictitiously and any resemblance to any actual person, living or dead, events or locales is entirely coincidental.

ISBN 9788184000313

Typeset in Galliard BT by InoSoft Systems, Noida
Printed at Repro India Limited

This book is sold subject to the condition that it shall not, by way of trade or otherwise, be lent, resold, hired out, or otherwise circulated without the publisher's prior consent in any form of binding or cover other than that in which it is published and without a similar condition including this condition being imposed on the subsequent purchaser.

www.penguin.co.in

FSC
www.fsc.org
MIX
Paper from responsible sources
FSC® C047271

This is a legitimate digitally printed version of the book and therefore might not have certain extra finishing on the cover.

For

R.

I wished for you before it all began. I'll need you after it all ends. In between, I'm giving life a chance . . .

'Sin is the only note of vivid colour that persists in the modern world.'

—Oscar Wilde

SCENE 31

Location: Mussoorie

'Film producers are like condom ads; they always want you to play safe. Those chutiyas don't understand if you want a baby, you can't play it safe,' the director said, noticing the young journalist sitting opposite him scribble something in his notebook.

'By the way,' he added, 'don't mention anything about the c-word.'

Arunodaye T. Manjrekar was known as ATM in the Hindi Film Industry and media for one simple reason: till date he'd directed seven Hindi films out of which five were among India's highest grossing films ever, inflation adjusted for all time.

'Aren't you afraid of certain extremist groups who are against nudity in your film?'

'I'm sure they understand it's all for the sake of art.' In his mind, Arunodaye had exhausted his dictionary of slang.

'Was it tough to coax the actors to do the nude scene being shot today?'

'Actors are adventurers. And an adventurer never says no to his fears.'

It was tough, but in the end he'd put together a dream star cast with which he had already secured the eyeballs of more than three-fourth of India and almost the entire NRI diaspora.

Arunodaye's walkie-talkie crackled with a voice, 'Sir, the shot is ready.' The journalist took his cue and left.

Inside the room where scene 31 was to be shot, Arunodaye noticed the first camera framing a tight close up from the right while the second was ready to capture the two actors naked in a master shot. 'Perfect!' he murmured and turned to the actors who had donned white bathing robes. 'Start whenever you two feel comfortable.'

He left them amid a quietude of their own thoughts.

As the actor advanced towards the actress, her heart started beating rapidly. 'I am not doing this. The character in the script is.' She prepared herself to enter the mind space of the character. Though the scene scared her, the character was still way simpler than the one she played daily—herself.

They came close, disrobed, and smooched. Placing his hands on her rear, he lifted her up and looked arrow straight at her. And just when the actress thought something that had kept her awake for nights was finally over, the actor gave her a compulsive kiss on her lips. It shocked her. A bigger shock happened when she kissed him back almost as an offensive reflex.

His warm breath felt like obnoxious insects crawling all over her face. It aroused her but also made her feel cheap. The moment he cupped her breasts, all the intangible and invisible entities within—her thoughts, her soul, and her will—froze momentarily.

It was when their tongues, once again, met and fought urgently like two sparrows fighting over the first piece of morning bread, that she felt the frozen entities melt.

She wrapped her toned legs around his waist tightly. Instead of the neat bed, he pinned her against the freshly painted wall in the driving-the-peg-home pose. With each push, she knew the paint on the wall was getting spoilt as much as the paint of her soul.

As her hands explored his back like an eager tourist, her heart rummaged through excuses—from rubbish to real—in order to justify her willingness to enjoy what he took for granted about her.

Her mind went blank with the first pelvic thrust of his. With the second, she heard her thoughts loud and clear.

When a man is desperate, he injures others. When a woman is desperate, she hurts herself the most.

His thrusts were switching thoughts on and off in her mind alternately. Third thrust, her mind was blank again. Fourth...

Sex is everybody's home, nobody's address.

Blank.

When we are young, our heart is like a village full of simpletons. As we grow up, it changes to a big, bad city. Its desires become stranger and darker.

Blank.

Our actions are our immortal version.

Blank.

Finally, they knew this short film with no dialogues and yet a plethora of subtitles had to end. She knew what he was waiting for. *A nod*. He knew what she wanted. *A burst*. They knew what they wanted. *A climax*. Orgasm was the prey they both were out to hunt with equal urgency. Not a sound could be heard and yet there was a stentorian sexual symphony audible to them.

It was the actor who opened the door and walked out. The first one to enter the room was Gita, the actress's girl Friday, followed by assistants, technicians, and spot boys. While helping her 'madam' wear a warm, furry overcoat, Gita heard her madam whisper to her, 'Get an I-pill. Quick.'

Amid all the chaos and chirpiness, only Guddu, a spot boy, happened to notice the haphazard blotch on the wall. And if what he thought was right, Guddu wondered, the media would have a raging hard on with this piece of juicy gossip. And when the media has a hard on, someone gets fucked twenty-four seven.

BOOK ONE: (1986-2010)

SECRETS OF A SIN

THE LEGEND

SHAHRAAN ALI BAKSHI

10:00 a.m.

If you want to give a woman an earth-shattering orgasm, I remember her confiding in me, first make her sit near you. Then look straight into her eyes till she gives you a confused shrug, slowly bringing both her hands onto your lap and holding them tight. Make sure it's a warm grasp, not a threatening grab. After which, lean towards one of her ears and whisper with all your honesty what she *means* to you. And then gently embrace her, allowing your nervous breath to kiss her vulnerable nape.

I was twenty-one. She was sixteen when I first saw her. Between two hearts of that age, there exist infinite possibilities. And there were. I swear. Whenever my today wakes up in the arms of my yesterday, those unrealized, unacknowledged, untraversed possibilities appear before me and streams of cold sweat drench my brow.

The world celebrated my forty-fifth birthday last month. And in all these years, I have come to realize that love is actually an act of sowing. Problems start when we convince ourselves into believing it's an act of reaping instead. Thereafter, we use love as a fertile farm land for harvesting whatever we desire from life and a relationship, assuming being in love is in itself eligibility enough to deserve whatever we thought, wished, and coveted for.

Today—October 21—is Mehfil's fortieth birthday and I am here, in this once famous brothel which was her identity and destiny. Fifteen years ago, I had bought this entire place along with the small lane which branches out from the main road to lead here, like an unexpected disappointment often does from the spine of happiness. Men came here from different walks of life with only one thing in common—an indomitable libido. Libido, Mehfil told me, is a drunkard's faith. They follow it blindly wherever it takes them. And prostitutes are the ones who encash on that faith. Much like what happens in most holy places around the world. Though she was young then, every word of hers made some kind of celestial sense to me. She didn't have what I wanted in my dream woman except for the outer appearance; maybe. But she had everything I never realized I would need in my woman. This also made me understand that there are two kinds of beauty—outer and inner. Everyone doesn't have the former since it's subjective. On the contrary, inner beauty is present in every one. It's not subjective but its exclusive; visible only to a select few. And love is about winning that exclusivity.

This house where I am right now was called Neela Makaan then for its vibrant blue colour. Though the colour has faded considerably, the public memory hasn't. It still is a forbidden place.

Neela Makaan used to house six prostitutes and a swarthy, foul-mouthed, middle-aged woman who was their pimp. Mehfil was the youngest. I used to visit her as often as a young couple visits the memory of their recent marriage. I remember at the funeral of one of the prostitutes, staring at the burning pyre, Mehfil had remarked, 'That's the life of a woman in every prostitute and the prostitute in every woman. Men come and light a fire in some corner of us and we keep burning till we turn into insignificant ash and thereafter a slave to the wind of destiny that carries us as per its desires.'

I don't know when and how she became my emotional dictionary. The moment something would torment me from within, I would scamper up to her to find solace. I loved the way she had, at her age, unknotted everything within her, around her. Compared to her, I was a dumb boy. Now, of course, I am a man...in between, I fell in love with her.

The reason why I haven't renovated this place is both obvious and personal. I can still *feel* her here, in this place. Not like a memory, but a premonition. In the weary double-sized bed where I am sitting right now; in the stained and smelly lime coloured bed sheet which still transpires the perfume of her love for me; in the frail and exhausted looking pillows which are still young with the phantasmal caress of her dense black hair; on the morose, old walls that now look shy with seepage but once supported her delicate shadow valiantly; the ceiling which has a thick layer of dust along with a cavalcade of cobwebs that, I know, have safely locked the echo of her smiles and cries in its heart, and that's the reason I don't allow anybody to clean anything here. In the half-broken window frame where she used to stand tying her hair and admiring either the blue sky above or the once busy street ahead, the creaking door, the discoloured mosaic floor, the broken ventilator and most importantly, in the emotion that connects all these inanimate things and makes them vibrate with life. I have carried their pain with me like generations carry a curse. Since her departure, I have been living in a vacuum, with time at a standstill.

Just like there was permanence in her temporary presence in my life, the spring that I find in these twelve hours acts as a good antidote to the winter I encounter for the rest of the year. Physically, I loiter around to start with. Emotionally, I drain myself as my past copulates with my present. And pleasantly it all starts flashing in front of me...

Once upon a time there was this beautiful prostitute princess and a penniless prince...

I glance at my Tag Heuer; it's a little past ten a.m. Like always, I'll lie on the bed now and close my eyes...

For the rest of it.

In the summer of '86, a nervous young boy stepped down on to the warm chest of one of the platforms in Victoria Terminus, Bombay. Seeing the fleeting clouds of people all around, he thought to himself, 'What the hell am I doing here?' His face then resembled a messy traffic jam with the vehicles of hope, fear, joy, disappointment, curiosity, and skepticism—all honking away simultaneously for attention. But he knew no one would look at him because one nobody for a mass of nobodies is a gigantic nobody; an invisible man.

The rush at the station seemed like a gush of sperms had been released into the womb of Bombay. As if everyone was on the run for having stolen something. Jerking his legs anxiously, he felt their numbness disappear. He had been sitting for twelve straight hours in squat position beside the train's door. It was after his best friend Avinash dropped him on his Rajdoot at the Ratlam railway station that he managed to board an already loaded train. It was also his rich friend, Avinash, who had given him fifty rupees to sustain himself before he met Bheem; Avinash's only contact in Bombay.

At thirty, Bheem was a super success story. He had his own biryani centre in one of the hungry bylanes of Bombay. But for his townsfolk in Ratlam, more than his hard work, it was the mysterious Goddess of verisimilitude called Bombay which changed Bheem into Bheem Seth. The name was a paragon of disgrace once. But the moment it slept with success, it became a metaphor for good times. It was Bheem who had promised Avinash he would do something for Shahraan. And in his 'something', Shahraan had sniffed the sizzling starters of his seminal dream of making it big in Bollywood.

When Shahraan had announced his dream to his parents—Dayanath Ali Bakshi and Ratna Devi—they had taken him to a Tantrik the very next day.

Dayanath was a former freedom fighter and a primary school teacher in Ratlam. The middle name 'Ali' was chosen by him for the men in his family to showcase a secular solidarity. His ignorant lust for Ratna Devi made them conceive seven children; Shahraan being the fourth child and the first son.

The Tantrik beat him left, right, and centre with a broom and stopped only when Shahraan accepted to study further. Satisfied, the Bakshi couple provided the baba a sumptuous bhog. Two mornings later, their insurance-for-old-age was well on his way to Bombay.

Shahraan got a push from one of the commuters, making him move forward. He noticed a man standing idle by a pillar.

'Beware of two kinds of people in Bombay; the ones who are idle and the ones who are busy,' Avinash had advised him. Following the commuters obediently, he reached one of the exits of Victoria Terminus.

Looking around desperately for a way out, Shahraan recollected Avinash's words. 'Ask someone about Parel and they'll help you out.'

He saw a man dressed in a safari suit dragging a suitcase. He approached him.

'I am Shahraan Ali Bakshi and...'

'You have a problem.'

'Yes.'

'Please carry this bag for me till there. And I'll help you out.'

Shahraan agreed. His 'there' came half a kilometer outside the station.

Keeping his bag down, Shahraan queried, 'How can I reach Parel?'

'Don't disturb me,' the man almost rebuked him. As a taxi came, the man ensconced inside while Shahraan, without losing on time, ran alongside it looking helplessly at the driver and asked, 'I am Shahraan Ali Bakshi. I need to go to Parel.'

'Ninth platform,' the driver quipped.

It didn't take much of an adventure for Shahraan to reach the ninth platform where a local train was waiting. As he intended to get in, Shahraan noticed a man in a vest and a khaki-colored half pant semi-blocking the entrance and doing some invisible calculations in the air. He seemed to be wearing high-power spectacles that magnified the size of his eyes. The man suddenly glanced at him and said, 'Hello, I am Unnisau Saitalis.'

A lunatic! God bless him, Shahraan thought and said aloud, 'I am Shahraan Ali Bakshi. This train is going to Parel, right?'

'To Thane. It will pause at Parel. Knowing the difference between a destination and a temporary stop simplifies things.' The man beamed at his not-asked-for wisdom and made way for Shahraan who hopped into the train.

There was an exhibition of bored faces inside. Faces claiming to have given up on their dreams long ago. Faces suggesting life is after all a betraying bitch. The faces brought a sudden rise of fright in him which made him promise himself: Shahraan Ali Bakshi isn't going to be just another face in an exhibition. He will be an exhibition for millions of faces.

Unnisau Saitalis helped him find the small yet busy Bheem's Biryani Centre by the Parel railway station. His lodging and food problem was solved immediately since one of Bheem's boys working at the biryani centre, Krishna, had already been informed about his arrival.

There were five boys who lived on the first floor of the two-storey semi-built structure, with the ground floor being used as the biryani centre.

At first Shahraan thought it would be difficult for seven to squeeze in. Krishna corrected him.

'Not seven. With you it'll be six. Bheem bhai doesn't stay with us.'

'Where does he stay?'

'Nobody knows. All we know is that he comes here every evening by four and stays till eight.'

It was on the third night that Shahraan finally met Bheem, though he had met him twice before in Ratlam. And each time Bheem's weight had multiplied. Now sitting on a floor mat in the huge hall room, Shahraan could see a trace of a triple chin on Bheem whenever he sipped the dull-looking country liquor in between his banter.

'No job for you in my biryani centre,' Bheem declared. Everyone noticed how his belly juggled to his movement.

'But I need to sustain myself.'

'Let me complete, bachcha. You'll work for me alright but on my new taxi business.'

'Are you going to sell this place off, Bheem bhai?' a concerned Krishna asked.

'No chhote. I have purchased three taxis and have fixed drivers for two of them. The third driver will be you, bachcha.'

Shahraan abhorred the idea in the beginning. He learnt driving from a fellow driver who also helped him get a license. Right from early morning to late night he was driving continuously. From Parel to Bandra to Ville Parle to Andheri to Pali Hills to Juhu Chowpatty to Haji Ali to the Gateway of India, he took everyone, everywhere. Eventually he started taking pride in driving the taxi since he realized that it was a true representative of a secular India that his father once fought for. People of every possible caste, creed, age, and sensibility availed his taxi. In the womb of monotony he discovered an overlooked adventure. He used to observe the passenger's body language, picked on their diction, and at times analyzed their thought process listening to their personal prattle. Soon the taxi became his four-wheeler acting school.

Of whatever Shahraan earned, sixty percent went to Bheem. It was a good proposition since the lodging and food issues were taken care of by Bheem for all his boys. Apart from his necessary expenditures, he used to buy popular film magazines, got stitched cheaper versions of the kind of clothes his contemporary crop of heroes wore then, or collected cheap audio cassettes of his favourite movies. His second home was the tenth seat of the third row in Regal Cinema at Churchgate. And the little money that was left went inside a small tin box kept under the taxi's back seat.

One afternoon, a harried looking man got into his taxi during lunch time.

'It's twenty past one by my watch. If you can take me to my destination by two, I will give you double the amount your meter asks.'

'Where do you want to go?'

'Madh Island.'

'It's not possible. I need to have my lunch also.'

'Arrey bhai, the whole film crew is waiting for me there.'

The mention of a film crew was enough to make Shahraan turn his head around swiftly. The man had a my-entire-dowry-cheque-bounced expression on his face.

During the formula-one-inspired drive, the man said he was from the production team sent urgently to the main office to bring extra film reels since the on-set ones had finished because of the heroine's innumerable retakes.

It was two minutes past two in the man's watch when Shahraan stopped his taxi. Good enough! Paying him double the amount as promised, the man, with the fluidity of an idea, disappeared into a dense and noisy crowd. Shahraan parked the taxi a little ahead and stepped out.

As he approached the crowd, Shahraan heard a few abrupt whistles and claps. It took him some muscle power to pierce through and reach the front. At a distance he saw superstar Shekhar Rai being explained something by a restless looking person. The bouts of whistles and claps happened whenever Rukmani, the heroine, waved at the crowd. The restless looking man went behind the camera and screamed, 'Start sound, camera, and action!' on a mic, his voice booming over the loudspeaker. Minutes later, the man cried, 'Cut!' voice beaming on the Shahraan remained in awe of everything around; the camera, the ambience, the stars, and the overall process. It seemed like a different zone all together. Before he knew it, the director called for a pack up.

It was only after reaching the biryani centre that Shahraan realized his mistake. He should have requested someone in the crew to give him a chance as well.

Next morning, he put on his best attire—a blue shirt and black bell-bottoms which were his first buy with his savings—and reached the place early, waiting all afternoon under the scorching sun. But there was no sign of any film crew and by dusk, he drove back with hundreds of knots in his stomach.

He told Krishna about it who in turn relayed it to Bheem later in the evening.

'Our bachcha wants to be a film star,' said Krishna, watching his boss kick start his Bajaj scooter.

'Every second boy in Bombay wants that,' said Bheem and he was gone.

'Don't worry, dost.' said Krishna earnestly. 'One day the scent of your success will be more intoxicating than that of my mutton biryani.'

Shahraan tried hard but couldn't smile.

Almost three weeks later, Bheem surprised everyone by arriving at the biryani centre during day, bellowing from his scooter, 'Bachcha, quick.'

Shahraan, who was in the middle of eating lunch, gave him a confused look.

'Let's make you a phillam-isstar,' Bheem added.

Shahraan swallowed the bolus he had in his mouth, got up, and hastily washed his hands under the nearby tap. He came running to Bheem.

'Don't I need to change?'

'Idiot, we have only two minutes. Get your ass behind!'

If Madh Island was a five-storey building, then this one was a skyscraper. Bheem and Shahraan kept walking past faces with an ascending blotch of tension on them. Finally, they reached a group of four sitting on red plastic chairs arranged in a circle. Bheem raised his hand to announce his attendance to a particular man wearing a half shirt, shorts, and a cap. *The director*, Shahraan concluded.

Nothing happened for five minutes. Then suddenly the group stood up and dispersed with a nervous energy. Bheem pushed himself forward. So did Shahraan.

'Sir, this is the kid I was talking about a few hours back.'

The director glanced at Shahraan once and shouted aloud, 'Someone explain this chokra how to operate the clapper.'

He then walked away.

'What is a clapper, Bheem bhai?' asked Shahraan.

It took him two days to realize what a clapper was. His job was diametrically opposite to what he had come to Bombay for; to be in front of the camera from action to cut. When Shahraan complained of the same to Bheem, the latter advised him: 'Bombay pehle leti hai, phir mood mein aaye toh deti hai. Bombay jeetna hai toh lage raho bachcha.'

Those words became Shahraan's primary religion for the next few months. He kept driving his four-wheeler acting school to earn a living and whenever a chance beckoned, he alternately played the role of a spot boy, clapper boy, errand boy, and the likes. He soon realized that the difference between a normal being and an artist is that the latter has two lives: one where he only exists, the other where he lives. Cinema for Shahraan was the other life he was striving for.

As days and nights kept switching their roles in a hurry, a fear, with all its sharp canines, started digging deep into the flesh of his hope; what if time, which supposedly was performing a striptease in front of his destiny, finally finished doffing every bit of its clothing? For in that nakedness, his fears convinced him, might lay his worst nightmare: that he had grown old by a decade and was still driving a taxi.

The year was finally ready to shed its final leaf named December. After dropping one of the passengers for the night, Shahraan parked his taxi by Juhu Chowpatty and looked around. There were people everywhere to celebrate the arrival of the new year with balloons and crackers.

'Bombay is a blank cheque. Everyday thousands of people fill it up with their aspirations. Most of them bounce.' Shahraan, consuming the on-going pandemonium, sighed. He could feel how pregnant the sigh was with the twins of dejection and loneliness. This was the first time he wasn't going to celebrate New Year's Eve with his younger siblings—Chotu and Golu.

'We shall wait to see you doing dhishoom-dhishoom with the villains,' they'd stated together.

Then suddenly the same thought that occurred when he first arrived in Bombay seven months back restated itself. *What the hell was he doing here?* This time it happened with all its nosy and manipulative relatives.

What if the rest of my life goes the way the last seven months did? Baba was right. After graduation he could have helped me with a job in the school. I would have lived a traditional life with a wife and children. What's so wrong in it? That's the best bet for people like me who are born to exist like cockroaches with our energies directed towards survival all the time. I'll go back. Yes! Baba shall forgive me. I shall re-enter college, complete graduation, and then...that's final!

Following his impulse to eject himself out from the bowels of the city he climbed back into his taxi. He was about to start the engine when, out of the blue, came a girl and boarded the taxi.

'Please drive. I am in deep trouble,' she said.

Shahraan switched on the small bulb inside his taxi, turned around, and saw her face for the first time.

1:00 p.m.

I woke up that night to something unprecedentedly special.

I open my eyes. A crow is cawing by the window. I need to shoo it off. I do. I stand by the dusty window frame alert about the crow's reappearance. How interesting it would have been, I wonder hypnotized by nostalgia, if I could have shooed time away too with the snap of a finger. Especially the time that separates us. When a woman leaves a man after gifting him the kind of filters that Mehfil has given me to look at the world, he has no choice but to turn weak.

What would have happened had she not come into my life that night? Maybe, I wouldn't have travelled the world nineteen times over, wouldn't have private villas in Bombay, Dubai, Cannes, Atlanta, or Sydney. I would have been a nobody to the universe, wouldn't have inspired a single soul to be like me, no eyeballs would have cared to get a glimpse of me, wouldn't have…her nervous face when she boarded the taxi flashes in front of me. A woman, trust me on this, is not an object. She is an *experience*. If you are lucky, that is.

At first glance, her face resembled an unsolicited manuscript. But with a bit of patience I realized her face was actually the omnibus of a celebrated author. Everything was there, if you were interested, else not a trace of anything. Facing someone with such a visage either makes you listen to her intently, thanking time, or you unveil your heart and prattle, forgetting time. That night, her presence made me hear a song. And I was desperate to know all such songs nested within her soul.

I smile. Who said exploring the dry yet beatific grassland of memory—even for the thousandth time—isn't a self-realizing journey in itself?

'I dropped her on Faras Road.' Shahraan said.

Krishna was busy transferring rice from a jute bag into a container with his back to him. Now he was staring at him, half-turned.

'Are you sure it was Faras Road where you dropped her?'

'Yes, why? What's in Faras Road?' Shahraan asked.

'The bar girls live there. It's near Kamathipura; Bombay's famous red light area. Bachcha, stay away from her,' said Krishna and turned back to work.

'But, I love her.'

'You said she was young, beautiful, and stays somewhere on Faras Road. She is either a bar girl or worse; a prostitute. So stay away and fly off now. It's an hour past your lunch time.' Shahraan suddenly jumped down from the bench he'd perched on, wore his slippers, and moved out in a rush.

Driving his taxi towards Faras Road, Shahraan was all consumed in the conversation he had with her the previous night.

'I am in deep trouble.'

'What happened?'

'I was here with my friends. Somehow I lost them and then that old, horny man...'

Shahraan looked into his rear-view mirror, only to see the girl put her hands against her eyes.

'Please don't cry. I'll drop you wherever you want me to and you don't even have to pay me.'

'Why? If I have boarded your taxi, I'll pay. I don't take anybody's charity.' The girl was still busy rubbing her eyes. The road was empty of beings and lights except for one street light under which Shahraan stopped the taxi presuming she was crying. For someone standing afar, the entire scene would have looked like a dark stage with a golden spotlight bathing the protagonists.

Shahraan got down and was about to approach the girl when the sky lit up with all kinds of spectacular rockets. The New Year had arrived. Both Shahraan and the girl looked up at the sky in admiration. It made them go into a collective trance. When the sparkles ended, Shahraan glanced at the girl. *Put all the jewels of the world on her and still nobody will care about the jewels*, he thought. Standing beside her, his real purpose of nurturing a dream all these years, and later coming to Bombay following it, lay crystal clear. They were destined to meet.

When the girl looked at him, he realized one of her eyes was shut, making it seem like she was winking. His smile dried.

'Why are you winking at me?'

'Uffo! Neither was I crying nor am I winking. There's something in my eye.' She brought her handkerchief near her mouth, blew air on it, and put it on her left eye for relief.

'Now get in and drive. I am already late for the night.' The girl blew some more air on her handkerchief.

'If you allow me, I can help you,' said Shahraan cautiously.

The girl paused and looked at him with her hand over her left eye.

'Okay.'

'Please come out. It's clearer here.'

There was another spectacular blast in the sky as the girl stepped out, waiting for further directions from her seemingly different taxi driver. It was then that she noticed behind the dusty and torn-at-places uniform, a person who had a boyish charm about him—something ineffably genuine.

'Now what?'

'Hold your left eye between your fingers and spread it... like this.' Shahraan showed her. She started laughing. Realizing he was looking funny, Shahraan stood in an attention position, feeling awkward.

'I am sorry,' said the girl and did as asked, with the hangover of laughter still evident in the twitch of her cheeks. Shahraan came closer and looked deep into her left eye. Alert that his skin mustn't touch hers or else she could misinterpret his intentions, Shahraan almost had an epiphany.

'Eyelash!' he said. 'Wait, don't move. Give me your handkerchief.'

Shahraan took the handkerchief from her, draped its edge around his finger with the tip pointing out and moved even closer. The girl's body went slightly taut. Within the space of a few small steps, both seemed to have made a leap across seasons. The girl was experiencing a summer within, as she saw their shadows on the road by the taxi from two heads and one body.

Shahraan skillfully pulled out the eyelash. In the process, her breath diffused into his, escalating both their heart beats.

'Shukriya,' the girl said in a soft voice, but in the silence it seemed heavy enough.

Shahraan only smiled awkwardly. They slowly stepped away from each other and got back into the taxi. What they couldn't walk away from was the vista of an alternate universe their chance proximity triggered within them.

Tearing through massive traffic, Shahraan finally reached the place where he had dropped the girl the previous night. He parked his taxi nearby and stepped out. It was about seven in the evening.

The place was busy with adults moving around, street children playing illogical games, and some of the shopkeepers—whose idea behind the rickety architecture of the shops was the same as a modern city's take on relationships—were focused on their daily business. Though Shahraan saw a lot of people, he didn't know what to ask and whom. He kept traipsing the place, looking around, hoping for the girl to appear suddenly in front of him the way she had the other night. In particular, he noticed some sick looking kids, anaemic girls, and a few women with a have-had-enough-of-life expression on their faces. As he paused by a crossroad, Shahraan felt a tap on his back. He turned in a flash.

'Bheem bhai!'

Shahraan noticed a pouch of country liquor in his hand and a bracelet of Jasmine around his left wrist.

'I couldn't believe it from the distance it's our bachcha. What are you doing here?'

'Looking for...' There was a pause and then it came out, 'a friend.'

'Friend? What's his name?'

'I don't know. It's a she.'

Bheem stared at him for few seconds trying to read him.

'Okay. Follow me.'

Shahraan followed Bheem through some identical lanes and bylanes, ahead of the crossroad. Finally they reached a house. It was difficult for Shahraan to guess the color of the house since there wasn't any light nearby. It was a two-storey house, with the ground floor sporting an abandoned look while a thin ray of light was visible through the edges of the closed window frame above.

'This is Neela Makaan. Nazakat Begum owns it. If your friend is from this area, she will know her,' said Bheem. They climbed a narrow but clean cemented staircase and arrived at a passage where a tightly shut door was staring at them. Bheem knocked twice before it was opened by a young girl. Shahraan was glad she was not the one.

'Salaam Walekum,' said the girl and moved in.

'Walekum Assalam,' Bheem bent his head slightly and stepped inside. He paused and turned to gesture to Shahraan to come in as well. Shahraan did as instructed, noting that the door opened to a small mosaic corridor. He noticed Bheem take off his black leather sandals that were shining like a celebrity, in the corridor. Shahraan too did the same with his wretched ones.

'Is Begum inside?' Bheem asked the same girl who opened the door.

'Jee,' the girl said without looking up.

The corridor gave way to a hall with a round solid pillar in the centre balancing it. All around it were neatly laid out mattresses covered with white cotton bed sheets, with cozy looking cylindrical pillows kept atop dressed in cheap white satin. There was a stifling silence all around.

'Begum?' Bheem had made himself comfortable on one of the mattresses by the side. Shahraan stood nearby trying hard not to think, judge, or presume anything.

'Begum has fever. She is sleeping,' said a delicate looking girl who came out in the hall.

'Oh, is it?' Bheem looked at Shahraan and said, 'Tough luck, bachcha.' Changing his pose a bit he said, 'Could you prepare a hookah for me, Mehfil?'

What he didn't notice was that the girl and Shahraan were staring at each other. There was a bite mark beside her soft, supple lower lip, a small purplish blotch on the left eye while a bigger blotch present on the right of her forehead. None of it was there the other night.

Looking deep into each other's eyes, they realized, the near perfect alternate universe that they'd together glimpsed just a night before was experiencing acute tremors.

4:00 p.m.

I remember in the days following my encounter with Mehfil in Neela Makaan I found myself in a dilemma. One side kept asking me: *How could I be in love with a prostitute? What would I tell my parents and friends?* And then there was this adamant other side that said: *She is only a woman, after all.*

I realized life has orbits too. But being in love with someone shifts and takes one away from the orbit one is born into. And it's this changed orbit that simplifies things in a complicated manner because it gives us that overview of life which we assume—rightly, wrongly, I don't know—is worth everything. It was perhaps because of this orbit shift that no amount of alcohol or degree of pretense or level of forced indifference could make me forget Mehfil.

Every time images of her on bed with strange, lustful men flooded my mind, I felt disgusted. There was this rage inside me which wanted to kill those men even though I was yet to know whether Mehfil at all liked me or not. Still, I felt like I was her man—her knight in shining armour—who, pushed by a moral responsibility, must rescue her from the shithole she was in. Funny, I had never even had a word with her till then about her profession, and here I was designing hopes of rescuing her from something that I didn't have a clue if she was doing willfully or otherwise.

There were times when I took my taxi to Faras Road and stood like a fool, too afraid to go to Neela Makaan in fear of what would await me. What if I went there and found her in the arms of someone? Or worse still, Mehfil opened the door and said she was busy with someone? I used to crib not at what options I had—to fight for her or to forfeit her from her world—but at the simpler fact that I had options. Life was easier before I saw her for there were no options, no roads to choose from, and certainly no preformed tracks. Then I saw her and I don't know how so many unnecessary flies of options started hovering over my conscience only to spoil my instinct and colour my impulse. Worse, I knew I had to choose an option else there would be no respite.

Something happened at the start of the third month since I first saw her in Neela Makaan which took my mind away from her temporarily. I bagged my first film role.

'Aren't you ashamed to ask for money from me?'

Shahraan turned, noticing his last passenger for the night for the first time. The immense growth of unkempt hair had disguised the man's facial structure. His neatly-combed shoulder-length hair were sticking to each other thanks to the pungent smelling hair oil. He had a cloth bag on his right shoulder and was wearing saffron-coloured clothes. He was a sadhu. In Shahraan's dictionary it read: asshole. There were plenty of them in his home town feeding on people's weak sapling of a faith.

'I'm not in the mood for nonsense.'

The sadhu leaned forward, looked closely at Shahraan's forehead, and murmured, 'There's a Sun on your forehead. You know what that means?'

Shahraan was still.

'You will be a big man. Successful man. Popular man. Mark my words. Baba Bholaji is never wrong, son.'

'Still, the fare is thirty-five rupees.'

Anger swapped inquisitiveness on Baba Bholaji's visage.

'You fool!'

'What did you say? You have had it now,' said Shahraan moving out of his taxi, opening the back door, and catching hold of the sadhu's cloth bag, pulling at it with all his energy.

'Help me!'

Hearing the ruckus, some fellow taxi drivers came running toowards them and separated Shahraan from the sadhu with the latter fleeing away quickly. The fare remained unpaid.

That night, the irony of the Baba's prediction didn't let him sleep properly. Sometime in the night, Krishna shook him up almost malevolently.

'Bachcha, get up!' said Krishna grasping Shahraan's vest. 'There's a boy here who wants to take you to a film set.'

'I don't want to be a clapper boy anymore,' muttered Shahraan, his sleep dictating his slurred speech.

'Idiot, he says there's a role for which the director wants you urgently on set.'

For a moment Shahraan didn't blink.

'Oh, God. Where is he?'

'Downstairs. He said you will get one hundred and fifty rupees for it.'

Shahraan almost crawled the distance to the open roof-top bathroom for he was still half asleep. He splashed water on his face five vigorous times and only then did he realize that the moment he had been waiting for all his life had actually come.

The messenger boy was a lean fellow who himself looked like he was fighting sleep valiantly. The moment he saw Shahraan, he blinked tightly and then looked at him again.

'What?' Shahraan asked the boy restlessly.

The boy took out a comb from his back pocket and gave it to him. Shahraan snatched the comb, went to a nearby parked scooter, and perused his reflection on the scooter's rear-view mirror.

'God, was I sleeping or getting my hair fucked in hell?' said Shahraan looking at his dishevelled hair in the mirror.

It happened the way things happen in a dreamer's life; by chance. One of the henchmen of the antagonist in the film was suddenly down with cholera. The absentee actor had a miniscule role to play in the night's action sequence that was to be shot in a sprawling replica of a dance bar. But the producer had spent quite a bit of money on the set and wanted everything to go according to plan. So, a quick replacement was asked for. The director bellowed at his assistants, one of whom had been bribed by Bheem to arrange for a role for Shahraan.

'What is the name of my character?' Shahraan asked the assistant who was standing beside him trying to arrange a bunch of papers in sequence, while a make-up man furiously dabbed some foundation on Shahraan.

'Shut the fuck up, okay?' was the assistant's first brief. 'You open your mouth only when the director shouts action, else nobody needs your ass here.'

Shahraan zipped his lips; a bit out of obedience and a lot out of fear. He heard the assistant say, 'Here, you are one of the villain's men and you have to say "haramzaade" when the hero hits the villain and then jump onto him. He will punch you and you shall fall on the ground.'

'That's it?'

'Did I hear you speak?'

'Absolutely nothing.'

The shot went well and Shahraan was able to impress the director by doing it right at the first take. It was pack up at five in the morning and Shahraan got the promised amount in cash right after.

Sitting by Juhu Chowpatty, Shahraan felt a strange emptiness overcoming him. At first he thought he must be hungry but later understood what it was. He couldn't share the news of his first film role with his siblings, nor could he show the currency notes to his parents. They would still be angry at him. And then suddenly Mehfil's face flashed in front of his eyes. *Will she understand my emotions attached to the currency notes? But why will she? What she is in my heart and in reality are two different things. Only if she weren't a prostitute...* his heart whimpered. The wind had suddenly picked up speed and as it hit him, gravid with sand grains, Shahraan turned his face sideways and saw someone at the distance. There weren't many people around apart from the few carrying a globe of a belly and running after their pets. Shahraan, after a fixed stare, was convinced it was someone wearing a white vest, khaki half-pants, high-power spectacles, and doing some calculations in the air. He instantly knew who it was—Unnisau Saitalis!

He got up, dusted his back, and walked up to Unnisau. It was when the latter heard someone breathing hard beside him that he turned.

'Remember me?' Shahraan smiled.

'Shahraan Ali Bakshi. Victoria terminus to Parel to Bheem's Biryani Centre.'

'How have you been?'

'Good. You want tea?'

'Is that what you do for a living? Sell tea?'

'No. I once befriended a foreign visitor here who happened to be a loner. He was suffering from cancer. After his recovery, he went back to the States but keeps sending me dollars off which I feed myself and keep writing to him. I am the only one he calls a friend, so he keeps me alive with money and I keep him alive with companionship. Do you want tea?'

For a trice Shahraan thought Unnisau would chant a magical mantra and make tea appear in front of him. He looked like he could do anything.

'From where?'

Unnisau flexed his waist slightly and a satchel with a flask came in to view. Unnisau opened the flask and poured hot, steaming tea on its plastic lid that doubled as a cup. Shahraan took the cup with a faint smile.

'Your cup?'

'We can alternate taking sips.'

They sat on the sand and together looked at the wide expanse of nature ahead, alternating their sips of tea. Time flew like the wind.

'Why is your name Unnisau Saitalis?' They were done with tea.

'I'm an orphan. The old aayi who raised me, goofed up the name and date-of-birth section in my birth certificate. She had written Unnisau Saitalis in the name section.'

Again silence. Shahraan felt the back pocket of his pant and took out a two rupee note.

'For taking me to Bheem's Biryani Centre.' Since he held the note by its edge, it was fluttering in the wind. Unnisau looked at the note for some time. Then he took it saying, 'First time I have earned money for taking someone somewhere. Usually love does that.' He smiled caressing the note.

'Are you married?'

'No, I'm not. Like you.'

'How do you know?'

'Married men never sit alone in the morning by the Chowpatty side.'

'Right,' Shahraan said averting his eyes and looked deep into the sea. 'Actually, I am in love with someone.'

There was no response from Unnisau. It didn't surprise Shahraan though and he continued telling him about her.

'Her name is Mehfil. She is a prostitute.'

From the corner of his eyes, Shahraan made sure to check if Unnisau was gawking at his courage of falling for a prostitute or his dastardliness? Unnisau didn't budge an inch; not even give a slight scowl. A second later, he asked with a steady poise, 'What is the point?'

'Problem, not point,' said Shahraan, surprised at Unnisau's lack of grasping power. 'I told you she is a prostitute.'

Unnisau finally glanced at Shahraan obliquely with a hint of a frown as if he still wasn't geting the point. 'But you said you are in love with *her*. And prostitution is only her profession, right?'

The comment squeezed out anger from Shahraan's impulse. 'Don't tell me I have to explain to you what it means.'

'A profession is a reaction to one's survival instincts. It means she sleeps with people to survive. Like I run errands for people. Like your Bheem bhai runs the biryani centre. And profession has got nothing to do with the kind of person one is because if it was so, then for a top-notch business man, driving a taxi would be as shitty a profession as prostitution. So would you appreciate him loathing you?'

Shahraan frowned. Why was he trying to read Mehfil through the literacy of her profession? Why was the nature of her profession challenging his newfound love for her? Wouldn't he have fallen for her had he not known she was a prostitute? Why the hell was he upset? Was it because she must have been carnally conquered on bed by other men? The thought shot bile up his tongue, almost. And that even if she agreed to his proposal, he would never be the first man to own her? *Her*? Really? Or *her* body? Was his love a euphemism for his lust to deflower her first? Shahraan abhorred himself for having such thoughts.

'Look Bakshi, if you are into her with an intention to conquer her, then all you will see are her good points, her beauty. But if you want to go from black to grey with her from here on,' Unnisau continued, 'then know her flaws. In doing so, if you come to terms with a few of your own, then give your possible togetherness a shot, a chance. And anyone's profession cannot be taken as a flaw, right?'

'But I am yet to talk to her properly.'

'Now, that's a problem for sure since that means you are only in love with the idea you have developed of her in your mind which, if and when you get to know her, may or may not be true.

There was silence.

'Have you ever been in love, Unnisau?'

'No, but I know what love is.'

'What is it?'

'Like reading a good story is about travelling without moving an inch, love is about winning even without caring to win.'

'How do you know this if...' Shahraan saw Unnisau make some quick calculations in the air.

'Hey, what do you keep calculating?'

'I have animated discussions with time.'

Unnisau Saitalis was different. He was weird. Informed. Confusing. And perhaps, right too. Shahraan had to know Mehfil to take a decision. He had to confront his mental spider so that it stopped spinning further web of assumptions unnecessarily.

And for that, he had to go to Neela Makaan, at least once more, to meet his prostitute princess.

It was exactly eight forty at night when Shahraan, perspiring profusely, knocked at the green-colored door of Neela Makaan. After smoking half a packet of bidis for the first time, Shahraan had finally given his courage preference over his cowardice.

Standing outside, he prayed hard for Mehfil to open the door. It would imply she wasn't busy. *Wasn't busy with*—he controlled the incorrigible spider in him knitting debilitating thoughts. The door opened. A sweat drop slowly trickled down from his forehead to his lips. He tasted it.

'Shahraan?'

'How do you know my name?'

'You have told me twice.'

How many strangers' names do you remember? He felt tempted to ask but restrained his stupid self.

'I need to talk.' There was this momentary eye contact and when it broke, Shahraan wondered: *Am I still living? Why?*

Mehfil shot a careful look behind her and said, 'It's not the right time for people like you to be here.'

'I know. But I need to talk to you about something important.'

'With me?'

Shahraan nodded. Her presence was hypnotizing.

'What is it?'

'I like you.' The words were barely out when there was an immediate correction, 'I love you. And I want to know you.'

For a few seconds nothing happened. Then Mehfil laughed out compulsively looking at Shahraan who stood there like a life-term prisoner with one helluva prison-break plan.

'Who is it, Mehfil?' A heavy sounding woman's voice called out from inside.

'Someone wants to know the directions to an address nearby, Begum.' Mehfil shot back, raising the pitch of her voice.

'Ask that motherfucker to get lost.'

'Yes. I have.' Mehfil turned her head and whispered, 'Shahraan, you better go away. I'll meet you soon.'

The door was shut tight. A confused Shahraan slowly retracted away from the place and muttered to himself, *I'll meet you soon. She must be kidding to get rid of me.*

One evening later when Bheem was about to get onto his Bajaj scooter, he said, 'Chhote, when bachcha comes, ask him to take a day off tomorrow from regular driving. Nazakat Begum wants her six girls to go on Bombay darshan.'

There were six places the ladies wished to visit: Mahalaxmi temple, Siddhivinayak temple, Marine Drive, Haji Ali, the Gateway of India, and Juhu Chowpatty. At first Shahraan thought Mehfil, being a Muslim, would not go inside the temples and that shall buy him an opportunity to talk to her. But to his disappointment and surprise, Mehfil was the one who led the girls inside both the temples. It was while leaving from Siddhivinayak temple that he asked her, 'Is Mehfil your real name?' He was glancing at her from the the driver's mirror above him. Mehfil's eyebrows came together while trying to grasp the quintessence of the query.

'Mehfil is my real name. And I am a believer. And a believer doesn't need a religion.'

While waiting at a red light, he kept looking at her reflection as if trying to read a book. She sure was a page-turner with every page taking a different story. But they were all equally intriguing. The more he tried to read and understand her, the more confused he became.

Their lunch session happened inside the taxi where all of them ate what Mehfil had brought in a big lunch box.

'The food is delicious,' said Shahraan.

'Mehfil cooks really well,' remarked one of the girls. They were all between fourteen and seventeen.

'It reminds me of my mother's home-cooked food,' Shahraan said and thought he would get another quick glance from Mehfil but she preferred to focus on the food instead. A woman's shyness can turn on a person more than any cosmetic make over, Shahraan realized.

'She also talks about...' The girl was about to say something when Mehfil, as if she knew instinctively what it was, put her hand on the girl's mouth. The rest of the girls began laughing.

'What is it?' Shahraan asked.

'Nothing. Let's get going,' said Mehfil sounding alert.

It was during their post-lunch visit to the Gateway of India that they spoke at length for the first time, standing against the cemented barricade below where some boats were harboured and several, others could be seen sailing afar in the sea. The other girls were busy giggling at scantly-clad foreigners.

'Congrats for your first film role.'

Shahraan was genuinely surprised. 'Thanks, but how did you know?'

'Bheem bhai told me a night ago.'

'It's only a tiny crumb from the huge bread of my dream.'

'And what is that huge bread?'

'I want to rule Bombay!'

His voice had the same raw ingenuity which Mehfil had noticed during their first meeting on New Year's night. As if he was not merely reading aloud his dream from the notepad of his wishes, but was authoritatively announcing what was already embossed on the iron slab of his destiny. When he said he *wanted* to rule Bombay, he meant he *knew* he would rule Bombay.

'But, do you know what it takes to rule Bombay?'

'Hard work!' Shahraan was quick to utter.

'A little more than that,' said Mehfil sporting a flirty smile.

'Sincerity—dedication?'

'Ummm, still a little more.'

Shahraan's face had a wait-I-will-crack-this frown, 'Luck?'

'Little more!'

'Money?'

'A lot more.'

'Why don't you tell me?'

'Love.'

The frown slowly migrated away from his face with the bird of admiration appearing in its place, fluttering its wings furiously.

'When did you open your eyes by the way?'

'You mean how old am I?'

'Yes.'

'When you met me in Juhu Chowpatty, I was sixteen. I turned seventeen the day you came to Neela Makaan with Bheem bhai. How old are you?'

'Twenty-one.'

There was silence. She was looking at a boat which was fast disappearing against the horizon while he was looking at the clear blue sky with painted white clouds.

'Where are you from?'

Mehfil turned to look at him.

'I—'

'Let's go now. We are dying to go to Marine Drive.' The girls were back.

Though neither Shahraan nor Mehfil traded a single word in the taxi, love letters of smiles were constantly exchanged between them via the mirror atop the driver's seat. Neither wanted to get down when they reached Marine Drive.

The girls ran along the cemented barricade guarding the coast while Shahraan and Mehfil made themselves comfortable on them. They were sitting close but not close enough like the other couples sitting nearby.

It was Mehfil who spoke first.

'I am from Shahjahanpur in Uttar Pradesh.'

'I am from Ratlam, Madhya Pradesh. When and how did you come to Bombay?'

'I was ten when my father sold me to a man for money. He had given me orange juice. I drank it and fell asleep soon after. By the time I regained consciousness, I realized I was here in Bombay having been sold to Begum by that man.'

'Didn't you try to run away from all this shit?'

There wasn't any immediate response. Shahraan thought he saw a tiny twitch under her eyes as if the question hit her instead of patting her.

'In the beginning I didn't know what was happening. And when I did, it was too late. The same age-old trick life pulls on everyone.' A pause later she added, 'Wisdom, you know, is something we buy with the price of innocence.'

'You never responded to what I told you that night.'

'Is it necessary?'

'I wouldn't have asked otherwise.'

Mehfil's face had the same edginess that's present on a student about to enter his examination hall while trying to peruse all his notes at once.

'If you don't like me then—'

'I like you, Shahraan.'

He knew she wasn't finished at that.

'But, I won't be able to leave Neela Makaan. Begum will never allow it.'

'Why? I'll marry you.' Shahraan couldn't believe how easily it came out. And while he said it, he was considering her and not her profession. He thanked Unnisau in his heart.

'You are a guy, Shahraan. All you'll see is the immediate solution. I am a girl. I need to look at the immediate problem.'

'I don't see any reason not to look at the solution. I want to be with you forever.'

For the first time, Mehfil saw a hint of resilience in Shahraan. She liked the way he was fighting to be with her. But she also knew what had happened to Jhalak, her late best friend. After a lot of explanation and emptying tears, Begum had allowed Jhalak to marry the boy she loved. Neela Makaan was decorated that day for a different reason and Begum herself had doled out money for Jhalak's marriage. Six months into the marriage, the guy ran away with all the jewellery. The news disturbed Begum so much, she declared the next man who proposes marriage to one of her girl's will be slaughtered first, followed by the girl herself.

'Even if I say I like your intention of coming back to Neela Makaan for me, what do I really know about you? Nothing. You are what you tell me you are. I am sure you'll put your best face forward to get me.' Mehfil was sure the last statement would crash his ego. But she forgot she was talking to a man who was deeply in love with her.

'In order to know each other, we will have to meet regularly. So when are we meeting next?'

'Begum never allows any of her girls to go outside even for a single day. Today is an exception.'

'Then?'

'We can meet if you come to Neela Makaan as one of my customers.'

Given a choice, she would have drowned in the sea in front. She was sure no lover would be brave enough to meet his love in a brothel. Still she was happy the words came out, for all through the day, she realized she loved him too much to stop him from loving her.

She had her reason.

Fifteen days later, Shahraan went to Neela Makaan again. The girl who smiled opening the door recognized him instantly. He followed her inside to reach Nazakat Begum who was leaning on one of the pillows. She looked like a giant. The loose end of her sari was evidently unqualified to cover her excess, water-filled balloon of a tummy, while the huge sagging breasts seemed they could divorce the blouse any moment. Her eyes were puffy and one cheek was stuffed with a betel leaf ball, the juices of which had painted her lips and tongue red. As Shahraan stood in front, he saw her patiently counting some currency notes. Once done, she put the money bundle inside her loose blouse and examined him bottom up.

'What?' Even an ignorant query sounded like a threat.

'I am here for Mehfil.'

'For?'

'Meeting her.'

'Gandu. I'm asking for how many hours?'

'Two.'

'Seventy-five rupees.'

When Shahraan presented the money to her, his hands were trembling. The notes vanished inside her mammoth grasp.

'Third room from the right. It's ten now. Get out by twelve, else you'll be thrown out.'

Shahraan nodded and proceeded towards a white curtain separating the main circular area from the rest of the place.

He moved the curtain and peeped beyond to witness five closed doors staring at him. *Third from the right*, Shahraan reminded himself and took a few steps towards it and knocked.

'Nobody knocks here. Just come in.' It was Mehfil. Shahraan slowly opened the door to find her standing with her back to him. She was busy trying to attach the hook of her brassiere. She was wearing a black petticoat below.

'Sorry,' Shahraan blurted out without knowing where to look.

The familiarity of the voice made Mehfil turn around in a flash. She sprinted for her dupatta and covered herself. Her flat stomach was still exposed. She grasped a pillow from the bed and covered the exposed portion. Being stark naked in front of strangers was something she did everyday and still exposing some skin in front of Shahraan embarrassed her.

'What are you doing here?'

'I am here to meet you. You'd told me this is the only way we can meet, remember?'

For a moment she kept gaping at him blankly, coming to terms with his zest for her. Shahraan shrugged.

'Close the door,' she said softly and saw him do so.

'Sit down.'

He ambled in gingerly and sat by the edge of the bed. Tightening the wrap of her dupatta around her, she went and sat by the opposite end of the bed. She saw him swallowing a lump. She followed his eyes and realized her panty was still on the bed. In another flash, she snatched it and put it below the mattress.

'Please don't look around much.'

'Okay.' Yet another lump.

'I thought you won't ever come.'

'Did you want me to come?'

'No.'

There was a sudden power cut of disappointment all over his face.

'But I wished for it.'

Power on!

'So?'

'So tell me,' Mehfil sat in a more relaxed manner, folding her legs by her side, 'what's up with your acting?'

'I've acted in three films till now; just a few small and insignificant roles.'

'Do show me your portfolio once?'

Shahraan seemed thoughtful for a moment and then spoke aloud, 'What's that?'

'Don't tell me you don't know! Portfolio is like a collection of all hero-hero style photographs to attract producers.'

She saw Shahraan bite his lip contemplating something. She smiled obliquely for he looked cute.

'It would cost a lot. Won't it?'

'Umm, it normally does. But for starters, you can try the one in Andheri. Wait, I'll give you the address.'

Shahraan's eyes followed Mehfil as she got up, yet again, tightening the wrap of her dupatta around her, took four steps before she reached a weak wardrobe. She raised both her arms to get to it and in the process, her waist was exposed. Shahraan's eyes were fixed on the exposed part.

'Don't you remember what I told you?'

'Not to look around.'

'Right.'

As Shahraan interviewed the floor, Mehfil took out a pen and a writing pad from the wardrobe. She took another minute to scribble something on it. Once done, she climbed down and handed him the paper slip.

'This guy, Rajesh, will do it for less or on credit. He helps strugglers.'

'Thank you,' said Shahraan, running his eyes on the address once and slipping it inside his shirt's pocket.

'The first film I acted in will be releasing next month. It's called *Insaniyat ke Khatir*. Will you come with me to Regal?'

'I told you Begum is strict. If we have to watch any movie, she comes with us. She snores, while we watch.'

'That will do. Just sit next to me.'

'We'll see.'

The next one hour passed by silently. But when lovers sit in silence, it's never quiet. The glances seemed like flying kisses, the abrupt eye contacts were tight hugs, and the averting of it was a love bite.

'I'll come here again,' said Shahraan as he stepped out of the room a minute prior to his two-hour quota. Mehfil only nodded bemused. She was not sure if she should like the course their relationship had been steered onto by the night, for she knew time was the most unpredictable chauffeur.

I'll wait, she couldn't say it aloud.

Rajesh indeed agreed to photograph Shahraan on credit. He was impressed by his looks and the splendid way in which light bounced off his skin. Shahraan was photogenic. Period. Perhaps the most of all the strugglers that Rajesh had shot in his studio so far.

'You have got it, man. Looks wise for sure. Acting, I don't know.'

'Thanks. What exactly do I need to do with this portfolio?'

'Make as many producers' and directors' lives miserable as possible. You are a dog now and they are your bones. Don't think about anything else.'

'I have been to some offices but the security guards don't allow me to go inside.'

'Oh, they will not. Catch them when they move out of their offices. Bribe the security guard if possible, take his uniform and substitute him so that you are there to open the gates for the producers and directors when they come, and in the process, present your portfolio too. Are you getting my point?'

'No!'

'Get mad. Crazy, my boy! You've got to be crazy for your bone. Remember, fate loves those who don't like being ass-fucked,' Rajesh winked.

For the next two to three months, Shahraan went to twenty producers across Bombay. Fifteen of them didn't allow him inside their offices and the rest that did allow him to get in, made him wait till his patience ran out.

One night, he saw Rajesh walking towards the biryani centre. Shahraan felt embarrassed.

'Rajesh bhai! Sorry I couldn't pay your last two installments. Actually I had to skip driving to meet producers. Neither anything positive happened there nor could I earn enough to pay you.' *Not even enough to go and visit Mehfil.*

'Hey, I'm not here for the installments. There is this director friend of mine who is making a big film with big stars. He might have some role for you. I'll give you the address. You go with the portfolio. Okay?'

'Oh, Rajesh bhai, how will I pay off this debt that you—'

'Brother, no man is ever a self-made man. When you dare to take on the scorching heat, you at times get trees for shade. I am just one of those. And believe me, you'll make it big.'

You'll make it big! The words of the sadhu ricocheted in his head. Hearing them again from Rajesh, he felt like an atheist who had just been announced a life imprisonment inside a Church.

Shahraan was made to audition the next day in the director's office itself. They asked him to visit the next day as well. He signed a sheet of paper, agreeing to do the role of the star protagonist's younger brother. He was supposed to be dead by the tenth minute of the film. His signature fetched him five hundred rupees. The other two thousand, he was told, would be given when the shooting was over.

Shahraan first went to Rajesh and paid him his dues, then he bought a Safari suit for Krishna, a duplicate bottle of scotch for Bheem, and finally, a set of colorful earrings and bangles for Mehfil. It was nine in the evening when he reached Neela Makaan. With both his hands gripping onto plastic packets, Shahraan stood in front of the green door which by now had become the vista for the alternate universe he so desperately wanted to belong to.

Mehfil was lying on the bed when he entered the room. Shahraan almost dropped the packets by the door, closed it, and pulled himself onto a bamboo-made stool. As he settled on it, he noticed dark circles around Mehfil's eyes. She looked weak and pale. Shahraan's mouth went dry.

'What happened to you?'

'That's why I said keep visiting,' she said trying to smile. In vain.

'Don't joke.'

'First I had fever, then caught a bad cough, and then developed malaria. Now I'm okay, so don't worry.'

'Thank God!' He stretched himself to reach one of the plastic packets and pulled it close, 'For you.' He took out the bangles and earrings set and gave it to her.

For a moment, she forgot her lips could move. Caressing the bangles with her own hand for some time, she found her voice.

'No one has ever gifted me anything, Shahraan,' she said, caressing the bangles as a mother does to a newborn. Then she wore the earrings and said, 'Congrats for the role.'

'How did you know?'

'Shopping packets, earrings, a shine in your face—they are all hints enough.' Mehfil wore some of the bangles now.

'Though it's a small role, it still is of some importance in the movie. Not like the earlier, insignificant ones.'

'Learn to appreciate the insignificant, Shahraan. It's the insignificant in life that bridges the gap between the significant and us.'

He smiled generously and looked at the bangles and earrings which looked even better now.

'I love these,' she said.

'I love you.'

Her facial expression changed.

'What happened?'

'Do you even realize which way we are heading?'

'I am trying to get my foothold in acting so that I can marry you and we can live together forever.'

'And you think that's possible?'

'Giving more importance to anything other than films was impossible for me. Getting into films was my dream. The end. And this life was only a means to reach that end. Then I met you and the means became an end and the end turned into a means. Now I want to be in films so that I can take you away from here and we can remain together forever.'

Mehfil took off her earrings and kept them back in the box. 'For a man to be happy, he needs a fantasy in reality. But for a woman, she needs reality in fantasy. And what you just told me is a fantasy with no element of reality in it.'

'Why?' Shahraan shrugged looking bemused. 'Don't you think I would be able to make it big in Bollywood?'

'Oh no!' Mehfil paused and looked at Shahraan as if he had committed a sin. 'I believe you'll become a superstar one day.' *Just that...* she didn't dare complete it in her mind.

'Then?'

'Nothing. Forget it. We'll see with time.'

Shahraan took out his wallet. 'Keep this with you,' he said, handing her two hundred and fifty rupees.

'But why? This is way too much. And I am not allowed to keep cash. Begum keeps it for us.'

'No, these are my savings. Earlier I used to keep them in a tin box in my taxi. But now I want you to keep them with you. If you had not boarded my taxi on that New Year's night, I would have gone back to Ratlam like a loser. And then when I met you again, my first role happened. You are my good luck charm.'

Mehfil looked at those notes and displayed her best smile.

Begum had started liking him because he seemed like a decent man and was always punctual for his meeting with Mehfil. She joined him and the girls to Regal cinema to watch the first show, second day of Shahraan's first release. Shahraan made sure he was seated right next to Mehfil. Every time he appeared on screen, either standing behind the villain or afar in the frame, Mehfil grasped his hand tight. As if she had associated herself with his dream from a long time. During those bliss-inducing grasps, Shahraan realized Mehfil had become a zoom-in process for him that magnified all his visceral elements to himself and allowed him to choose the person he wanted to be, select the traits he was comfortable with, and neglect the ones he was not sure about.

The monsoon arrived on time that year. It was raining morning, noon, and night. Streets, along with their numerous dimples of potholes, were filled with water most of the times. From a bird's eye view, Bombay would have looked like an omnivore's digestive tract with everything—from snakes to human infants—swimming in water-filled lanes, streets, and roads. And the bouts of power cuts and load shedding became a regular problem to put up with.

Shahraan was late for his meeting with Mehfil one day. He ran from one lane to another, drenched copiously in the rain that was beating the streets incessantly like politicians beat up common men in a democracy. He soon reached Neela Makaan totally drenched.

'I am sorry to have come like this,' said a shivering Shahraan as he entered Mehfil's room.

'Are you mad? Come inside quickly. And stand in the bathroom.'

It was the first time Shahraan had stepped inside her bathroom. It had a tin roof on which the rain was drumming mercilessly. A second later, Mehfil came in with a towel and switched on the light bulb at the corner. The bathroom suddenly seemed smaller.

'Here, dry yourself quickly.'

Shahraan's unsteady hands took the towel. He asked, 'Where's the door?'

'Sorry, there's no door here. Wait—'

Mehfil disappeared momentarily and came back carrying a bed sheet.

'Let me try this.' She attached two ends of the bed sheet onto the two junked nails on either side of the wooden frame which looked like it had once supported a door. It wasn't perfect, but it worked. She sat on the bed outside. She couldn't help but notice his shadow on the bed sheet. As he doffed his clothes, Mehfil felt warm within. Perhaps for the first time she was aroused in the place where it mattered the most—her heart.

'I'll need something to wear,' Shahraan said.

She took a deep breath and said aloud, 'One minute.' Stretching her right hand to the switch board above the bed's head rest, she turned off the light in the room. It took her a few seconds to strip herself. A lightening struck and for a trice, Mehfil fluffed seeing herself standing naked in front of the mirror. Ordinarily, she loathed her naked self since it was a reminder of the hell she was in. But in that particular sorcerous capsule of time, she admired it.

Shahraan switched off the bathroom light and stood in front of the bed sheet that separated them both. As he stretched his hand and pulled it, the bed sheet fell down. Even in the darkness, he could make out her form standing in front of him. He walks towards her and ended up touching her wet lips. There were instant goosebumps all over her skin.

Shahraan picked up Mehfil in his arms, gently placed her on the bed, and came to lay beside her. Their fingers teased each other and finally locked themselves. And they stayed in that position till it stopped raining that night. After a while, there was a knock on the door by one of the girls. 'Two hours,' she relayed.

'You know why I didn't make love to you tonight?'

The fact that a man lying naked beside her asked her such a question in a brothel of all places amused her.

'I didn't want to touch you amorously here and become one of the many. I'll work hard, and when we will have our own house, own bed, own night, then...' his voice trailed off.

It was dark and thus she could cry. Eight years in the brothel had taught her how to cry without letting the person right next to her know about it. She wondered what it was that transformed the larva of her prayers into the butterfly of reality. Was it her sincerity towards the dirt she was in? Was it her courage to commit something as serious as love being a member of a world where flesh was all there was to a being? Or, was it Shahraan's passion for her? Whatever it was, her heart declared, it was something that didn't happen every day. Or in every life.

'Tonight, you made me feel what heaven really is,' she said, hiding the choke in her voice.

'What is heaven?'

'Heaven is nothing but hell, but, with *you* by my side.'

She was on his arm. She looked up. He looked down. Their eyes linked. Time seemed amputated of motion.

Following that rainy night, when all doubts of the heart were coronated with assurance, Shahraan suddenly found himself running from one film set to the other. All were short, minor character roles, but the volume of work was high. And Shahraan's passion, punctuality, and dedication impressed whoever he worked with to an extent that regular recommendations kept flowing in.

'After all,' Mehfil responded when he told her of the developments, 'it's not you they are appreciating. It's my choice that they are.'

'But this is not the news I came here to give you.'

'Then?'

'First tell me why are you turning pale day by day? And these dark circles around your eyes?'

'Oh, this is nothing. It's the month of Roza. So I'm fasting. It's taking a toll on my health.' She looked at Shahraan's still-not-convinced face. 'It's okay! Now tell me what is it?'

'I believe you.'

Mehfil averted her eyes and bringing his right hand to rest on her lap, she caressed it softly.

'I have been selected as one of the main characters in a Doordarshan serial called *Jai Jawaan*,' informed Shahraan.

'Doordarshan?'

'Yes. Lots of talented people are working in it. It's about a bunch of military boys' personal lives. I play one of the boys, Captain Abhimanyu Sen.'

'But how did you bag the role?'

'I was playing yet another non-consequential role in a film, when one of the ADs asked if I was game for television. I said I was game for anything that would take me forward in my quest to attain stardom. He asked me to audition. I did and they chose me.'

'Who was this AD?'

'A boy of my age called Ravi.'

Mehfil looked lost for a moment, biting her lip slightly.

'But there's a problem.'

Mehfil looked up with a questioning look.

'I'll have to go to Delhi for its shoot since the production unit is based there. It will be a month-long shoot. They want to wrap all the thirteen episodes in one schedule.'

She looked at him as a tree looks at its leaf just before it drops onto the ground and merges with the earth forever. She had an intuition Shahraan would belong to the world more than he ever belonged to anybody before.

There were ten boys who had been given basic military training by an experienced Army Major just prior to the shoot.

During the shoot, Shahraan heard about a young boy whom the people referred to as AD on the set. The boy seemed a little different from the other ADs. He always used to see things and people through an instrument around his neck which, Shahraan was informed, was called a 'Director's Eye'. And the guy wasn't around everyday too.

It was only after the shooting of ten episodes that he was told the person's initials were AD—Aditya Dev—the only child of Bollywood's most happening producer and distributor, Veer Raj Dev of VRD Films Pvt. Ltd.

'You know what he is doing here?' asked one of the actors. The bunch was having evening tea with samosas.

'He has learnt filmmaking from abroad and has worked as

an assistant in a Hollywood production. He is here to make documentaries.'

'Documentaries, my ass!' the same actor belched before continuing, 'These film kids need a different shit hole to flush off their extra money.'

'I agree.'

When the others left, the actor sitting beside Shahraan said, 'Motherfuckers! They think nobody knows why AD is here.'

Shahraan slowed his masticating of the samosa and shrugged.

'Of course, for checking us out for his debut film. I mean all of us! The director of *Jai Jawaan* is his father's dear friend, and he showed our auditions to him. Now don't tell me you didn't know that?'

'Oh, of course I knew,' Shahraan lied.

The fact that Aditya was there to check the actors out himself and not trust an audition was reason enough to believe he must have only one thing in mind: performance.

For the rest of the episodes, Shahraan doubled his sincerity towards his character. In the beginning, he would snap out of the character when the director called 'cut', but now he embodied it even after each pack up.

Diwali coincided with the wrap-up party for the serial. Shahraan was sad since he hadn't been able to connect to Mehfil in so many days. Not even on her birthday. He chose a corner where he simply sat thinking nothing and everything alternately. He was soon joined by Aditya.

'Hello, myself Aditya Dev.'

'Shahraan Ali Bakshi.'

'Oh yes, I know all that I should know about you.'

Shahraan's heart skipped a beat.

'Day after tomorrow you'll be in Bombay, right?'

Another beat. 'Yes.' Shahraan did not have a clue where this conversation was headed.

'Then make sure you come down to my dad's office in Santa Cruz. That's my office as well. We will do a look test on you for the character of Shekhar Rai's illegitimate brother.'

Something about the way Aditya spoke told him he was about to reach the *light* in search of which he had left his home, driven a taxi, lived in a wretched place, and went through whatever he did in the last few years. He wanted to jump, to strip, to yell, and run from Delhi to Bombay naked. Damn, civilization!

Shahraan's urgent steps slowed as he saw a crowd of people gathered outside Neela Makaan. As he stood at a distance separated by the crowd—with both his hands clasping onto packets full of Diwali crackers, sweets, and a dress for Mehfil—he thought something had happened to her. He took all the packets in one hand and moved ahead in the crowd to reach an undertaker's van where a dead body lay covered with a white cloth. Peeping over some of the busy shoulders, he spotted Mehfil leaning her head on one of the other girls. He had never seen her eyes so empty of life. Nor her face so famished of hope.

She told him the turn of events at Neela Makaan as they walked together with the body to the nearest burning ghat.

'A middle-aged business man had promised Lata a home, family, and a life outside the biased walls of Neela Makaan. And she dared to believe him. She eloped with him fourteen to fifteen days ago. We were all concerned. Her body was found two days ago on the railway tracks in Virar.'

Shahraan was silent throughout the walk. He heard Mehfil

next when Lata's body was laid on the pyre and introduced to fire.

'That's the life of a woman in every prostitute and the prostitute in every woman. Men come and light a fire in some corner of us and we keep burning till we turn into insignificant ash and thereafter, a slave to the wind of destiny that carries us as per its desires.'

As the fire started licking Lata's deceased body, Shahraan looked at Mehfil; first through the corner of his eyes and then almost straight. She was unaware of the chaos around her. Her hands, he noticed, had gone slimmer and the face seemed dry as if it was thirsty for something. Her eyes looked tired and even the blinks, he was sure, took pounds of energy from her. There was a strange wilderness in her poise that seemed desperate to turn itself into a civilization. He wanted to inquire about her health. Instead he said, 'Let's get married, Mehfil.'

'Hmm?' Mehfil turned probed by an instinct. Her facial ruggedness requested him to repeat.

'Let's get married.'

Mehfil stared at him, too afraid to accept she had heard them for her own good reason.

'Shahraan, you've got to leave me, forget me.'

'What are you saying? Why?'

The people by the pyre threw a when-will-people-have-manners glance at them.

The reply came when he was in Mehfil's room in Neela Makaan later in the evening from Mehfil herself, 'When a wife sleeps with another man, she is a whore. But when a whore decides to sleep with only one man for the rest of her life, she still remains a whore. Look Shahraan, you say I matter to you, but you are on the fringes of giant success. I know it. And then what? You won't be able to afford to be associated with me. The world judges everything by two things: one, their eyes and second, the things they themselves are missing out on. And that world which will soon shower love and accolades on you would not want to see me by your side. If you remain adamant and still choose me, then that very world would replace their tongues with blades and shall lick you up. Are you getting my point?'

'Yes. The point is there's another man.'

'What is it with you men? Whenever a woman wants to end a relationship, why is it you think it's because of another one of your species?'

'Then what the hell is it?'

'Our love is doomed. From the time we met or perhaps, from the time we wished for something like this.'

'I don't understand.' For the first time Shahraan had raised his voice before Mehfil. He was standing up now with his hands on his waist while Mehfil continued to sit on the bed eyeing him.

'Why do you keep saying these negative things about our future? I am trying hard. You know it. I came here to tell you about Aditya Dev. Yes, Aditya Dev of Veer Raj Films! He is making his directorial debut and I am supposed to do a look test for it tomorrow. You getting it, Mehfil? This is something I was waiting for! That's why I asked you to get married to me.'

A supremely irritated Shahraan came and sat on the bed opposite Mehfil. He was glaring at the floor as if he could drill a hole in it with telekinesis. A gentle smile touched Mehfil's face and she dragged herself towards him and held his face in her hands. Shahraan tried to stare at the floor.

'I have never seen such a big tomato!' she said and laughed out pinching his face. 'I only wanted to see how committed you are to me. Can you promise me one thing?'

'I have promised my life to you, Mehfil.'

'I want you to promise me that you'll put the red vermilion, on me if we marry.'

'I promise.'

'And you'll burn me, not bury me, when I die.'

'What nonsense!'

'Promise me.'

'Okay, I promise.'

There were five more actors who competed for the look test and auditioned for the role of Shekhar Rai's illegitimate brother. It went in favour of Shahraan. This time it was a legal contract he signed, with a whopping thirty thousand rupees as the signing amount. Another forty five thousand were promised when shooting would end after two months. Shahraan couldn't believe the number when he read it in the cheque he was issued.

The first person he went to with the cheque was Bheem. The latter hugged him with pride. He announced free for all Biryani at his centre for the evening. Krishna requested Shahraan to make him his assistant once he became a star. Shahraan hugged him for a good five minutes, unable to hold his emotions in. He could well imagine how happy Mehfil would be.

Yukta, the new girl in Neela Makaan, opened the door.

'I'm here for Mehfil.'

'She is not here.'

'Not here? Where is she?'

'She has gone to her home.'

'Home? Shahjahanpur?'

'Yes.'

'When will she be back?'

'I don't know.'

Shahraan looked at Yukta for some time. Her face was like an undecipherable dream: too simple and too straight to make any sense.

'Okay, I'll come after some time,' he said and left.

Shahraan was taken to Kashmir at the end of the week for the first phase of the outdoor shoot. Though he was shooting potent scenes with superstar Shekhar Rai and learning new facets of acting each second, something inside him was not at peace. That something kept playing a requiem no matter how much he laughed, partied, or made merry on the sets with others.

The night before New Year's, Shahraan was alone in his hotel room while the rest of the film crew was busy partying in the banquet hall. There was still one more week to go for the shoot. Though Shahraan wanted to celebrate the arrival of yet another year, the elegy inside him made him lie down on his bed by the fire in the room and play hopscotch with his memories. One year had gone by since he first saw Mehfil. *Only a year? No way!* he thought. The image of Mehfil and him together under the street light lit road was fresh in his mind as if time kept engraving those moments deeper and deeper in his heart. And whenever he visited them in his mind, they would seem like it all happened yesterday. He was sure by now she would be back at the Neela Makaan. And no matter what she told him, this time he would marry her, and they would shift together somewhere.

In the first week of January, the first outdoor schedule came to an abrupt end.

All through the shoot, Shahraan kept nailing every shot in one, two, or at the most, three takes. But on that particular morning, it had gone up to six retakes. The scene had one of the goons drive in a van towards Shekhar while Shahraan's character would jump in time, push Shekhar away from the line of fire, and it would be a cut. Aditya, standing behind the camera with his technicians, was getting a bit worked up. Finally, the seventh take started: the man drove in the van, Shahraan jumped in, slipped, and fell down while the van hit Shekhar right on his pelvis. This scene had gone horribly wrong.

Shahraan escaped with minor injuries but Shekhar had to be taken to a nearby private nursing home as he was bleeding profusely. The shooting was called off for the day. Shahraan enquired after Shekhar's health from the director who told him Shekhar's injury seemed to be of a serious kind. He was urgently flown to Bombay early at night while a dejected Shahraan accompanied the production people on their way to Bombay the next morning. Everybody knew it was an accident, but the kind of glares and hush-hush talks Shahraan saw the production people involved in, suggested they doubted his slip during the shoot.

Shahraan reached Bheem's Biryani Centre in the afternoon. He was surprised to see Krishna sitting on the broken stairs.

'Bachcha!' said an unshaven and lean Krishna standing up, dusting his trouser.

'What happened?' Shahraan paused.

'Mehfil…'

The only thing Shahraan heard next was a thud in his heart which he was scared to interpret.

10:00 p.m.

I'd promised her I would burn her body. I didn't comply. In fact, I didn't even attend her funeral. The most audacious thing, however, was that I read a short letter she left for me with Begum. I opened the letter on her birthday the following year. I still have it. I slip my hand in my pocket and take it out. An old, wrinkled page from some random notebook on which she had written the night before she died or so Yukta had told me. I open the letter.

I never told you about the kind of men who visited me. They all had strange urges to quench. One used to paste the photograph of his wife on my face and then slap me while doing me; another wanted me to act dead as he kissed me all over; and then there were the ones who wanted me to call them papa, chacha, and other family names. But you came with the weirdest of all urges: to make me fall in love with you.

When you looked at me for the first time in the taxi, my core felt the pulse of a poignant promise. When we got talking, my existence woke up to an eventual commitment. And when we finally got to know each other, it was like an irrevocable deal to go on a journey together—far beyond forever.

The worst thing that can happen to a kid is the realization that this world is a cruel and manipulative place. I knew it when I was nine. The only thing that kept me going was a wish that someone would come and respect me because of the sacrifices I made for the woman that's inside me, for the woman who helps me survive. Thanks for fulfilling my wish.

I know you will be angry with me since I never told you about my uterine cancer. But I can die with that. Since I know by then you'll be on your way to become what I know you will one day: the king of Bombay. Don't worry, nobody here will ever tell anyone that we were in love. What will people say? The king in love with a prostitute! I don't think anyone would believe it either.

Anytime soon my death will whisper to my life that it's all a dream and I'll have to wake up. I won't be able to see you one last time. And I have accepted it all, Shahraan. And I want you to accept it too. From now we'll be each other's secret. And mind you, only a lucky man becomes part of a woman's secret.

Do you know, Shahraan, what is a smile called when it falls in love? A tear drop.

I fold the letter. It only tells half the story. The other half was later told to me by Bheem bhai. She had requested him to bribe an AD to look out for a role for me. Rajesh, the photographer, was Mehfil's 'client'. It was on her insistence that he had agreed to do my portfolio. Mehfil lied about how he helped newcomers fearing my reaction. When I didn't see her for two to three months, it was she who'd sent Rajesh to me with an opportunity. And in exchange, she fulfilled his carnal kinks.

God designs our lives. Love redesigns it. That's what Mehfil did. She secretly redesigned my life while I was busy assuming it was all a result of my hard work and luck. *How did she do it?* I didn't ask because the *why* was already weighing on me. I had talent in me. All Mehfil did was help that talent get noticed. In the end, that's what makes the difference between winners and losers.

I decided to leave then. As I open the door and look out, there are a myriad faces waiting to get a glimpse of me, but my vigilant security that accompanies me wherever I go has everything under control. Stardom was always a place that I wanted to reach till I arrived there and realized it was actually a price I would have to pay. I no more belong to myself. I am as much the paanwalah's who has my photo right beside his God as I am of the teenage girl who lusts for me or the housewife who covets me, and perhaps also the pious mother's who prays for my well being without ever meeting me. I put on my dark shades even though its night. And I get out of Neela Makaan. Another year gone by. As I walk the small lane towards my black Mercedes parked outside, I remember the earrings worn by a girl with whom I had an ad-shoot recently.

They looked similar to the ones I gifted Mehfil once. For some reason the girl's face has stayed with me. This has happened the second time in my life. The first time had changed my life in the 80s.

As my car makes it way out, I ask Krishna, my secretary from the last nineteen years, 'Could you please call up that girl with whom I did the watch advertisement recently?'

He gives me a what-to-tell-her shrug of his.

'Tell her, Shahraan Ali Bakshi wants to meet her.'

THE ICON AND THE HEART THROB

REVA GUPTA AND NEEV DIXIT

Reality winked at him whenever he glanced at the bloated condom lying on the toilet sink beside him. It was only after the fuck ordeal that he realized the condom had perforations. He flushed it down the toilet sink, praying his sperms don't turn out to be as irresponsible as him.

He joined the other actors in the small drawing room of a one-BHK flat in Mayur Vihar, New Delhi, where there were now seven final-year students—four men and three women from the National School of Drama—rehearsing for a play.

'Reva!' the guy heard Amjad holler, 'You should have made your entry by now.'

Reva Gupta swallowed the lump in her throat. Since morning she wanted to tell Amjad—her boyfriend and the writer-director of the play—she was neither interested in this drama nor in his mindless shit anymore. With Amjad staring at her for a response along with the rest of the cast and crew, she realized now was that moment.

Several kilometers away, within the campus of Progressive College of Engineering and Management, Ghaziabad, regular rounds of job interviews for the final year batch of engineering students were being conducted. Most students resembled molestation victims. Except Neev Dixit who was happy to have screwed up his group discussion. But to his horror, he was shortlisted for the technical interview round. He tried sounding stupid and was chosen for the HR interview which was currently in progress. Given a choice, he wouldn't have even cared to appear. But his not appearing for the campus selection exams was improbable because the placement coordinator was a friend of his father. And their family reporter too.

'Why do you think we should take you?' asked one of the interviewers. Even though he seemed the youngest, his skin was loose. *The man could very well be the next model for Godrej hair dye*, Neev wondered looking at his fiercely-black hair.

'Sir, honestly,' said Neev, 'I don't want to get picked.'

The interviewers exchanged quick glances.

'Would you mind telling us a little about yourself?' asked the same person. The others were sitting so tight and straight that to Neev they looked like fart balls waiting to explode.

'I am Neev Dixit. And I want to be an actor. That's all I know about myself. Everything else about me, except my sexuality, is in a state of confusion.'

'Do you know we can blacklist you for this kind of talk?' It was a lady this time. Her visage made Neev conclude she was suffering from PMS.

'That would be my pleasure, Ma'am,' replied Neev, his smile having a hint of mockery.

The first interviewer immediately pushed back his chair, pressed a bell, and stood up. A man came running in within two seconds.

'Please take this gentleman outside.'

Neev stood up, took a bow, and left the room with such pride as if he had signed a major peace treaty with a neighbouring country.

'This is the twentieth time we are performing today,' Amjad howled, beating the script wildly against his thighs. Reva looked at Amjad and saw a stranger. In the last few months, seldom did he praise her acting skills like he used to. Earlier, whenever she promised him a smooch or a quick love-making session, he would raid the nearest Archie's gallery to bring her the perfect gift. Not anymore. As if now he wasn't grateful for any intimacy she agreed to, simply taking things for granted. Was she at all in love with him? At times she thought her friends were right. She was a shameless opportunist and the only reason she was with Amjad was because it would get her good roles in plays. But then an opportunist only seizes the opportunity and forgets the person on whose behest it came. She had given him everything—from her vagina to her heart. What else does a man need from a woman? What else does he deserve?

The real problem was: Amjad was not her only problem. The three years at the National School of Drama made her realize she wasn't cut out for the stage. She had to be the on-screen Goddess! Theatre was long shot, whereas Cinema was close up. And Reva Gupta loved close ups. Plus the attention, the pampering, the fawning it garners, always helps. From the second year onwards she realized her priorities were different. Priority decides intention which influences a decision and dons an action. Of course, there was so much to learn in NSD—India's premiere drama school—but they were all dwarfed by what all she aspired, dreamt, wanted, urged.

'Amjad, there's something I need to show you,' said Reva holding her middle finger up.

Neev knew his parents would act as if they were asleep. But parents are always awake, he knew, especially when their only child comes back from a campus interview. And because he didn't wake them up either, Neev hoped they themselves would reach the obvious conclusion. But in the zest to throw himself on the bed and sleep peacefully, he forgot the dawn that was about to break would bring with it a Sunday—that day of the week when he met his father at the breakfast table. And yet another cold war shall follow.

'So now you are going to humiliate me in front of your batchmates; my juniors?' Amjad banged his hand on the wall against which Reva was standing. There was an inhuman condescendence in his eyes like never before which, though unexpressed verbally, reprimanded her for what she said. His only bad luck was she read it instantly. It enraged her.

'Humiliate? You really want to know what humiliation is? You lying to everyone about me and our relationship; that's humiliation. For me! And you want to know humiliation better?'

Before Amjad could take her into another room, she was divulging their relationship's secrets to an all too eager audience, directed by an unadulterated anger towards him.

'Keep your ears open for this one guys; as open as we girls keep our legs to fit your insects in us. I have never slept with Amjad irrespective of whatever shit he has been filling you up with. And why you may ask?' she glanced at Amjad's pleading eyes. Reva, whose first tear drop was falling down now, said, 'Amjad can't even get it up even if he wants to. So in reality he has been finger fucking me all this while, and that too because it comes with a bone.'

The second stunned silence of the night followed. The only positive thing for her in this three-year-old relationship was that her mind had been dressed with the correct fashion of experience.

'How many students did they select?' asked Mr. Dixit, an Indian Railways employee, soaking half his bread into the hot tea the following morning.

'Twenty students.'

'Two thousand students and they selected only twenty?'

'Everyone is taking it easy after the WTC attack last year.'

'And you couldn't make it to the list?'

'No. They wanted engineers, not actors.' Neev first ate the edges of the bread and then bit the soft middle part with the tranquility of a spiritual guru.

'What about the second company?'

'All I know is that they didn't select me.'

Hiatus. Neev always knew what existed on the other side of his father's hiatus. Allegation.

'You must have presented yourself like an ass.'

'Why would I do that? And papa, it's high time that you realize my passion lies elsewhere.'

'You mean in acting.'

It was an old war between his wishes and his father's desires. When he was ten, Neev wanted to learn swimming, but his father made him learn cricket. At twelve, he wanted to play the guitar, but his father forced him to attend an art school. At sixteen he wanted to study arts, his father coaxed him to study science. At eighteen, when Neev finally realized what exactly he wanted to be all his life—a movie star—his father pushed him into the engineering bandwagon. Neev could never understand why people were judgmental about any kind of aberrant. Even if the tradition stank like shit, they would like to lick it more than give the aberrant a chance.

'What do people do if they want to become an actor?' Neev heard his father speak. It was unlike him.

'Amjad and I had to end, who cares how it ended. Are you listening, slut?'

'Like fuck I'm listening, bitch. Shimit told me the condom had holes in it. I don't want to get fucking pregnant right now.'

It was seven in the morning. Reva chose to be with her best friend Sheetal in her room after the group dispersed clueless about the play's future. Reva called Sheetal a slut, with love, while the latter referred to the former as a bitch, with admiration. Their undeclared rule for sharing secrets and worries was that they would prattle about their own without listening to the other.

'Get over it, slut. God allows girls a safe period as well. You are on one.'

Sheetal relaxed realizing Reva could be right.

'And listen,' Reva continued, 'I want to go to Mumbai.'

'What? Are you out of your mind? Do you even know anybody in Mumbai?'

'I'll get to know people only when I go there, right? Theatre is so not for me.'

'Then why did you opt for NSD?'

'It's only after being here that I realized the big screen is my calling.'

'You are mad, bitch. Bollywood is like a secret society where you are invited only if your genes belong there!'

'But the stalwarts of all the previous generations were outsiders. From Dev Anand to Amitabh Bachchan to Shah Rukh Khan to Shahraan Ali Bakshi, all came from outside the industry and made it their pet, didn't they?' The mention of Shahraan made her heart skip a beat. Reva had a strong crush on him from the time she traversed the park of adolescence.

'They were all men!'

'Madhubala, Madhuri Dixit, and...'

'And?'

'And Reva Gupta, you never know! And please, don't tell me what I am. Tell me what I should do?'

'Alright! Six more months and our NSD stint gets over. Why don't you talk to Raghu Sir? He keeps going to Mumbai.'

There was silence. And it stretched for another four hours. Sheetal fell asleep while Reva remained wide awake, with the pendulum of decision oscillating between her mind and heart. Finally it stopped at her heart.

Six months and then I'll be in Mumbai. That's it! She finally stretched herself on the mattress, relieved. She woke up, took a paste-it slip from a nearby table, and wrote:

Sorry Slut, I was kidding. You are not on your safe period. Get to a doc first thing tomorrow. She pasted the note on the door of the refrigerator and went out to run a few errands.

It was twenty past eleven at night. Neev was busy playing FIFA on his desktop. His room's door opened and Mr Dixit stepped in.

'You awake, beta?'

In the last ten years, he had never seen his father come in his room. He haphazardly stood up switching on the tube light. *Is he throwing me out of his house already?*

'Yes papa, what is it?'

'I need to talk to you.'

Neev gave his chair to him and himself preferred to stand.

'After talking to you in the morning, I kept thinking about what all happened in the past. I don't think you know this: when you had applied for FTII, they had replied back but...' Mr. Dixit took a pause, wiped some dust from a corner of the computer keyboard with the tip of his index finger and said, 'Just because you are my son doesn't mean the course of your life is my prerogative.'

Neev's mouth went dry and his throat drier. Parents at times do things which you least expect them to do. His father was looking around at his only child's room as if he was discovering him for the first time. There were five posters in the room: one was of *The Godfather* movie, then there was Tom Cruise, Clint Eastwood, a small computer print out of The Beatles, and a full-size Charlie Chaplin poster.

'Your grandfather never allowed me to do anything against his wishes. As a result of which, many desires of mine remained thwarted within me. Locked forever into obscurity.' He gesticulated by crisscrossing his fingers. 'And when you were born, I thought those desires had been granted wings. My mistake. I wanted to live not through you but through thrusting myself onto you. My foolishness. If you think you can act well and are sure you want to make it a career, then go ahead. I will not stop you. I simply came to tell you that you have my back, son. The only piece of real advice I can give you at this stage is complete your graduation first and then steer your life in whichever direction you want to.'

His father left the room. Neev sat down on the chair, letting himself loose. *Six months and I am done!*

Life was waiting for both Reva Gupta and Neev Dixit in Mumbai.

REVA GUPTA

A day before, Mumbai had been hit by monsoon. Monsoon and Mumbai make a classic love story, she was told by a co-passenger. Reva stepped down from an express train at the Borivali station. She had been craving for this moment all her life.

Reva had a few relatives in Mumbai. But she knew a girl alone in the city who had come to become an actress would be gossip fodder for them. They would criticize her to start with and then end up accusing her father, Shirish Kumar Gupta, of not being a good parent. In his hay days, Shirish Kumar Gupta was a name to reckon with in the theatre circuit of Delhi. Many famous contemporary theatre personalities owed their skills to him. People called him 'master sir'. All this came to an abrupt halt when cancer snatched away his wife. After which, he withdrew himself from theatre and all other futile things in life that other mortals, at times, deliberately magnified in order to give them a reason to live. Shirish would have been as okay if Reva had chosen to become a housewife as he was when he heard she wanted to be a cinema actress. Reva had an elder brother residing in the US, married to a Chinese woman. Reva and he never really connected.

Making her way towards platform one, Reva was already scanning the faces around. She was supposed to meet someone with a hard stubble, well-oiled hair, and wearing old-fashioned spectacles.

Amit was Sheetal's Mumbai-based cousin whom Reva had met twice before during his visit to Delhi. At first she thought Amit was a nerd because every time they talked, he gave her an unwanted lesson on all the upcoming gadgets in the market. The second time she realized he was a psycho, because whenever Reva excused herself to join a group of girls, he would shoot at her a straight-wide-eyed-open-mouthed ogle. And as destiny would have it, of all the people to help her in Mumbai, it had to be Amit scouting to help her. Sheetal had told her he had taken care of her accommodation. That was the first major concern in a big city where she knew nobody of consequence.

Reaching the first platform, she again face hopped. She was about to call Sheetal from a nearby PCO when she noticed a guy—clean shaven, wearing shades, and with fluffy hair—gaping at her from a corner. She looked at him. It encouraged him to come forward.

'Reva Gupta?'

'Amit Garg?'

'Yes, how are you?'

'Good.'

Reva was pleased to see he had used the time since they last met to work on his nerdy-psycho thing. By the looks of it.

'Let's go,' he said trying to get her suitcase.

'No, it's okay.' Reva intentionally loosened her grip on the suitcase for Amit to snatch it easily.

'Sheetal said you have finalized the rent.'

'Yes, I have. It's six and a half thousand a month. But—'

'But?'

The explanation happened inside an autorickshaw. Amit had arranged a one-room-kitchen flat for Reva through a dealer who had promised him the room from the fourth Friday of the month. But a day before, the dealer had told Amit the room would be available from Sunday instead of Friday since the owner has stationed some of his relatives there owing to some medical emergency.

'Then where will I stay?'

'If you don't mind, you can stay with me.'

So the psycho has become a super psycho, Reva thought, and said, 'I'm sure Mumbai has hotels.'

'Don't get me wrong. I know you are from Delhi and all that, but a big city is a big city.'

'Which means?'

'Girls are never safe, especially one as beautiful as you.'

And the nerd has turned into a subtle flirt, Reva concluded.

'Moreover, I stay with three guys, not alone.'

'Three guys? And you want me to stay with you people?'

'I have already had a talk with them. We have a two-bedroom flat. We shall give you your own room. You can even lock your room for the three days of your stay if you want to. Nobody will disturb you.'

There was a genuine concern in his voice which Reva couldn't sever herself from.

'I want to check out the place first.'

Amit confirmed with a thumbs-up.

If this apartment was a person, Reva wondered standing right outside it, it needed a birth-control pill. It looked fucked up from all sides. There was not even a security guard.

Inside, she was surprised to see an elevator. As Amit closed the elevator door, he pressed on the seventh floor button.

'Top floor is always better,' she quipped.

'We stay on the second. The elevator stops only on the top floor. We'll climb down.'

Reva gave him a what-the-fuck gape.

The flat was a typical bachelor pad with everything lying scattered everywhere except in the bedroom they had vacated for her. It was neatly done. Amit asked her to settle in, after which he left for work. After a prolonged siesta, she woke up feeling hungry. While searching for food in the kitchen, she heard the main door being unlocked. She rushed there.

Vishal stared at her for a moment, looked around the room as if checking if it was the same one he lived in, and then recollecting something smiled awkwardly. 'Oh yes, Amit did tell us about you. This shooting and all is taking a toll on me. Reva Gupta, right? I am the second flatmate here.' Vishal entered the flat.

'Yes,' said Reva smiling faintly and said, 'By the way, which shooting is it?' She wanted to churn out more.

'An ad film. I assist Shubash Anand.'

Reva's mind raced. Shubash Anand had made three films till date. Two flops and one hit. His latest one was supposed to be an ensemble casting.

'Great. I was wondering if there's a good place to eat. I am so hungry, I can almost eat a horse now.'

'Tell me about it. If you give me two more minutes to freshen up, then I can prepare the world's best Maggi noodles.'

Sucking in the steaming noodles a few minutes later, Reva inquired, 'Do the rest of your roommates also work in the film industry?'

'Amit and another one are both engineers, while the third works in a bank.'

So out of the other three she met the one working in the film industry the first; a good omen. And he prepared dinner for her; a better omen.

'Amit said you are here to be an actor.'

No, I want to be a star.

'Right.' It was better for her to state the milder version of her dream.

'It's a bad, bad place, mind you. You'll be given what you need only when you have something more desirable to offer. Exceptions are but rare.'

Reva eyed him intently as he ate his food.

'Are you an exception or the rule, Vishal?'

He looked up at her in a way as if someone had taken out his battery after switching on the surprise mode. Then he laughed out. A few seconds later he asked, 'So where are you from?'

Before Reva replied she made a mental note: Vishal hadn't answered her.

NEEV DIXIT

It was all pleasant: the train and his taxi ride from Panvel to Vashi till he climbed the five floors to his friend's apartment. Then he saw a big, shining Godrej lock on the door and a paper slip taped on the door addressed to him:

Neev, my granny is not well. I'll be back in a few days. SORRY!–Mohit.

Neev took off his shades to read it again. It read the same. He stomped the floor in angst. One of the neighbours opened the door and peeped out. Neev turned to face her. She looked middle-aged.

'Excuse me, can you please tell me—'

The lady locked the door on his face. Anger, which was his Achilles' heel since birth, clouded his mind. He pressed the calling bell and showed his two middle fingers at the peephole.

Downstairs, standing by the security guard's bamboo chair, he realized it had started raining copiously.

'Excuse me bhaiya, is there any hotel nearby?'

'Where are you from?' said the guard, busy scratching his groin.

'I've come from Ghaziabad.'

The guard suddenly looked interested.

'I'm from Allahabad.'

Neev gave him a good-to-know-that smile which he didn't really mean.

'Here for holidaying?'

'No. To act in films.' Neev's pride was evident.

'Phillam?' the guard looked at him up-down-up. 'Why don't you sit?' he got up.

'It's okay. I need a hotel for myself.'

The guard looked lost for some time. He rushed across the road to the only open shop opposite the apartment. A minute later, he was back gasping for air and drenched in rain.

'I had a talk with my son-in-law. He works as a boy in a good hotel in Goregaon.'

'Goregaon?'

'Where Phillam city is.'

Neev's attention got a punch. The guard told him the address and directions.

'Take an auto from here, go to Vashi station, and then take a train. Get down at Wadala station and then take a train for Borivali. Goregaon will come in between.'

'Thanks.'

'Uttar Pradesh zindabaad.' Finally, the reason for the guard's sudden behavioral change registered with Neev. It's ethnocentric attitude like this, Neev wondered, that integrates people at one level and disintegrates them at another.

The humongous crowd made the train seem like a monster's belly, with loads of shit ejected and refilled regularly at each station. He was literally mauled by the crowd and was all too glad when his destination finally came, allowing him to disembark from the horror of a journey.

He eventually located the place in Goregaon. As soon as he checked into his room and saw the bed, he surrendered himself to it. He got up late, ordered food from a nearby restaurant, and ate it on his bed. It was while finishing his food that he heard a woman's voice. The second time it happened, he knew it was coming from the adjacent room. There was a common door between the two rooms and by now Neev had placed his ears on it. The quiet surrounding helped him listen more clearly.

'I hope you know what you are doing.'

'Yes. And I'm sure you want it as much as I do,' said a man. 'Want to smoke?' he added.

There was silence. Perhaps the girl had said yes and the man was lighting a cigarette for her.

'You can make a great heroine,' remarked the man.

'Really? Thanks. This will bear result,' said the woman.

'What will?'

'Whatever we do tonight.'

'I hope so,' said the man.

'What are we waiting for?'

There was a loud noise. As if a vase had broken. Next, he heard the girl moan.

Casting couch! Neev finally knew what was going on in the other room. And he wondered—if this woman is sleeping with the man for a role, it means the man must have some good connections in the industry. That's the whole point of casting couch anyway—give and take. *If I can locate this man then perhaps he could lead me to...'* Neev sighed and went back to his bed. The erotic sounds were still audible but Neev wasn't listening anymore, too preoccupied with his own thoughts. He had to get in touch with the man. *His name with the receptionist would be a fake one. Better to keep an eye on the door lest the man slips away.* Neev stepped out in the empty corridor, tiptoed to the adjacent door, and sat down on the floor. It was a stupid thing to do, but this could be an opportunity for him as much it was for the girl moaning like a kitten inside. In no time, Neev fell asleep outside their door.

It was the sound of shoes walking past him that woke him up in the morning. Rubbing his eyes he saw the door was ajar and the man inside was arranging his bag. A closer look and he thought the man could easily be of his age. He knocked.

'Excuse me, Sir.'

'I have given the tip.'

'I'm from the next room.'

The boy now turned to face him.

'I'm sure you are from the film industry,' said Neev exhibiting his best smile. The one that floored girls in college.

'So?'

'I thought if you could give me a chance. I have my portfolio with me.'

A moment later, the boy laughed in a demeaning way.

'Dude, I don't know what your problem is, but I'm no producer or anything. I was here to secure a one-minute role myself.'

'You got laid for a half-a-minute role?' Even though he said it aloud, he still couldn't believe the girl was actually doing the casting couch on him.

'It's a Shahraan Ali Bakshi movie, bro. There are people ready to give their organs for it.'

'Who was the woman?'

The boy seemed to take offence at this.

'Who the hell are you anyway? Now you get going or I'll call someone to—'

'Hey chill! I happened to hear you people have fun last night, so I thought of—'

There was a nostalgic smile on the boy's face now.

'Yeah. Her moans told me she liked my tool.'

'Is it that bad?'

The boy shot an obnoxious glance at him.

'I mean the competition.'

The boy nodded. 'Only the luckiest get the roles.'

'And the rest?'

'We call them "talented artists".'

REVA GUPTA

The best thing about the flat was that from one of her windows she could see a medium-sized billboard where Shahraan Ali Bakshi's latest film's poster was put up. It made her feel as if he was her neighbour now. Over the years, her relationship with Shahraan had gone from pure admiration to lust to love to respect, and now it was devotion. Now that she was in Mumbai, the cloth of her hope of seeing him in person once was somewhat ironed.

Reva shifted to the one-room flat with help from Vishal. He arranged for the auto rickshaw, took her bags, and even arranged most of her things. Her deliberate inclination towards Vishal was an investment. If it paid rich and quick dividends, she would stick to it, else she would move on. At twenty-one, Reva knew that for a girl like her—with curves that qualified her as any man's fantasy doll—it's easy to pocket a guy. The only thing she had to do was show she was interested.

'How do I get to know where the auditions are taking place? Reva asked walking into the kitchen.

'I know some casting coordinators,' Vishal said as he straightened his back on the single mattress he got for her the previous night. Reva appeared from the kitchen with a glass of water.

'Here.'

'Hey, when did you get the filter?'

'When you were out to get the mattress for me. Thanks a lot, Vishal.'

'Don't mention it.' He gulped the water and said, 'Can I ask you something. But don't mind it please.'

'Sure.' Reva sat down beside him.

'Amit told me that you have already paid the rent of this flat for eleven months. Sorry, it's not that I am prying, but did you pay for it yourself?'

'Dad did.'

'Hmm. Just out of concern; why don't you do a job first and meanwhile keep pursuing for roles in the industry?'

'But would a job leave me with enough time to run around securing roles?'

'True. Perhaps you can give it some months before deciding.'

'For how many years have you been in Mumbai, Vishal?'

'Five.'

'Five? How old are you?'

'Twenty-nine. Why?'

'Nothing. And you have been an assistant director for?'

'A year. I came here to be a star,' Vishal laughed out loud. Reva realized his laughter cocooned a pain so unsorted that she didn't dare to stick to the subject anymore. She wondered why she was entertaining a guy who, as she learnt in the last few days, didn't like girls smoking, drinking, coming home late, or wearing revealing, western outfits. She sighed realizing it was all for her own sake. The only thing she had learnt before coming to Mumbai was that one can't realize one's dream and be human at the same time.

'This Wednesday, I am supposed to meet someone,' Reva said softly.

'Who?'

'I know this Raghu sir from NSD who has acted in some serials and has done a few movie appearances as well. Raghu Janardan?'

Vishal gave her an I-have-no-clue shrug.

'Anyway, so he is a good friend of Arushi Sachdeva. She is a casting director of a leading production house here. You know her?'

'Not really. But it's nice to know you've come to Mumbai with an appointment. And I thought I was the one who would set you up for something.'

Vishal's hurt was evident. *Three days he has known me and look at him*, she thought. She had read him right. Vishal loved to own his women. But at this point, she had to behave like she was indeed owned.

'Come on. It's just an appointment. Okay, let me promise that when I become a star, I'll do your film for free. I'm sure you'll be a director by that time.' She gave him an enduring smile. This was her future investment. In case the present investment didn't bring immediate returns who knows, when the future one might come in handy.

The production house was on the fourth floor of a tall building in Versova. After passing three uniformed security guards, one had to push open a thick glass door to arrive at the reception.

'I have an appointment with Arushi Sachdeva.'

'Your name?'

'Reva Gupta.'

'One second.' The receptionist picked up the intercom,

punched a double digit and spoke, 'Ma'am, Reva Gupta is here. Certainly.'

She kept the receiver down and said, 'Please wait there.'

'Thanks.'

Reva turned and saw a guy already occupying half the couch. He had long curly hair, was clean shaven, and judging by the fit of his clothes, she knew he had a good physique.

'Excuse me,' Reva said.

The guy looked at her and said, 'Yes?'

'I too have to sit here.'

'So sit down. Why are you asking me?'

Who the fuck is this shit?

'I'll need more space,' said Reva, still clutching onto her manners.

The guy leaned and threw an obscene glance at her hips.

'Just perfect.'

'What do you mean?'

'You'll sit perfectly in this space is what I mean.'

Asshole! An irritated Reva muttered and preferred to stand.

The minutes that followed, Reva tried to calm down and return to her normal, confident self. Come what may, she couldn't afford to let this opportunity go. Raghu Sir had told her that if Arushi took a liking to her then she could arrange some roles for her. *Not the leading ones*, she imagined, *but not bad ones either*. She took out her small mirror and a small brush and gave her face a retouching. The next instant, she saw the guy who was sitting next to her a while ago being pushed out by the security guard. He was hurling abuses at him but the guard didn't care. For a moment Reva was scared. And then she smiled when the guy glanced at her. It was her opportunity. She showed her nicely manicured, lavender-painted middle finger to him.

'You are next, girl,' Reva heard the receptionist say.

She took a deep breath and stood up. Something told her this was her moment. She could feel her instinct whisper to her that she would be the first outsider who would make it big without much of a struggle. She entered the thick glass door.

Fifteen minutes later, Reva came out—her eyes red and glistening with tears. She had met with her worst humiliation inside.

NEEV DIXIT

Mohit located the hotel with help from the security guard of his colony. He apologized for his absence, but Neev's arrogant self couldn't take it. Unable to convince Neev that he was really sorry, Mohit left. A day later when outside food caused him diarrhoea, emptying him of body salt and arrogance, Neev found himself in Navi Mumbai once again.

'You said you don't need me,' Mohit mocked.

'I am sorry. Now move—'

He ran inside and locked himself in the toilet. It was only three to four days later that he could converse with someone without excusing himself in between to go relieve himself.

'So what's the plan?' Mohit said.

'This is my plan,' Neev was looking at a piece of paper.

'Tissue paper? You said you are okay now!'

'This has the name and address of the person who slept with a woman with connections. All I need is the woman's name.'

'What the fuck! How did you get the guy's name?'

'They were fucking in the other room where I was staying. I got the guy's name there. Sanjay. Fifty rupees and the guard at his place gave me his surname. Chopra.'

'But the address?'

'I followed him from the hotel to his place in Malad.'

'Unbelievable!'

'He scared me actually with all the talks about competition and all that. It's like everyone comes here like a pumped-up rockstar tyre and one day at a time, Mumbai empties him of the air.'

'And you want to get to the woman, sleep with her like this Sanjay dude did, and get a role. Is that it?'

'Pretty much,' he winked.

To reach the woman, Neev had to wait for six more days. Every morning, he used to wait near Sanjay's apartment and follow him around. On the sixth day he saw him enter a production house and, at lunch, come out with a woman. The moment he heard her voice, sitting behind them in a restaurant, he knew he had got his target. It took one hundred rupees this time to know her name: Arushi Sachdeva. She had her own casting agency – Right Role Casting Agency—which she ran from her husband's production house itself. From advertisements to television shows to films and, as the grapevine went, to providing male and female escorts to bored housewives, curious corporate men, depressed socialites, and adventurous foreigners—everything was on offer. Neev visited her office the very next day, mentioning he was a small time television producer to make an appointment with her.

'I had a talk with Sanjay. He said you were there with him at the Gold Leaf hotel. Actually, I too am interested in acting and was—'

That was the last Neev spoke inside Arushi's office. Had her husband not been present there, she would have at least allowed Neev to finish. Unfortunately he was. Arushi made sure Neev was thrown out.

Standing by the production house, an enraged Neev did what he always did when he was angry: first break something and then eat. First he bought a plastic mug and broke it with all his power and then ordered six bananas from a roadside fruit vendor. He was already on his fourth when he saw the same girl who acted cocky in the reception come out. He noticed her stand by the iron railing demarcating the footpath and the road. In no time, she broke down into tears. People around saw her but nobody cared. Standing still, Neev wondered why he was rude to her in the first place. Perhaps he was too worked up about the meeting. *What the heck*, he thought, *it's all over now*.

With his fifth and sixth banana in hand, he crossed the road and reached her.

'Want to have a banana?'

The girl rubbed her eyes and said in a choked voice, 'Stay away from me.'

'Oh, what happened to the fire you showed me inside?'

'I don't know what her problem is! She started barking at me from the moment I entered. She abused me. Fucking bitch! She said people like me enter and leave Mumbai every second and nobody gives a damn. She didn't even hear a word I said.'

'I am afraid I should take the blame here.'

Reva shot a surreptitious glance at him.

'I screwed up her mood before you went in. I should have known one shouldn't mention a woman's flings in front of her husband. But how would I know that faggot was her husband?'

Reva didn't respond.

'By the way, I'm an aspiring actor and you?'

This time Reva looked up at him and said, 'Same here.'

'I understand whatever happened with us,' Neev paused as he got a piercing glance from Reva, 'especially with you...is inhuman. But then let me tell you we aren't the only ones with whom this has happened.'

'Keep the philosophical shit to yourself. Maybe you have come across failures often. I haven't!'

'Oh, don't you go by my outer appearance. I'm hurt too. I eat a lot when I'm hurt. Wanna have this banana?' He showed her the last one with him.

Anxiety had made Reva skip her breakfast and now it was two in the afternoon. The sight of the banana made her realize her hunger. She snatched it. Half of it was gone at one go. Her cuteness while doing so amused Neev.

'What?' She quickly took out her mirror and saw herself in the mirror with half the banana stuffed in her mouth and dried tear marks on her cheeks. She looked at Neev who by now was having a tough time controlling his laughter. Reva laughed out.

'By the way, I'm Neev Dixit.'

'Reva Gupta. NSD graduate,' she said.

'Oh! That means you are a good actor.'

'A theatre actor. I believe movie acting is different.'

For lack of knowledge, Neev preferred not to turn the statement into an argument. For him, acting was acting. Theatre or movies—it did not matter.

Uninvited, he accompanied her to a nearest pav bhaji centre. Standing by a wooden counter they were served few soft pavs with some hot bhaji.

'Why acting?' Reva asked.

'Hailing from a middle-class family, money is the only ugly thing I find sexy.'

Reva was impressed to know the same snobbish asshole who deserved her middle finger an hour ago, had a pragmatic mind. Along with a raw appeal about him as well, she noticed.

'I started lusting for emotional power over others. Something which will make people listen to me and only me.

In a way I believe acting would take care of these weaknesses for me. Of course, I love it too.'

'Hmm. You can eat the last pav. I'm done.'

'Thanks.' said Neev finishing off the food on her plate. 'What about you? Why acting? Why films?'

'Acting is in my blood. My dad is a thespian. But cinema turns me on more than theatre.'

'Nice.'

Soon Neev was done as well.

'Sorry, I didn't get you before. Why were you here actually?' asked Reva.

'I was here because shortcuts are tempting when a dream is big. Let me give you my friend Mohit's number. It'll be good to be in touch with a fellow actor.'

Neev took a napkin and was looking for a pen when Reva gave him her lipstick to write.

'I guess the mobile phones people are talking about these days would be a boon for communication.'

Neev smiled affirmatively and asked, 'I was curious to know if you have any seniors from NSD here?'

'I don't really know many.' Her best senior contact was Amjad. And he had made sure nobody helped her.

'Okay. What shall be your next step?'

Vishal's face flashed in front of Reva.

'I don't know,' she lied.

REVA GUPTA

Time became a restless kid for Reva. From the time she shifted to the rented flat, she hardly got time to do what she wanted. One minor work triggered a series of other essential works. The result was that from the last four months she didn't even get a chance to watch one single film at the theatre. Apart from the one film starring Shahraan. And even if she wanted to go out and have fun, there was nobody she could go with. Vishal was away for an outdoor shoot in Kerala. Being alone in a big city, she felt someone was peeling her sanity off each day. There were times when she talked with herself; speaking aloud the monologues she recollected from her NSD days. And cried. And laughed. And stared at the empty night sky with Vodka by her side and a cigarette between her fingers. Though Vishal's shoulder was there to lean on when he was in town, she didn't want him for her emotional support yet. Guys like Vishal, she knew, wouldn't be able to handle it. If she verbalized or even projected the emotionally vulnerable side of hers, he would assume himself to be her savior. Professionally, Vishal did help by informing her about certain auditions for all kinds of roles in films, advertisements, and television, but nothing bore any fruit. In most of the auditions, Reva was appalled to see fifteen- to nineteen-year-olds—with bony structures, wearing padded bras, and accompanied by their parents—secure the roles simply because they were younger and leaner. Frustrated one night, she went to a PCO and dialled Sheetal's number.

'Hey, what's up?'

'Nothing! You say.'

'Loads up. I am no more into acting. I'm going be a housewife soon.'

'What the fuck happened?'

'Dad had this friend of his who wanted to get his son married to a decent, well cultured, perhaps a virgin bride. And you know how well I fit the profile.'

'Sure slut, I do.'

There was a momentary giggle.

'He takes me to all the sexy, posh places. It's fucking awesome. I think every Indian girl should marry a rich guy. And even if I don't accompany him on his foreign trips, I'll have his credit cards for company. Anyway, what's up with you, bitch? Hello?'

Reva cut the line. She felt her organs converging at the centre of her body creating space for jealousy. She drank her heart out that night.

She woke up the following afternoon with a throbbing headache. Lying on her mattress, she switched on the television. She casually kept changing the channels till the local cable channel came on. It was showcasing Shahraan's debut film—the one that triggered his journey into superstardom. She wondered how Shahraan who came from a small town made it big here. Being here she wondered: Forget about stardom, even if she bags some decent roles that would be a lifetime achievement. She happened to glance at the ad-scroller which ran left to right with numerous colourful advertisements ranging from how to improve on one's sex life to a Kaamdhenu Babaji to a mosquito repellant to...Reva eyes were momentarily fixed on it: Lalwani Jewellers wanted a model for their jewellery advertisement. Only a contact number was given.

Fifteen minutes later, she was in a PCO talking to a man who asked her to bring her portfolio to their office. Reva came home, showered, did a bit of make-up, picked up her portfolio she had made in Delhi, and scampered out. She couldn't care less about the headache now. Twenty minutes later, she reached the desired office.

It was a small still-photo studio. The man looked at Reva's portfolio with a mix of interest, lust, and appreciation.

'It's good. I think you'll do great. Here's the offer. We'll give you three thousand rupees, shooting will take place at the jeweller's shop itself, make-up and clothes will be yours, and the jewellery you'll wear will be provided by the jeweller of course. Shooting will happen this Sunday, at three in the afternoon sharp. Is that okay?'

That's fucking awesome! she thought. 'Yes,' she said.

'You'll be paid in cash on Sunday itself.'

When the initial excitement wore itself off, Reva realized nothing worth telling had actually happened. The advertisement would probably be viewed by people like her who had nothing to do except watching movies on the local cable. The insignificance of it started weighing on her.

She had no idea what this 'insignificant' Lalwani jeweller's advertisement would do to her career.

And how!

NEEV DIXIT

With Mohit's family returning from Surat, he was forced to share his room with Neev while his younger sister shared it with her parents. They adjusted hoping Neev would shift soon to another place. But five months later, he was still with them.

The wait for good, substantial roles went on for a few months, till one day Mohit took an important call for Neev when he was out.

'Arushi Sachdeva wants to meet you this Wednesday.'

Neev had never mentioned to Mohit what actually had happened in Sachdeva's office. This time he did.

'Buddy,' Mohit responded, 'beggars can't be choosers.'

Neev agreed. Perhaps one of his photographs with his contact info had reached Arushi as well. It could mean his photographs were circulating and that definitely was good news.

The only thing that had changed in the last few months was Arushi's office address. The guard at the older address gave him the new address with the accompanying news that she no longer worked with her husband. Neev prayed it wasn't because of him.

The new office was a modest one and lots of wooden work was going on at different corners. There were a total of five employees sitting outside Arushi's cabin. Next he noticed Arushi from inside a glass cabin, gesturing him to come in. He did.

'Neev Dixit?'

'Good afternoon, Ma'am. I am really sorry for that day.'

'For the records, my husband and I have filed for divorce. So thank you very much.'

Neev didn't know what to say. He stood still.

'Anyway! I have this supporting actor's role for an action movie. I think you fit the bill.'

The words sounded like music to Neev.

'Your character is of a male stripper and the producer wants to audition you and a few others at her place tomorrow night. Are you on?'

'Male stripper?'

'Yes or no?'

'Yes, of course.'

In order to prepare for the audition, Neev went to a cyber café and saw some pictures of male strippers on the internet. He could see himself thrusting his pelvis in his jockey underpants. With his long curly hair, sharp features, and a toned body, he hoped of bagging the part.

Neev was on time in Gulmohar Villa in Napian Sea road. As a servant welcomed him into the main room, he saw two more guys already sitting on the couch. *My competitors*, Neev eyed them well. *No match!*

As Neev sat down, some loud, peppy music started playing. A few flimsy lights came on next from the four corners. An atrociously fat woman came out from the bedroom, clapping for no reason.

'Come on, boys. Hit the stage.'

Neev was hesitant at first, but seeing the other two lead,

he summoned all his confidence. There was a raised wooden platform at one end of the huge hall where they took their position. One minute later, it seemed to Neev as if the other two had been stripping all their life. As the music started to pump up, some more excessively obese women, in uber party mood, came out with drinks and cigarettes in their hands. Few threw money at the guys while a couple of others came close to them and slapped their butt. Neev's hesitance made him an unwilling centre of attraction. They eventually forced him out of his t-shirt and jeans.

That night while returning home in a lonely train, Neev realized, he had been raped in the most corporate manner possible. Arushi Sachdeva had taken the revenge of her divorce.

For the next one month, Neev didn't see a mirror. The debilitation that incident had subjected him to, convinced him he wouldn't rise ever. He wanted to kill Arushi and the other women but he knew it was only wishful. Every morning, he headed toward Marine Drive, sat there till late night, and then returned home. He avoided the gym and lost seven kilos in a couple of months. Over phone, he lied to his parents that he was making headway in the industry and looking forward to all the goodness he was born for. He wasn't sure if doing so, he was cheating his parents, or worse, himself. Soon the same sense of insignificance he encountered as a teenager engulfed and brutalized his core.

Mohit recommended a change of place and suggested he should either live alone or with a partner with similar tastes. Neev agreed to the former. A few months later, one of Mohit's friends helped him get a small flat in Goregaon.

The night he helped Neev to shift to the new pad, Mohit decided to stay on. They were not versed with the water timing and hence decided to knock their neighbour's door for some water.

There were three other flats in the corridor. The first one was locked, nobody answered at the second, while someone seemed to be dragging furniture inside the third flat but didn't answer the calling bell. Neev was about to turn his back when someone opened the door.

'Yes?'

'Mother of god!' Neev exclaimed. 'The Lalwani jeweller's girl.'

From the twitch in the girl's eyebrows, it was obvious she was trying to remember.

'Who is it, Reva?' Vishal appeared behind her.

REVA GUPTA

It had been three months since Reva shot for the Lalwani jewellers. But what happened thereafter remained the most popular tea-time gossip among Mumbaikars for months to come.

It was a Sunday when Reva shot for the Lalwani jewellers. They had hired a private security team to supervise the entire shooting since they were using real and their best designed gold and diamond jewellery for the shoot. Once done, Reva was duly given three thousand rupees in cash. Repeated failures had taught her to find joy in small things else there wouldn't be much happiness to talk about in life. It was the next day when the police arrived at her flat for interrogation that she came to know what had happened.

One of the security guards from the private security firm had held the others at gun point and fled with all the jewellery minutes after Reva had left. The fact which turned this small piece of news into an intra-state matter was the security guard had shot one customer—a girl of sixteen years—who was the granddaughter of the leader of opposition of the state. And

Reva's promotional video was the only source for the police to identify the thieves. News channels—first the regional, then some of the national ones—started tracking the incident while showing the promotional video again and again and again, till one young producer venturing into television realized this was the face he wanted for his low profile, debut kid's game-show host. He contacted Reva and soon she had something to look forward to from nine to four every day.

Vishal, a tad down on spirits, was over to visit her when the door bell rang.

'Whom do you want?' said Vishal standing behind Reva.

'Reva Gupta? This is Neev,' he tried a smile. He was sure the loss in weight had confused her.

'Neev Dixit? Oh my God, what happened to you?'

'Life!' he said and laughed alone.

'What do you mean? And please come in. What are you doing here?'

The banter lasted for an hour and a half. There was a spark between Reva and Neev which disturbed Vishal because he was yet to see it between Reva and him. And now this guy would live next to her as well. He felt he clearly had no place in their conversation and went back into the room. He felt empty within. Once Neev left for his flat with a bucket of water, Vishal asked, 'Am I just a friend, Reva?'

Reva sighed wondering why this dreaded conversation had to come so soon.

'Of course we are good friends,' she intentionally feigned innocence.

'I love you, Reva,' said Vishal sounding serious.

'I know.'

'And?'

'I don't know.'

'Do you like Neev?'

He suddenly sounded like those brain-between-legs assholes she had met all her life in Delhi.

'I don't even know him, dude.'

'I'm sorry. But don't worry, I won't force you because for that, I'll have to be honest.'

'Honest about what, Vishal?' Reva's interest was suddenly piqued.

Vishal stared silently at the floor for some time and then, covering his face with his hands, he started wailing like a child.

'What's the matter, Vishal?'

'I'm a failure, Reva,' he blabbered in between his short breaths. 'I came to Mumbai to become an actor, but I still am nothing.'

'But you are an AD for chrissake!'

'I lied to you. I lied to everyone. I work the day shift at a call centre to sustain my life. I was an AD for a week, years back, but I simply couldn't take the kind of shit treatment my director gave me. I complained. It became an argument and I was thrown out. With his connections, he made sure I was never entertained anywhere in the industry. I did try. I tried a lot, damn it! The people I sent you to were the ones who were struggling with me and now have become first AD, with famous directors by licking their asses. I couldn't do that'.

Reva only sat still. A minute later, he rubbed his eyes saying, 'Instead of outdoor shooting, I actually went to my hometown—Palakkad. Mom has tuberculosis so I have decided to shift there permanently. I can't bear this lie of a life anymore.' A few silent minutes later he asked, 'Will you mind if I don't meet you ever again?'

Reva didn't reply. Vishal didn't wait.

As she sat on the floor, Reva felt bad for Vishal because it could have easily been her story. Whatever good happened in her career till now was because of serendipity. Was it only serendipity that took one up amid the clouds? How many of those 'by-chance' events have been designed for her?

Wondering about Vishal again, she knew he loved her, but she only cared for him like a person cares for a new dress. She felt weak and cheap. With Amjad, she'd used love to secure the good roles in college plays and further understand the nuances of acting. With Vishal, she only had to churn out some decent contact in the industry and in exchange she made him believe she could be his. Reva sighed wondering why no one had come up with any anti-thought pill yet.

Amjad...Vishal...what will the name of her next level be?

REVA AND NEEV

Even little money, when one earns it for the first time, feels like one has made a difference somewhere in the whole celestial set up. Reva received her first payment after three months of the first telecast of the children's game show. She gifted herself a mobile phone and took Neev out to dinner.

A total of three months had passed by since they became neighbours. And it was enough time for Reva to understand Neev was basically a kid who could one second inspire awe by stating something profound and the next second be fastidious for the silliest of reasons. If one day she saw him down with frustration about his incapability of earning a penny since his year-long arrival in Mumbai, then next week she also saw him borrow money from his father for a mobile phone. Once seeing Reva arguing with an auto driver who charged her extra money, he had pacified the situation by paying the auto driver from his pocket. A week later, Neev was at her doorstep for medicine since he had injured himself while fighting with a fellow passenger who had pushed him while boarding the local train. At times he was overprotective about her and sometimes he was awfully careless. Though Reva made other contacts during her shoots, everyone on the set remained too busy to show concern for anyone unless pushed by some personal need.

The game show somewhere had calmed Reva's desperation for films since it gave her something secure to hold on to. Risk excites passion as much as security allows it to settle. Her plans had suddenly changed. She thought of continuing with television, allowing her bank account to gain weight till she got a chance in the movies. It was Neev, like Brahmins of the yore who used to show cattiness towards the lower castes, who refused to do television.

'Have you seen the standards? Master shot—reaction shot—master shot; that's it!'

'I know. But how long do you want to last on your father's money?'

'Once I start earning, I'll pay him back.'

'That's not the point, Neev.'

Television being the small screen was not the only issue Neev had. Since Reva had made her foray into television first, he wanted to do so in films. He was happy about her progress, but deep inside he was envious too. He had seen some of her episodes as a host and he knew she was good. Bloody good. And her consistency of being that good made him feel, in a way, insignificant to himself. A feeling he loathed.

Though Reva made him meet certain fellow actors, ADs, and line producers, he never followed up. He didn't want to give Reva a chance to think that even an inch of his success was because of her. He didn't hate her. Just that her good luck made his bad luck uncomfortable. The worse was he couldn't ignore her. At nights when he felt alone and depressed, it was Reva who comforted him like a burning fireplace on a chilly winter night. She had become a forbidden necessity for him.

The good thing was it was mutual. The bad thing—neither knew what to do with it since they were as much a curse for the other as they were a blessing.

In order to not beg from his father too often for his own comfort, Neev decided to take in a room partner and save on the rent. Reva was against it.

'You anyway get frustrated once a fortnight. In case the person is not of your profession, you won't be able to gel well. And if he is an actor, then your frustration might start happening once a week—if you know what I mean.'

'Shut up!'

'You know that's true.'

'I do. And that's why I'm moving in with a girl. Girls know how to manage boys.' It was supposed to be a joke. But the mention of it made Reva's heart beat faster. She had no clue why. Was she possessive about him? Were they really that close to owe each other a heart break if the other went around with someone else? The answer turned her face red in parts.

'Which girl?' She didn't want him to answer.

'Reva Gupta.' Neev's face read amusement. 'If she doesn't have a problem.' He still thought they were stretching a joke. But during the silence that followed, he thought she would slap him hard for this.

'She anyway lives with you more than she stays with herself,' Reva's statement revealing more than it hid. And Neev immediately knew it wasn't a joke anymore—their companionship.

'One, the bedroom is mine. The drawing room is yours. A girl needs a more enclosed space to live. Two, we won't bring any of our friends here; neither separate nor mutual. Three, if one drinks, the other has to drink; the same drink, the same amount, so that neither takes advantage of the other. Four, no porn here. Five, I may add other rules with time,' said Reva after Neev asked if she has anything to say about their living together.

They initially presumed Reva's landlord might have a problem with their decision since Neev was suppose to shift to her place. But the landlord only had two things to tell them: rent should come on time and no complaints anytime. Both were okay with it. When the other residents started visiting them on silliest of excuses only to know if they were married, Reva considered pasting a statutory warning on the main door stating: 'We are NOT married. Visit at your own risk.' With time, people lost interest in the forbidden space they thought constituted their live-in relationship.

On the other side, not only was the house rent shared, but the mundane household chores were also divided to their relief. Neev used the money he saved to join kick-boxing and salsa classes the following month. He realized he had to do something during the day apart from waiting impatiently for his dream to come true on its own. On weekends, they used to watch three back to back films, sponsored by Reva, and discuss its nuances while Sunday was their official booze day when they recorded their drunk selves on Reva's newly-purchased digital camera.

One night when they were drunk, their prattle took a sexual turn.

'I swear I have never seen a real girl naked in front of me. What about you?' Neev was fighting hard to stay in his senses.

'What would I see a naked girl for?' burst out Reva. She was laughing at every spoken sentence.

'I don't know when I'll see one.'

Reva looked at him and stood up. She was laughing and stripping simultaneously. And soon she was naked except for her underwear.

'There you go. Happy?'

For a moment Neev only kept staring at her and then he collapsed on the floor; asleep. The next morning, Reva deleted the video even before Neev was awake. She was embarrassed, but thankfully he didn't remember much of the night. It nevertheless made her introspect: what was their relationship? Were they in love? Why was she living with him if it wasn't love? If wanting to be near someone was love, she definitely was in love with Neev. If love was about sharing the defining side of one to the other without being afraid of any judgment, she was again in love with him. But if love was about living a life together, then she was clueless. Sometimes, Neev's presence bored her. She didn't take him for granted but often he left her with no choice. It was scary. She never confessed it to him in case he felt hurt. But she had started nurturing a feeling that she wouldn't mind another guy. The reason was not to have a fling outside what she shared with Neev but to erase the boredom she felt while with Neev. Being with someone else, she believed, would make her miss him. And her connection with him would forever remain young. Or was it the philanderer inside her giving excuses? Deciding on one concrete choice seemed complex, but then Reva Gupta was always a paragon of complexity.

Almost three years had passed since Reva's arrival in Mumbai. The game show had ended six months back and her producer, Akhil Nath, had already started the pre-production for his next project. She could have taken up another serial in the meantime, but she'd saved enough for her to take it easy till Akhil started his next. Meanwhile, the kind of roles she was offered in film auditions had a screen time of three to ten minutes maximum. After being a bit of a known face in television, she wanted more meat in her roles and preferred patience to desperation. Though there were instances of production assistants and some ADs indirectly offering her a short cut which went via someone's bedroom. But that, at best, was the last resort. If at all!

Neev, meanwhile, had joined his Salsa teacher as an assistant. It didn't leave him time to chalk out a plan for his numb film career, even though it did give him a constant earning. And girls. The Salsa class had all kinds of insanely hot girls as students. A few asked Neev out directly while some waited for him to take the first step after dropping enough hints. By the fifteen months of his role as a dance assistant, he had dated close to eleven girls. Nobody was interested in any prolonged affair. Since life was short, they wanted to keep the affairs shorter. It triggered a polygamous instinct in Neev which he never knew existed. Though he wasn't in any declared relationship with Reva, yet there was a sharp guilt lurking in the shadow of his lust for others. Reva could tell there was a presence of a third person in the flat whenever she was back from work: two coffee mugs in the kitchen sink, one plate but two forks to wash, Neev's crumbled mattress and once a used condom in the dustbin as well. She never complained, hoping he would at least have the courage to inform her himself he was done with her. She didn't want to behave like some love-struck teenage doll. If a girl makes a guy realize he has the capacity to disturb her in any way, he will then stop at nothing.

One evening, Neev came home with Ahana. They were busy undressing in the drawing room when they heard Reva speak aloud from outside, 'Hey dear, I came early. Not feeling well today.' Seconds later she was in the drawing room. Disgust engulfed her.

'Are we having a threesome?' asked Ahana. Reva dashed to her room. Neev got up and quickly donned his clothes when he saw a harried looking Reva marching towards the main door. It was the insult wrapped in the shock she got seeing him with a girl that angered her.

'Reva listen, please, where are you going?'

'None of your fucking business.'

Reva went straight to a pub and drank till she threw up. But still the anger remained. When she saw a young guy glancing at her from a corner, the anger uncorked a bottle of sexual rage within her. Ten minutes later, she was getting her brains fucked out in the male washroom as if by destroying her purity for Neev she was punishing him after all. This was necessary, she coaxed her after-casual-sex guilt, to keep her from drowning into the lake of sorrow that an attachment often throws one into. Now Neev and she were equal in terms of betrayal; no heartache. She knew she had destroyed something within her in the washroom. But then what else is love's business if not to destroy what you thought you would own all your life?

She came home at three.

'Where the hell have you been? I have been calling your number for the last seven hours,' asked an enraged Neev.

'I was getting fucked just like you,' she laughed with a sense of Pyrrhic victory.

'You are such a whore.'

'Trust me, you are no better, you man whore!'

Enraged, Neev impulsively slapped her. Her jaw dropped in disbelief. She pushed him in and, sitting by his mattress, started sobbing.

'We are not in a relationship that I need to justify my acts,' he said, knowing well enough he was bullshitting himself.

'Then why did you stop in the evening? You should have continued fucking her. Don't tell me you felt ashamed!'

'I thought you'll be hurt.'

'Hurt? Me? How?'

'How? Then why did you react in this stupid manner?'

'Really? Stupid?' She hurled her mobile phone towards him. He ducked and it crashed on the wall.

'You are an asshole,' she declared.

'And you decided to stay with me. Now what does that make you?'

Reva stood up, went to him, caught his hair hard and standing on her toes, took his lip between her teeth and bit it hard.

'If you still don't get why I chose to stay with you, then keep fucking that bitch. And every other bitch in the world,' said Reva and locked herself in the bedroom.

One hour later, Neev picked up her phone which had crashed on the wall and assembled the pieces to realize it was still working. He placed it at the bedroom's doorstep along with his stereo playing Whitney Houston's 'I'll Always Love You' and left after a knock. A minute later, the bedroom door opened and the phone was taken in.

I am sorry. Neev's message read.

This never happened. Reva replied almost instantly.

Are we in love with each other?

If we are, we are.

Okay.

A minute later Neev messaged again.

Did you really get fucked tonight?

No. Reva lied.

Thanks.

Why do you ask?

I knew my girl isn't a bitch.

Reva didn't reply but realized men refer to a different dictionary when a woman does things they take pride in doing.

The next morning, Neev saw Reva take out a pain-relief ointment from the first-aid box kept atop the refrigerator and move in to her room. He followed her and noticed she was trying to apply it on her neck but wasn't able to do so. When he knocked, Reva reacted with a silent glance. It emboldened him to come up and sit behind her.

The whole flat was consumed in a haunting silence. Without a word, she gave the ointment to him. He took it and started massaging her neck, alternating between slow and hard presses on her muscles. She tugged her top down her shoulders slightly. The next moment, it was torn from behind. The fact that she wasn't wearing a bra was now a shared secret. What followed was an intense love-making ordeal, where their naked bodies seemed like instruments that made the amorous sounds within them distinct. They had heard the cliché—love happens once in life, but devouring each other under the morning sunlight taught them the opposite that life happens once in love. In that moment, they understood what they were and what all they could never be. They stopped around lunch time. The silence after seemed relaxing, for it wasn't concrete, wasn't direct. Both were ready to say 'I love you *too*' but neither wanted to say 'I love you' first.

In the evening, Neev had his Salsa class. Reva got up, took a shower, ate and was about to open her purse for her eyeliner, when she came across a slip of paper. Only a mobile phone number was written on one side. Reva crumbled it and threw it in the dustbin. Seconds later she picked it up, happy she didn't tear it. Meanwhile, the moment Neev stepped inside the Salsa class, he went straight to Ahana and gave her a tight hug.

Being in a more clear relationship, with time, made them verbalize their opinions on whatever the other did. Good, bad, or ugly was mood and security dependent. If she wore a mini skirt or a hot pant, he would inform her that her legs looked too fleshy. If he had a deodorant which was mesmerizing, Reva would never recommend it to him. If red suited Reva, Neev intentionally asked her to wear green feigning better appreciation. If Neev looked the best with his long curly hair, she made it a point he got it straightened. The entire pretentious attitude was because they never wanted to lose the other to someone else. As if agreeing to be in a relationship had suddenly given them the right to put their emotional canines on their individuality. They didn't trust the other because they saw the other through the spectacle of their own flaw. They were possessive, protective about the other, but at the same time craved for some space for themselves. Neev's insecurity reached an all-time high when he pasted a picture of his face on a small, topless poster of Shahraan by Reva's bed.

'Isn't it better?' Neev said.

'Fuck off, darling!' she ripped off his picture and smiled at Shahraan's.

A few months later, Neev's film career finally saw a glimpse of dawn. He met Suparna, an aspiring actress herself, in his Salsa class. As Neev and Suparna got to know each other, they realized they had a common wound: both needed a break. Sometime during the third month, they slept together. Post coitus, as a prize to Neev's expertise on bed, she confessed she had signed a Bhojpuri film as the lead. She said the producer was looking for a male lead and she could recommend Neev to him.

Back in their apartment, when Neev told her what he had signed up for, Reva seemed shell shocked.

'Do you even know Bhojpuri?'

'My voice will be dubbed.'

'Listen Neev, just cancel this contract. You have waited so long. Can't you wait for some more time? You are good. You'll have your opportunities.'

'This is my opportunity, Reva. I know it's a Bhojpuri film, but it's a film nevertheless.'

'What's the movie called?'

'*Tarzan Lautath Ba* or something. It means Tarzan returns. It's an emotional father-son story.'

Reva kept looking at him and then chuckled indecently. Seeing her laugh made Neev mad.

'Why don't you say you are plain jealous that I cracked the film thing before you did.'

Reva's chuckle went missing in a trice.

'I can't believe you said that.'

'I'm sharing my joy with you and look at you! You don't have any film experience anyway. So why don't you keep your opinion to yourself for a change.'

Reva stood up and faced him.

'Shut up and listen. I haven't done any films till now not because I haven't got any offers like you, but because I'm smart enough to know which ones to let go and patient enough to wait for the roles made for me. Moreover, you know how the offer for girls comes with a hidden offer.'

'Roles made for you? Who are you? Fucking Marilyn Monroe?'

'Ha, ha, ha! Neev has such a nice sense of humour! Happy?' Crossed, she went to the kitchen. The more she wanted to get this guy, the more churlish he behaved. She knew he was making a blunder and yet he would not give her perspective a chance.

She scrolled down the names list in her phone. She had to call someone to talk about nothing in particular. Her thoughts paused till she reached a name: 'Raima'. The fake name was to spare Neev from reaching any undesirable conclusions which he seemed to have a real talent for. She messaged:

Are you free tonight?

Going by the diversity he gave her every time they met, she thought he was India on bed. They only knew each other by their moans. They never saw each other or even tried to know the other's identity. Even the first night they made out in the washroom, Reva was too drunk to remember him. In the past eight months, they had copulated three times. Either she booked the hotel or he did. They connected through messages and once in the hotel room, they intentionally kept the light off and eyes blindfolded. It was an undecided but affirmed agreement.

For Reva, the sessions were an escape from the quandaries her relationship with Neev put her into. During one such session she also understood why artists, like her, were incorrigible philanderers. They are a rare awakened-mind-in-an-aroused-body species, inherently more aware of their inner dimensions than a normal person. And no matter how much those dimensions crave, it's impossible to find the magical compliments of those dimensions in one single person.

The fuck sessions were a cheap, hence easy, way to replenish herself to face Neev again. Moving away from him was out of question because a space within her thirsted for him, irrespective of his faults. Conditions of love and consequences of sex—both in the end were necessary evils. There were times when she wanted to tell Neev about the mystery man because it would have made him suffer and in that suffering he would have understood her worth. But her courage gave way because confession was a double-edged sword: it could destroy as ruthlessly as it could build spontaneously.

The physical roof under which they stayed was still the same, but the emotional roof under which they connected suffered. Reva accepted a mythological serial while simultaneously also doing auditions for advertisements arranged for her by an elderly casting co-coordinator, Vinod ji, with whom she had developed a good working relationship over time.

Neev was busy building his chemistry with Suparna as per the producer's wish. Finally, the outdoor leg of the film's shooting commenced. With Neev gone, Reva decided to visit her father in Delhi. She was welcomed with a series of smiles and waves of hands in her neighborhood. The recognition was her first taste of a spoonful of stardom. She also caught up with her old friend Sheetal who was now a mother. Sometimes others' achievement reflects one's own void in life. As Sheetal excitedly talked about how marriage and motherhood changed her, Reva seemed lost. Was it okay to cry because what Sheetal had already gained was what a person actually lives for; a family? Or, should she be happy Sheetal couldn't gain what she had; recognition? She knew how unfit a family man Neev would be. Some kites should simply be left alone and their movement admired from a distance. Neev was one such kite. She was another.

Once home, she slept straight for eighteen hours. She got up feeling sick to get a call from Vinod ji.

'Beta, this time it's a big advertisement.'

When she heard why it was a big one, all her sickness flew right out of the window.

The next morning, Reva flew to Mumbai. She went straight to Siddhivinayak temple in Dadar after landing, prayed hard, and refused to move out until the women security personnel pulled her out. It was for the first time she had gone to any religious place in her life. Back in her apartment, she was flipping the newspaper when her eyes went to the daily prediction section: *the next five days will be bad*... And she didn't read the rest. To numb her mind, she plugged on her iPod and played all her favourite Whitney, Avril, Rihanna, and Britney numbers. On the second day, Vinod ji rang her again

'I have got a connection.'

'Oh, Vinod ji. Please, make it happen. Please!'

'I'm trying hard, beta.'

Three days later, she got a confirmation mail for the advertisement. A bit of recommendation and a lot of her good past work was behind it. A draft contract was attached for which she had to reply ASAP. But how could she? Reva was in heaven reading the mail since it stated she would do the ad-film with the endorser of the watch brand: Shahraan Ali Bakshi. And life after the allegorical death seemed so underrated.

There was a constant buzz on the sets were the advertisement was to be shot, till it was reported Shahraan was arriving in a few minutes. People calmed down while Reva, who was in the make shift make-up room, felt her limbs go numb. An AD came running in to confirm if she was ready.

'I am.' Her entire body was shaking.

Outside, the director—Sanjiv Advani—came to her.

'I know you have a television background. But right now, forget melodrama. I want you to be as subtle as possible.'

'Sure.'

They were supposed to shoot in front of a green screen which would be substituted with some African scenery later during post production.

Finally Shahraan entered wearing a camouflage shirt and trousers with hunter boots and a tactic vest look alike.

'Everything set?' he asked. There were five nods. Shahraan noticed only the director's.

'Where is the girl?'

Reva was emotionally high, sexually aroused, and spiritually confused—all at the same time.

'There. Reva Gupta,' said the director introducing her to him.

'I am Shahraan Ali Bakshi. Nice to meet you,' he offered his right hand. The handshake felt warm and protective.

'God, you are cold!'

'Yeah,' Reva managed a stupid smile.

'Just calm down. I am sure this ad is more important for you and your career than meeting me.'

How easily he'd said the truth. Her senses were finally anchored.

Everything was approved in the third take itself. A moment after the pack up, Shahraan came up to her and said, 'Where are the red and golden earrings you were wearing in your photographs?'

For a moment she didn't know what he was talking about. Then she did.

'Those are my mother's. They are at my place. Why what's wrong?'

'Those earrings got you here,' he smiled and went away. As Reva stood there, uncertain if he was joking or not, a man came running to her.

'Reva Ma'am?'

'Yeah.'

'Shahraan sir wants your number. Could you please write it here.' He gave her a slip of paper and a Mont Blanc pen.

What the heck is happening? Reva's hands shuddered as she wrote her name and mobile number. The man scampered off.

'This did not happen. THIS did not happen!' The first time she said it in her mind. The second time she said it aloud. Vinod ji, who was himself present during the shoot for Reva's sake, came to her smiling.

'What are you mumbling?'

'I said the man didn't take my number on Shahraan sir's behest.'

'Of course he did. Have you gone mad?'

Once home, she called Neev. Nobody picked up after two full rings. She messaged him instead.

I met and shot with Shahraan Ai Bakshi!!!!

He replied after an hour.

Really??? (Sorry was shooting so couldn't pick up)

Yes, yes, yes!!

He is twenty years older to you.

Shut up, jealous.

On the following weekend, Reva got a call from an unknown number. It was Shahraan's secretary.

'Sir wants to meet you.'

'Me?' Reva was immediately apologetic for the way she must have sounded.

'Yes. Are you free tomorrow night at nine?'

'Am I free?'

'I am asking you.'

'Yes I am free. Why?'

'I told you sir wants to meet you. Could you meet me near the entrance of Hyatt? I'll pick you up from there.'

'Okay.'

The line was cut. *Tomorrow night at nine near the Hyatt entrance*. She kept repeating softly under her breath and then suddenly shouted at the top of her voice, 'Tomorrow night at nine near Hyatt!'

She bought for herself a black ruched LBD, matching lingerie, a clutch, a tiny diamond pendant, and matching heels.

Reva was on time. As soon as she got down from the hired cab, she saw a black Mercedes standing by the Hyatt hotel's entrance. A man waved at her. She recognized Krishna—Shahraan's secretary. She got in and the chauffeur wasted no time to hit the road. He parked at a corner by Nariman Point.

First she saw a panipuri wallah. Then she saw the man standing beside him wearing a cap, black track trousers, and a tight turquoise-coloured t-shirt. It had a signature on its chest which she knew dearly. The clothing line was in the name of Shahraan. Realizing he was dressed in casuals, she hoped he wouldn't mind her dressed-for-party attire. Seeing Reva step out of the car, he came up to her and said, 'Hope you didn't have any problem?'

'None at all.' It was then she realized he was sporting a fake beard and a moustache too.

Shahraan smiled reading her confusion. 'Without this, I won't be able to walk with you here. Come,' he gestured as if requesting her to lead. She did and they started walking alongside the cemented barricade lining the Marine Drive. To their left were couples lost in their own world and to the right there was steady traffic.

'I am sorry to have dressed wrong. I thought—'

'Not your fault. Anyone would have dressed like this. But we wouldn't have met here if you were just anyone.'

That was the first clue for Reva to understand it was a dream. She sighed, preparing herself to wake up soon. She was not walking with the legend himself. No way!

'You look beautiful with those earrings.'

'Thanks. If you don't mind—what is it about them?'

'They remind me of someone. They were a rage some twenty years ago. And I'd gifted them to someone with my first income.'

'Your mother?'

Shahraan nodded negative.

'The prostitute?'

Shahraan threw a curt glance at her. She realized it came out rude.

'I'm sorry, I didn't mean it that way. Anyway, she was a lucky girl.'

'Why?'

'I don't think anyone would ever love me so much to remember my birthday, even after I'm gone like twenty years.'

'Would you do that for someone?'

'I don't know,' she smiled compulsively. 'It sounds beyond my emotional capacity.'

'So I thought too. Then of course I fell in love with her.'

'Sorry for being personal, but what actually changed you; her arrival in your life or her departure?'

'Her departure changed my priorities.' A silence after, Shahraan continued, 'Her arrival helped me to discover myself. As life went on, I realized how important those discoveries were. It actually kept me going. And what else is love but a tool to dig, to discover what all you need from within you to lead a life of your choice.'

In the quietude that followed, Reva could hear her heart screaming out to her in beats.

'May I tell you something?'

'Sure.'

'Your eyes remind me of her. It's like a time machine where I want to go, but I can't.'

Reva had an instant attack of goosebumps. Until that night, she had no idea she could inspire a man like that.

'Why didn't you get married? You are like forty—'

'Six.'

'Yeah.'

'I guess I've become so used to the reactions she once had to my imperfections, my incompleteness, that I fear someone else's reaction would not be favourable enough.' A pause later he added, 'Are you married?'

'No!'

'Committed or engaged?'

'Not really.' The lie was so compulsive that it scared Reva. With those two words—not really—she had so easily disowned the last few years spent with Neev. Why? What for?

'Why do we have to tag everyone as something in our lives?' she said, swallowing a bit of her own saliva to quench the sudden dryness in her throat.

'The bottom line is, people are need based. And when you have lots of needs, you'll have to prioritize them lest they confuse you. Tagging people, I guess, helps us subconsciously prioritize our needs.'

She let the essence of it register with her. Half a minute later she said, 'Why are we here, Sir?'

'Call me Shahraan. And we are here because I haven't had pani puris in a long time.'

It sounded so cute she could have kissed him then. A smile twinkled in her face. 'When was the last time?'

'With her.'

'Twenty years! You were a cab driver then, weren't you? I mean, are these stories real?'

Shahraan laughed out.

'Let me tell you something. Its only when you are successful, people at large realize you are there, existing somewhere. But when you are super successful, people want to know you. They will treat you like an alien for, whether you agree or not, this earth is full of losers and failures. And when they want to know you, just to keep them interested—don't reveal yourself. So, maybe I was a cab driver. I'm not confessing.'

Reva smiled feeling emotionally high, sexually aroused, and spiritually confused—all at the same time. Again!

Reva initially presumed it was just a surreal one-night affair she had with him. But soon she started getting calls from Krishna requesting for some more of her time. She never found herself saying no.

One night after several such meetings had taken place over the past few months, a message appeared in her mobile phone from an unknown number.

I think I'll need you for the rest of the nights that bracket my life. Are you game? It was written Shahraan underneath. Reva only stared at the message for as long as she could. It was a Hobson's choice for her. She couldn't take the risk of rejecting his proposal outright. It was *Shahraan Ali Bakshi*, not some psycho who claimed to love her. A 'no' would undoubtedly upset him. Vishal's story flashed in front of her. Should she upset a man with connections just like that?

Accepting Shahraan as her lover would be too much for her to handle emotionally. It would invariably make her a weak and biased person. She knew she would be emotionally blind towards him. And that's suicidal for a relationship. They may have met months back, but she wished for him since her childhood.

'God help me!'

Precisely then the door bell rang. Neev was back from his outdoor shoot.

'Do you even know how many women Shahraan has slept with?' Neev asked sitting on a lazy bag sipping coffee. Reva was sitting opposite him. It was a rare instance for him to advise her. He made sure he did it rather well.

'Everybody knows why Shahraan never married. He had some true love shit with a prostitute or something. Christ, what's that even supposed to mean? It's all PR, damn it! They mess with the common people. And what never happened with Shahraan in the last twenty years, you are trying to tell me, happened after he saw you donning an old pair of earrings? I haven't heard anything more stupid than that. It's a ploy Reva to add you to his use-and-throw bedmate list.'

'But girls like me will happily sleep with him. He doesn't have to try.'

'Wow! Some lucky sonofabitch he is!'

'Watch your language, Neev. You know what he means to me.'

'Sorry. But I think it would be a mistake to say yes because it can ruin your career.'

'Or take me to greater heights.'

That sealed Neev's residual arguments. Reva got a call from Vinod ji who informed her about another audition and she went to her room to get ready. Neev knew if Reva agreed, she would invariably make it to Shahraan's good books. And then there won't be any stopping her. But he wanted to make it big before her. Not as a revenge but as a matter of fact. He had seen in her eyes love and care for him, but only till he remained subjugated to her. His secret wish was to make it big in the film industry, marry her, and thereafter burst all her ambition balloons by making her pregnant.

His Bhojpuri producer's words ricocheted in his head: '*We'll gift India its next Shahraan Ali Bakshi*.' It had given Neev an emotional hard on. Just the thought of it. The next Shahraan Ali Bakshi who would hold girls like Reva by their hair and they wouldn't complain. Money, power, and fame: the concoction can take care of every moral fibre in the world.

'I am going to take a shower first,' Reva locked herself in the bathroom. Neev stood up, went to the bedroom, and picked her mobile phone. He read Shahraan's message. His thumb shook vigorously as he pressed on the reply option and then typed:

Please don't mind this, but you disappointed me by bringing this up.

Neev felt his body temperature rise as he put his thumb on the send button.

Inside the bathroom, as cold water trickled down her naked body, unabashed and unrestrained thoughts started trickling down her mind. What happened to her smart, pragmatic self? She should have accepted Shahraan's proposal with a jig. Whom is she trying to kid? This was a once-in-a-lifetime opportunity. With one yes, she would be catapulted right up there where her dreams inspired her to be once upon a time.

But why was she even thinking about all this? Neev? Is he the reason for her introspection? Why is there this disturbance when two people in their own coordinates in your life, in their own right, demand your heart's attention?

As she came out after her shower, she saw Neev standing right outside. If fear was fever, she had one hundred and five then and there.

'I tried but couldn't fuck your relation with that bugger. I couldn't send a simple SMS! You know why? I love you. So finally, I say it. I love you, Reva.' He scurried out of the flat. *It would have been better if he had not said it*, thought Reva, *not now*.

In the days that followed, Reva and Neev saw less of each other though they still lived in. Neev was involved with the post production of his film. Reva didn't inquire what he actually meant. She didn't want to present her concern like a Christmas turkey on a platter where he would have a choice to reject it. She only wished him luck.

Reva didn't hear from Shahraan either. Had he realized what a fool he had been in wanting her at his side for the rest of his life? Reva tried to remain positive and waited patiently for any news from his side. A fortnight later, Reva read in the newspaper about the opening of a new restaurant in the suburbs. Shahraan was supposed to do the honours. The tagline of the advertisement read: *Thousands of fans are coming. Are you?* Was she still a fan? According to Shahraan, she was only the second woman who had the choice of becoming his. *Fuck you, ego. Double fuck you, self-respect.* Her impulse made her fit into a pair of jeans and a top and reach the mall in the next half hour. En route, she had made her decision which was troubling her since the night she read the proposal message.

She intentionally remained behind the huge crowd. When Shahraan was leaving, hogged by media and fans all around, he saw Reva standing with Krishna beside his red Rolls Royce. He got in. She got in. The Rolls Royce drove away.

'Why did you stop talking to me?' she said.

'Your silence to my message told me to.' He wasn't looking at her.

'Why is silence always taken to be negative?'

'What do you mean?'

'I mean what you inferred just now.'

Due to the soundproof glass separating the front and back seats, their discourse remained between them. Shahraan smiled at her through which she understood that it's love that makes one jealous, it's love that makes one sacrifice, and it's love that teaches one how to accept. Love only transforms; whether to a saint or a slut, is your destiny. It takes care of your journey. The destination is your call.

'I have been living in with someone,' said Reva.

Shahraan turned sideways and said, 'Past! I have had enough of it myself.'

Once home, she started packing. Shahraan had requested her to accompany him to a shoot in New Zealand. But before that, he had also requested her to move in with him. All she had to do was pack, the rest Krishna would take care of. Once done, she waited impatiently for Neev to arrive. She owed him a goodbye kiss at least.

He arrived at around midnight, totally drunk. His eyes were red and his visage frightening.

'God, what happened?' Reva almost shrieked seeing him.

'I am in deep shit, Reva,' he embraced her tight and started wailing like an infant. As they sat down on his bed, he still didn't leave her.

'The producer had a fight with the distributor over some money issue and now the film has to pay the price. It would be released only in one theatre. My hard work, my dreams, everything has been stomped upon.'

'Oh. But can't the producer and the distributor call a truce. It's their loss only.'

'I don't know. I begged them. I almost touched their feet, but nothing happened. Those motherfuckers don't care. They have loads of money but I don't have loads of faces. Once this film releases, it would be next to impossible to secure other films. No release is better than a super flop release.'

Reva couldn't agree more. But in that moment, she felt a sadistic happiness invade her.

'Now do you realize I only cared for you?'

Neev looked up at her and for the first time noticed the packed suitcases kept in one corner.

'Where are you going?'

'I am leaving, Neev. I'll stay with Shahraan from now on.'

Neev rubbed his eyes once and said, 'No, you can't leave me Reva. Not now. Not for ever. I don't have anyone here. That bitch, Suparna, is going around with the producer now.'

Reva tried to get up, ignoring his ranting.

'You can't leave, Reva.' With a sudden aggressive thrust, he pinned Reva on the bed. He pounced on her like an opportunist scavenger attacks a corpse.

'Move away, Neev,' Reva exclaimed, but all he did was force his lips onto hers. She started hitting him as hard as she could.

'Neev, I don't want this, so get the fuck away from me.'

'I can't let you go, Reva.' He made himself comfortable on top of her on bed and started lifting her top.

'I want you.'

She slapped him with all her energy. He stopped. Reva climbed down the bed pulling down her top. Neev dropped to her feet next.

'I beg you Reva, please don't leave. I know you don't love Shahraan. You love me, right?'

Reva realized he had no idea what he was doing. She stooped down, held his face and said, 'Listen Neev, and listen to me good. I am going to Shahraan not because I love him and hate you. It's because I have a moral obligation towards my dream of becoming the top actress as much as I have the same obligation towards my feeling for both of you. Even if I'll be with Shahraan, we shall be emotionally close, because no one will ever understand us the way we do. But we also need to be physically far from each other, for no one will ever destroy us the way we do. Get that?'

Neev didn't.

Finally, Neev had to strip off every inch of arrogance, chivalry, and emotional chastity and adhere to the beg-borrow-steal mode to bring his fledgling career on track.

Going by a baba, recommended by his parents over phone, he started visiting Hanuman Mandir every Tuesday and recited the *Hanuman Chalisa* daily. According to the baba, Neev's stars would soon enter the *Sade Sati*, the feared astrological phase, after which anything was possible.

He had seen humiliation before, but that was when he bullheadedly did things. Now he had willfully doffed off his moral robes and pursued people everywhere for work. One casting co-coordinator with whom he managed to strike a chord over whiskey told him a wise thing.

'You are lucky. If the movie had released all over and then bombed, you would have had it. Everybody would have known you then. Now nobody does.' It was just the confidence Neev needed. With his decision to abuse his till now dormant 'yes sir' attitude, Neev started making places in people's heart.

Though it didn't fetch him any acting assignment, he got the opportunity to assist a director for three months in the absence of his normal assistant. From helping him clean his ears to taking his calls for him on set and from making his drink at his home to identifying his ridiculous handwriting and making a fresh script out of it—Neev did it all. And for free. The director was so impressed by his newfound slave that he recommended him to another director, Pranav Khatri, whom Neev served with the same fervour. Soon he became his permanent assistant.

For a year, he worked with him on his advertisements and television serials. It was during the wrap-up party of his latest serial that Pranav took notice of his features after he was ten whiskey pegs down.

'Neev, do you know how sexy you look? Why don't I see you with any girl ever?'

'Just like that, Sir.'

'Just like that? Or...'

Neev managed a smile because he thought that would make Pranav happy.

'You naughty fucker,' Pranav laughed without any reason.

'How many have you had till now?' He meant boys.

'Few sir.' He was talking about girls.

'Wanna have me?'

'Sir, I have had only girls till now,' Neev wanted to state it as a fact but it ended up sounding like a sorry statement. Pranav felt bad for him.

'Sad. Come, let me change it for you. Come on.' He got up and ambled towards the washroom. He paused, turned, and barked, 'Come on now!'

Inside the washroom, Pranav made him turn around and stand with his legs apart. Then he asked him to strip till his knees. Neev closed his eyes and started chanting the *Hanuman Chalisa*. If there was something like karma-yields-results, then he prayed this one would bear some good ones for he couldn't go beyond this.

'Nice ass, partner,' Pranav said and took out his flaccid penis.

'Did it enter?'

Neev realized Pranav was too drunk to understand what was going on.

'Yes sir,' Neev hissed. Pranav gave a few thrusts, enjoying the process which in reality was nothing except for Neev standing with his ass exposed to his groin.

'Can you feel it boy? I'm about to—'

Neev turned around to see him on the floor, snoring.

Next morning, Pranav apologized to Neev and asked him not to divulge it to his wife. He was as much repentant as he seemed disturbed.

'I am not gay. Just that this alcohol makes me bisexual. Damn, I am sorry Neev. This is so bad. I think I owe you one.'

'It's okay, Sir.' He preferred to play the victim.

'It's not! Tell me what do you want in return? Anything, just shoot!'

'Sir, I actually came to Mumbai to become an actor but...'

Pranav perused Neev in a different light for the first time. He had the material. And Pranav was anyway done with Rajiv Tiwari—the tele-star from whom the industry got to know Pranav could be gay. He could do with a fresh face for his fresh story.

'Can you face the camera?'

Neev's karma finally seemed to be yielding results.

When he messaged Reva about his leading actor assignment, she was ecstatic. She wanted to meet him once but couldn't because of her pre-marriage cruise retreat with Shahraan. Though they were in touch via mobile texting, every time her picture appeared in print media with Shahraan, something burnt inside Neev beyond repair. But he kept quiet because Reva had promised she would talk to Shahraan about him once he had some exposure. In another time, another lifetime, it would have hurt his ego. But in this life, Neev Dixit had encountered enough shit to realize if you want to hunt success, go ahead, bereft of everything except determination.

The test pilot was a success. The channel green lighted the project—*Hum, Tum aur Pyar*—a repackaged *Romeo and Juliet*. Importantly, the audience lapped it up. The TRP of the show ascended, as did Neev's popularity among girls. By the time Reva returned from the cruise, he was slated as the heartthrob of the small screen.

The serial ran successfully for the next year after which Pranav was bored. He wanted to make something else with a fresh face against Neev.

Waiting for Pranav in his office, Neev was going through the entertainment supplement of a popular national newspaper. He read about Reva being voted as the Youth Icon for the year by a popular youth channel after her three back to back blockbusters. Though the opportunity happened because of Shahraan but, Neev agreed, it was her talent which fetched her fans across the nation.

His own journey flashed in front of him. In the end, he too reached where he belonged. That was the whole point. Unlike Reva, he was only a tele-star, but he was happy. But if it was written he was supposed to shoot to fame instantly on television, he wondered, then why didn't he listen to Reva before?

Pranav came in excited. 'Boy, I shortlisted a new girl against you for our new project. She is mind blowing.'

'What's her name?'

THE DIVA

NISHANI RAI

Shekhar Rai—the Prince of the Mumbai Silver Screen. That's the title media churned out for the unprecedented popularity of Shekhar Rai. A leading British tabloid had termed him a one-man industry because the last nine years saw Shekhar give five platinum, three golden jubilee, and two silver jubilee hits.

On screen, Shekhar was the ideal man for women across ages who believed in true love. Off screen, though, he was a notorious playboy. He had slept with models, supermodels, photographers, fashion designers, socialites, activists, authors, actresses, politicians, and painters. Until Ashlesha came along.

She had come to interview him on his latest film. When asked what she thought of him, Ashlesha had replied curtly, 'Actors are fake, celebrities are werewolves, and stardom is overrated.'

There was a raw arrogance in the middle-class Maharashtrian journalist which Shekhar, in a forbidden manner, swore to dominate.

'Would you like to go out with Shekhar Rai, neither the actor nor the celebrity but the man he is?' It was a ploy.

After dating for a record five months, Shekhar realized the middle-class Maharashtrian was clever than any other woman he had been with. She had placed a non-negotiable price for him to take her to bed. It was called marriage. But little did Ashlesha know marriage was the best bet to install a geyser of guilt within women which exploded with the slightest of mistake, but it could never be as innovative a ploy to comatose men against straying. For Shekhar, the marriage was again a chance to project his on-screen image as real as he could by marrying a simple journalist. Ashlesha will be the face of the Shekhar Rai people knew through his films.

It was in the sixth month that their 'happy' marriage bubble burst. It's dangerous to know too much about someone too soon. The philanderer inside him popped its ugly head. He only needed a way. He got one.

Ashlesha was the happiest when she learnt she was pregnant. She gave up her job as a journalist and remained home bound most of the time while Shekhar was out doing three shifts a day and one woman a night. The cockroaches of mistrust slowly crawled into the room of their companionship. In the eighth month of her pregnancy, Ashlesha lost her cool when one of the tinsel town actresses claimed Shekhar would marry her. Ashlesha threatened to abort their child, leading Shekhar to promise her he would be more responsible henceforth. She found a glimmer of the same earnestness in Shekhar's eyes as she did when he proposed to her. The countdown for their baby began.

Shekhar was in Kashmir shooting for Aditya Dev's directorial debut when Ashlesha went into labour. Five hours later, as Ashlesha tried to smile at the miracle for which she had undergone nine months of alternate life, Shekhar was involved in an on-set accident in Kashmir.

From the time the media learnt about Shekhar's accident and the subsequent irreversible paralysis of his lower portion, there were prayers and rituals performed by his well wishers throughout the country. Shekhar's condition remained the same though. Four months and everybody moved on. The same media for which Shekhar Rai was a sweetheart and his life a credit card which they could swipe anytime to buy eyeballs for their respective newspapers, suddenly developed a conscious amnesia towards him. The last film of Aditya Dev in which Shekhar acted, was completely reshot with the newcomer—Shahraan Ali Bakshi—in the lead and was released with a special note of thanks for Shekhar. It went on to smash all box office records of its time.

In the years that followed, spool by spool, the star named Shekhar lost its shine. He even tried committing suicide once or twice, but each time he failed miserably, which only further punctured his confidence and zeal to live and pulled him away from Ashlesha, himself, and his daughter.

Nishani Rai was six when she talked to him for the first time.

'You are my papa, aren't you?' she said, smiling at him with an I-am-all-yours twinkle in her eyes. She looked into her father's eyes which, with time, had pronounced dark circles around them. Shekhar only caressed her face from forehead to chin as if trying to guess the theme of a book reading the first page itself. Yes, she did have his features, he thought. Especially the sparkling eyes that could grab a person's attention by its throat and turn it into a voluntary slave, and the slightly longish nose which bulged a tad whenever arrogance pushed it, along with the elongated chin, the high cheek bones and the thin jaw line, all reflecting how much she was a part of him.

'I am sorry, kid.'

Shekhar abruptly turned his chair and wheeled into his room where Nishani was never allowed. The fact that he had bothered to even look at her with affection made her run happily out to her closest buddies—the clouds, the sun, the moon, the stars, rain, flowers, and anything which her innocence could coalesce with.

One day at a schoolmate's house, she saw a movie featuring Shekhar Rai. That night, neither the clouds nor the flowers could give her any plausible answer to why inside the television her father was like everybody else's father, perhaps better, but outside he was a loser.

When she queried it to Hema, her grandmother, the latter made sure Nishani never visited any of her friends' houses again. The same night, there was a tumultuous verbal duel between Ashlesha and Hema. The former wanted Nishani to grow in a natural atmosphere since the poor soul had already been subjected to hell since birth and the latter demanded her schooling be done either privately or from abroad henceforth. Hema's attitude toward Nishani was like a birthday girl's attitude toward someone who'd gifted the worst gift to her. She had a new rule every month for Nishani which irked Ashlesha. But that night, her anger simply plunged out of her emotional lap like a curious cat and turned into a lioness.

'I don't like all these rules for my daughter,' she said.

'Nishani is my granddaughter. And she'll live the way I want her to. Don't forget you are nothing beyond these Rai bungalow walls.'

Without caring to respond, Ashlesha walked straight to her father-in-law's room. Bharat Mohan, unlike his wife, always wanted Ashlesha and Nishani to have a life. After discussing the issue with him, Ashlesha decided to rent a flat in Andheri. Bharat Mohan, as a responsible father-in-law, suggested a free spirited Ashlesha save her earnings as a journalist for Nishani while he would take care of the their living and other expenses. Initially, Ashlesha's ego acted as a predicament. But when one has a child, she understood, one can't always be rigid.

A few winters later, when Nishani turned thirteen, Ashlesha gifted a computer with a dial-up internet connection to her. And the first word she typed was: Shekhar Rai. By now she knew her father was not a loser. He was a superstar before and now an invalid. Perusing one website after another, she finally learnt that Shekhar Rai was involved in an accident on a film set with a newcomer. The incident had not only paralyzed Shekhar's legs, Nishani concluded, but also the relationship that she could have shared with him. A beatific and pure father-daughter relationship like the ones she saw during the annual functions or the parent-teacher meetings in school. Oh, what a feeling it would be, Nishani's heart full of hope used to wonder.

Then there were those mornings when she used to quietly stand by the main gate of her school and gape at students who were dropped by their respective fathers before the school's entrance. Her eyes used to be fixed on the grasping of hands, the intermingling of their fingers, the way a father helped her daughter with the school bag, the way he waved his hand to her with a smile. Well, it wasn't a smile, Nishani concluded, it was a shade of security. It was a promise that her friend's world was beautiful. It was a sense of protection which could easily numb any fear one ever had. It was a reflection of solidity which prophesied that one's life would never fall apart. It was a concoction of all this that came out as a smile when a father waved at his daughter standing by the school gate. And then one day, she saw Shekhar doing the same. But instead of smiling at her, he was crying. She too started crying. In between the sugar-coated illusion and the stringent reality stood a thorny, wry realization. In all these years, 'papa' had only been a word for her to which she had associated a billion meanings, desires, and wishes. But no magic or conspiracy in the world could get the man behind the word kiss her cheeks, give her birthday gifts, or tell her a story of a charming prince whenever she cried.

Sitting in front of her computer, Nishani started crying compulsively. What could she do to get her father back? More tears welled up. And finally an answer punched her: *nothing!*

What's gone is gone. And what's gone was her childhood. She was thirteen now; a teenager. Nishani kept her head down. Then after a few minutes, her head was up again. If she couldn't get her childhood or her father back, at least she could get to the person who did this to her father, to her, to their relationship. She didn't waste a minute to reread the incident that happened in the film set as documented in one of the archives of a website. It said people did suspect foul play, mainly because the director went on to make the film, which now has a legendary status in Indian cinema, with the newcomer who was directly involved in the accident. The article stated it was precisely because of the carelessness on the newcomer's part that Shekhar Rai lost out on his golden career. And that the incident will always be interpreted as an accident didn't change what the truth was.

Nishani stared at the computer screen like a tigress whose cubs have just been snatched away.

'Shahraan Ali Bakshi,' she told herself, 'Nishani Rai *will* destroy you.' It sounded like a promise. But for Nishani, it was a premonition.

At fifteen, she had devoured all the English classics. To her English teacher's surprise, she'd come out with a thirty page casual criticism on Ayn Rand's *The Fountainhead*, presented her views on why Madame Bovary should be in every high school syllabus, had a crush on Henry Miller, propagated how listening to soulful music since kindergarten can humanize the mind, and held the belief that euthanasia and surrogate motherhood—like prostitution and politics—should be an individual's choice. Morality, she considered, was society's shit. Boys were scared of her because when she opened her mouth, all their grey cells turned to coal, while the girls thought she was too haughty to even approach and discuss anything which they considered normal and fashionable. The teachers gave her a 'keep it up' smile trying to look busy during classes, hoping her knowledge about the subject didn't surpass theirs. Not that Nishani didn't know it. She could tell from the slight twitch in a person's face if he was putting forward a false face, farting secretly, or was about to act smart. But she changed for nobody for she realized early on that one's own happiness, and life, is not someone else's perception. For her it was more personal than one's religious practice or sexual orientation.

Coming home early one day, Nishani was happy she would have to spend the next seven hours alone till Ashlesha came home from work. Of late, she had noticed her presence turned on a particular radio station within her mother who kept repeating the same thing again and again: *Nishani, make some friends. Nishani, why don't you join an art class or a dance class or perhaps some sport or even swimming would do. Nishani, I am tired of you being locked in your room. I fought for you with your grandmother. Not because I would allow you to stay indoors always!*

It was when Nishani kept her shoes in the shoe rack by the main door that she heard certain slurping sounds coming from her mother's bedroom. She tiptoed towards the bedroom and peeped in, only to find her mother and Gaurav—her mother's colleague—smooching passionately cuddled on the bed. The squeaky sound of the door stopper made them pause and stare at the intruder. By then Sonnet, Nishani's pet cat, had popped in its head from in between her legs and was alternating its sight from its mistress to Ashlesha as if expecting either of them to do something.

'Next time, try the door latch, mom.'

Nishani picked Sonnet up and went to her room.

Over the years, things had changed between them. Though Ashlesha kept a track, or so she thought, of every development of Nishani in her school and personal life, at times looking at her she felt she didn't know her girl at all. She was too unresponsive on some subjects considering her age and too smart at some others. She was like a calm lake inspiring life on the face of it but under, Ashlesha had a slight inkling, there were strong currents of confusion driving the quietude.

'How about having a father, Nishani?' Ashlesha asked during dinner one night.

Nishani glared at her icily and said, 'I have a father.'

Shekhar and she had finally undergone a divorce the previous year. Considering the negligible interactions that Nishani had with Shekhar, it was as good as not having a father.

'With Gaurav, you will be able to talk literature, films, theatre all the time.'

Nishani had just placed a piece of the butter paneer—her favourite—wrapped in a small crumb of roti in her mouth and for the first time that night, it tasted sour.

The following weekend, Gaurav dropped in. It was Nishani who opened the door.

'Hey Nishani! Don't you have school today?'

'Saturdays are off.'

Gaurav closed the door with a hint of disappointment. Nishani was always an untamed fire for him.

'Where is your mother?

'Bathing.'

'Okay. Beta, could you please give me a glass of water.' He was skeptical if she would agree.

'Okay.'

Gaurav's hope got the necessary air to flutter. An instant later, he saw Nishani come out with a glass of water and a plate.

'Mom asked me to give you this eggroll.'

Something about Nishani's endeavor told him that soon he would have a family. He took a joyous bite from the eggroll.

Few minutes later when Ashlesha came into the room, an ugly shriek escaped her. Gaurav was on the floor carpet with white froth oozing out of his mouth while Nishani was helping Sonnet with her milk.

St. Jones Senior Secondary School was the most 'happening' school in Mumbai. Whatever new teenage fashion initiated in Mumbai, it already was a trend in St. Jones. The kids studying there were the offsprings of deserving, hyped, and overhyped achievers. And thus, the annual sports event of St. Jones was always a well-publicized event.

Nishani's classmates and teachers were surprised when she enrolled for all the athletic events for the first time. Little did they know that from the time she learnt Shahraan Ali Bakshi was supposed to be the Chief Guest of Honour and would award the Sport Girl of the Year award personally, she had been jogging a good nine and a half kilometers to her school every morning.

'Mom.'

A tensed Mrs Sehgal turned to see her son standing beside her. Looking at his one hundred and twenty kilo self, it seemed someone had twisted the number eight in such a manner that the lower portion formed his hips while the upper one formed the stomach.

'Kaash? Isn't your event going to start now?' Mrs Sehgal was up on her legs.

'Yes, but my teacher told me that I am not ready for it.'

'Didn't you challenge him?'

'No.'

Mrs Sehgal held her son's hand like a soldier holds his gun and walked with such pugnacity that people on their own moved away from her line of gait. Finally she reached his teacher.

'Did you say—'

Kaash heard the announcement instead. *The Gold medal for the one hundred meter girls' race goes to Nishani Rai.* Kaash's eyes rested on the girl on the fifth track who was taking a breather with her hands on her hips. Nishani Rai. Bathed in sweat, she looked all the more attractive to him. She had already won four Gold medals and five Silver medals out of the nine events she took part in. This was her tenth and last event.

'Kaash, Mr Ingle is ready to give you a chance.' He heard his mother shout his eardrums out.

The whistle was blown for the race and every one sprinted ahead. So did Kaash and tripped a quarter of his way to the destination. There was an instantaneous roar of laughter among the spectators. This had happened so many times with him in the past that even a sense of embarrassment wasn't natural for him. He limped up to his mother by the track.

'Go, clean yourself up,' she told him.

While making his way to the boy's toilet, Nishani stopped him.

'Hey Balloo, just stand still.'

'Why Nish?'

Nishani suddenly took out a toy gun from her pocket, aimed it on Kaash's face, and fired a streak of water.

'Hell, what are you doing?' He wiped his face taken aback.

'Testing.'

'It's not Holi yet.'

'I know.' She kept the toy gun back in her pocket.

'Then?'

'You promise not to tell anyone?'

For a moment Kaash didn't know how to react.

'Promise.'

'I'm going to gift this to someone.'

'Who?'

Instead of answering, she pulled his cheeks as wide as she could. It irked him, but he was forever lenient with Nishani.

After all events were done with, Nishani was declared the Sports Girl of the year, triggering jealousy in all fellow students except Kaash who kept clapping non stop. Right after, there was another announcement.

'Ladies and gentlemen, bring your hands together for a resounding round of applause for our Chief Guest of Honour this year—Mr Shahraan Ali Bakshi.'

A charismatic man was seen in the central podium waving at the spectators. Nishani's jaw tightened. She could see him, like other awardees, from a close distance. He was wearing big brown shoes, a torn-at-the-knees blue jeans, and an untucked chalk-white full-sleeved shirt rolled up to his elbows. His Ray Ban aviators were clasped in his left hand. He was requested to say a few words.

'Hello everyone.'

Someone from the crowd screamed, 'I love you, Shahraan'. There was roaring laughter.

'I love you too, darling,' he said and continued, 'Kids, I feel, are the only reason why the world is still beautiful.' Applause. 'Thanks for inviting me here. Lastly, to the kids—don't give up if you didn't win today and certainly don't give up if you did because someone somewhere is working hard as you are celebrating. Cheers!'

There was another round of applause as Shahraan took his seat.

'And now we start with the first award. The Sports Girl of the year is Nishani Rai of Standard Nine, section D.'

As her name was announced, Nishani took a step into the central podium and Shahraan got up from his seat taking the giant cup in his hands. Nishani slipped her hand inside her skirt's pocket and gripped the toy gun. Instead of water, it now had acid.

Shahraan was waiting for Nishani with a giant cup and a smile which had won all the hearts it came across.

As Nishani took her steps, time seemed to have gone for a vacation. As if the entire world had leaped ahead and she was left behind. His eyes, which she had been so passionately sketching all her life, were locked with her own now. But there was something beyond them that she couldn't ever bring forth in her sketches. They didn't look evil. They were rather apologetic. And forgiving too. She couldn't grip the toy gun inside her pocket. Perhaps she did but didn't realize. Her hands were too numb to notice. As if his eyes had injected some tranquilizer in her blood stream.

One more step and she would be near him. She had to decide now. She had to destroy him. She felt the toy gun this time and was just about to pull it out and shoot all the acid on Shahraan when she heard him speak, 'Congratulations. Your eyes tell me you will go a long way in life. Keep it up, kid,' he said handing her the giant cup as she impulsively pulled out her lifeless hand from her skirt's pocket and accepted it. *Kid*...Only her father used to call her that.

'God bless,' he touched her head in a manner of blessing her. She only kept looking at him with dry, shivering lips as people burst out applauding. But her ears, much like her other senses, failed her.

Sitting in her room, she was staring at her shining achievement—the cup—as Shahraan's words ricocheted within her, colliding with the clouds of excitement, interest, arousal, hatred, obsession, passion, and love for the man whom she wanted to destroy. Hitherto.

She scribbled the sketches of Shahraan's eyes she made at

different points in time beyond recognition. She no longer needed to sketch them. They had now been imprinted on her soul. Was she defeated in her purpose? Will her father be ashamed if he gets to know this? Next time, she won't commit the sin of looking into his eyes. *Next time*!

The aftermath of her self-claimed defeat made her skip school for five days straight, claiming sickness. In reality, she was down with emotional and moral confusion. Shahraan was an out and out enemy till then whom she wanted to kill at first sight. Now there was an indomitable urge in her to know her prey before the kill. *Am I wrong? Am I being unfaithful to my father and my own wounds by desiring it? But he was my prey after all. And it's up to me how I killed him. By knowing what he is or imagining what he could be or fantasizing about him.* The last thought shocked her. She had never, but for this moment, realized there were hormones within her which suddenly seem to manifest a sudden insatiable physical need. The door bell rang.

When she opened the door, Kaash handed her a yellow and a white rose with an I-know-you-know-I-am-stupid smile.

'I had called last night. Aunty said you were not well. And my mother says whoever remains sick for at least five days should be visited and given flowers. How are you, Nish?'

'Come in, Balloo,' she said accepting the roses. Though he'd followed her often to her place, this was the only time he came inside. They went to her room. He made himself comfortable on her bed. 'What happened to you?'

'I am in...' Nishani took Sonnet on her lap and sat on her study chair.

'In love?' Kaash blurted.

'No stupid.'

Kaash relaxed. A 'yes' would have made him the youngest to die of a coronary thrombosis.

'I don't know. I am in hate.'

'In hate? What's that?'

'People fall in love. Similarly, people fall in hate as well, right?'

'Right.' Kaash had no clue what she was talking about. 'What happens when someone falls in hate?'

'The same thing that happens in love, I guess. You become obsessed about a person. He doesn't leave you in peace at all. Infuses weird thoughts in you and you unknowingly fall sick.'

'For five days?' Kaash had to prove he was getting her.

'But what's the difference between falling in love and falling in hate?' Nishani was looking intently at Sonnet's eyes.

'I... I don't know,' Kaash wished she asked something easier.

'Yes, you are right Sonnet. The heart gets ransacked in case of love and with hate, it's the mind... where sex resides as well.' She shifted her eyes to Kaash. He swallowed a lump.

'Have you ever kissed anyone, Balloo?' There was a strange eeriness in her eyes which made Kaash hear his own heart beat aloud.

'Only mom.'

Nishani placed Sonnet on the floor. She didn't budge an inch. She stood up and ambled up to Kaash and sat right beside him.

'Open your mouth.'

'Mouth? Mom kisses me on the cheeks.'

'I'm not your mom, Balloo.'

He obeyed and opened his mouth wide.

'I'm not going to enter through that hippo mouth of yours. Do it like this.' Nishani said and demonstrated. Kaash aped her. She came closer. Her breath was on him now.

'I shall put my upper lips on your lower lip and you purse my upper then.'

Kaash nodded. And they kissed. Kaash noticed Nishani

had her eyes closed. Presuming it to be protocol for kissing, he too closed his eyes but kept opening them to know if it's over or not. But it never got over. Two minutes, three minutes, four… Nishani kept sucking his lips while Kaash sat stiff like a painter's muse not allowed to move. Finally, he pulled himself out of it with a shriek when Nishani bit his lips hard.

'Damn, what are you doing?'

'That's what people do when they fall in hate.'

Kaash went to the full-length mirror by Nishani's study table and checked his wound.

'What would I say if mom asks me about it?'

'Oh, you are too innocent Balloo. I love that.'

Kaash kept looking at her.

'I shall nurse you. By the way, do all lips taste the same?' asked Nishani.

She wondered how Shahraan would have reacted if she bit him hard and deep. If she dropped molten wax on him after she had bitten his naked self red all over. She suddenly felt as satiated as a sixty-year-old impotent man would feel waking up to a raging hard on.

'I don't know,' said Kaash.

Nishani preferred English for her Graduation. She also joined a small advertising firm as a junior copy editor which she went to after college. She had the least qualification but the best knowledge which impressed Ravi Kumar of Kumar Advertising.

With a job in hand to take care of her pocket money, Nishani was further disconnected from her mother. They seldom talked. After being discharged from the hospital, Gaurav informed Ashlesha he wouldn't ever accept Nishani. Ashlesha didn't blame him for she knew her daughter was a natural calamity; hard to predict and impossible to tame. The choice in front of her was simple: either change Nishani according to her cognition or live her own life before she attains menopause. Ashlesha made the smart choice.

'Did you ask your grandpa to gift you a Royal Enfield?' Ashlesha was working on her computer in the drawing room.

'So?' Nishani was helping STS with its dinner patting and squeezing its back from time to time. Sonnet died a year ago. This was her kid: STS; Sonnet, the second.

'Guys ride that!' Ashlesha's fingers stopped tapering the keyboard.

'Bikes are not gender specific. If you can control it, you can ride it.'

'And what do you need a bike for?'

'College and everything else.'

Ashlesha suddenly realized her rebellious little daughter had actually grown up and she should start keeping an eye on her before she brings a problem with the complexion of shame.

'Everything else?'

'I work now.'

'Oh! What work are you doing?'

'I'm a junior copy editor in an ad firm.'

Before Ashlesha could knit her next question, Nishani went to her room with STS.

'I thought we were having a conversation, Nishani.'

'We were having a Q and A round. And you know I don't like those.'

Sitting in her room, Nishani wondered about the real reason for getting the bike: she was being stalked.

It started one day when she took a train from Andheri to Santa Cruz for her college. She had seen the man in an auto rickshaw at a traffic signal and then again at the station. And when he ended up in the same first-class bogie as her, Nishani knew something was wrong. Right through the journey, they stood separated by a young guy. He was constantly looking at her. He was of average height, a thick moustache, deep eyes, thick eyebrows, stout build, and dark complexion. He looked middle aged. The relief came when he didn't get down at Santa Cruz like her.

Three days later, she saw him standing opposite her college gate, smoking. Then he sat right behind her in the BEST bus that she took to reach her office. It was then she knew she better own a private vehicle.

A week later, as Nishani was preparing to leave the office on her shining new Enfield, she saw the man yet again. He was standing leaning onto an electric pole at the opposite end, looking arrow straight at her. She quickly sped away on her Enfield.

A little ahead in the road, her rear-view mirror showed an autorickshaw following her. Was this man head over heels for her as they show in the movies—an obsessive lover of sorts? The thought turned her on. Could someone she didn't know become obsessed with her? Did he fantasize about her too? It made her feel significant, filthy, important, trivial, supreme, and ordinary; all at once. She wondered how people like her father, Shahraan, and other stars of the magical world were definitely stalked, hounded, sought after morning, noon, and night. How interesting and special a life that would be! Her turn on became an indomitable emotional arousal now. Before she knew, it she was driving at a speed which could be easily followed by the autorickshaw. In that pleasurable home-bound bike ride, Nishani decided what she wanted to become in life: a professional attention seeker, a dream instigator, an obsession initiator, a fantasy propagator, a mass inspirer…

A *movie star*!

If Shahraan Ali Bakshi was an adolescent excrescence for Nishani, he turned into a compulsive disorder by the time she drove into the one-way lane of adulthood. He was a means to an end. But what the end was, Nishani never knew. She visited Neela Makan twice just to witness the man she hated was indeed capable of loving someone as selflessly as the media said he did. Since Shahraan was preparing for his home production on Genghis Khan, for some time now, he was going numb on publicity. Though occasional tidbits in print media was duly read and recorded by Nishani in a scrap book, nothing substantial came out apart from some rumours of him falling for the recently tagged youth icon—Reva Gupta.

Opening one of the fashion magazines to the page where Reva's recent blistering hot photo shoot in a white negligee was published, Nishani held it near her mirror and altered her glances between the photograph and the mirror's reflection.

Loads to catch up, she concluded.

Next she took out a fat yellow pages book, flipped to the beauty parlour category, and called the one named Madame Rizvi's. A lady answered.

'Good morning, Madame Rizvi's here. How may I help you?'

'I need a makeover.'

'For what purpose? Marriage?'

Nishani was silent for few seconds and then said, 'Yes, marriage.'

*With Shahraan...he'll have a bride who would kill him on the first night...*The thought gave her an evil kick.

A day after her makeover, one of her colleagues at Kumar Advertising, Rakesh Parekh, surprised her by asking, 'Are you free for coffee in the evening?'

Till that moment in life, she considered herself to be an invisible entity who at all times wanted to know what Shahraan was doing, forgetting the fact that there are other people too who could be seeing her; a well formed, nineteen-year-old girl. *But someone asking me out for a coffee... Was it the makeover effect or was he interested in the person she thought I am?*

'Why suddenly?' she asked. Looking at her eyes, Rakesh fumbled for words, 'I... I...'. Nishani only stared back at him the way a gun stares at someone as if saying, 'You know I'm going to shoot you and yet you are scared. Funny!'

'I always wanted to ask you.'

'Umm, alright. I don't mind coffee.'

At three the same night, she pondered about her rendezvous with Rakesh in the cafe.. He seemed to be a nice guy whom every normal girl would want to see by her side forever. And Nishani knew if she played on the way she was during their coffee session, he would in no time propose to her. But did she really want that? *What do people usually think about when considering getting into a relationship? Do they think at all?* she pondered. Her mobile phone beside beeped with a message from Rakesh: Hey, sorry for it's very late. Our conversation today felt more refreshing than the coffee. What say?

She was about to type a reply when she paused. *Let him assume I'm asleep*, she thought. As she closed her eyes, different thoughts played together to form a symphony of questions.

Another message from Rakesh arrived: Seems you are asleep. Do let me know if we can go out for a movie tomorrow. It's Saturday after all!

Before she had time to respond, the mobile phone beeped again with a message from a college friend.

Sweets, we all are meeting at Farhad's uncle's place at Worli for his birthday bash at eight.

At least her reason for not going out with Rakesh would be a genuine one now.

The party at Farhad's uncle's place was a usual one: peppy music, cake-smeared faces, beer, dancing, and a performance by Farhad's best friend, Rehan, who was the lead singer and guitarist of a rock band called Cloud 9. During his performance, he noticed Nishani eyeing him. While the other's eyes read enjoyment, appreciation and cheer, her's read like a life-insurance advertisement: *you shall need me even if you don't know it now.* Once done, he went straight to her.

'Hey!' Rehan pulled a stool to sit beside her.

'Hey!' Nishani almost echoed back.

'A beer after your life's worst performance feels just right,' Rehan smiled. To sound dejected in order to make it to the girl's he-needs-sympathy-so-must-be-harmless list was his favourite ploy. And with his experience, Rehan knew once a guy is in a girl's he-is-harmless list, then he can harm her however he wanted to and she would not even complain.

'I don't know. I'm yet to give my worst.' Nishani stated.

Rehan paused while sipping his beer. Nishani intentionally avoided looking at him. Rehan's next sip was a slow one. As she looked at him suddenly, he smiled as a reflex.

'So, you are Farhad's friend? Why haven't I seen you before?'

'We are meeting for the second time.'

'Really?'

'Yeah! If you can imagine me with a thin moustache and a little more facial hair, you may hit the right memory cell.'

Rehan stared at her. She was right. She was the girl with a thin moustache.

'Never knew behind those facial hair, hid such a sexy diva.'

'And hence this conversation, is it?'

'Why don't you punish me by saying you are single?'

For a trice, Rakesh's innocent smile flashed in front of her.

'What if I am?' Nishani's voice had intent.

'No hard work for me and all play for us,' Rehan winked looking amused. Nishani maintained her poise.

'What if I am not?'

'Well,' Rehan finished his beer. 'I'll have to work harder and make you wish you were.' He thought he had cracked a wise one. Nishani only stared at him.

'So, what are you?'

'I'm, let's say, accommodating.'

This one is actually easier, Rehan thought.

'What am I doing here?' she said throwing a questioning glance at Rakesh.

She chose to keep her voice down. Nishani was sitting in the drawing room of a one-bedroom rented flat in Malad. It wasn't small but due to the lack of proper ventilation, the walls seemed to close in like pesky neighbours. Apart from the usual furniture, she noticed, the walls sported several pictures of Hindu Gods and Goddesses.

'Meeting my mother, of course.'

'But why?'

'I told her about our coffee thing. Then she wanted to meet you.'

'Coffee thing? What's that?'

'I mean I told my mother I wanted to settle in life with someone like you.'

There's the subtle proposal along with a distinct destination: settling in life!

Nishani was about to open her mouth when his mother came in with a glass of water. Nishani pushed down the water and immediately spit it out; a bit on the table and a lot on her dress.

'It's hot.'

As Rakesh went to bring a towel for her, his mother came out of the kitchen and spoke, 'Rakesh always drinks warm water. It's good for the system.'

'Well, I don't. And this is hot, not warm.'

'You will get used to it.'

Nishani threw a surprised look at his mother. She had only gone out for coffee with her son twice and the woman wanted her to get used to her son's ways? God bless her!

Her mobile phone rang flashing Rehan's name.

'Hi. Yes. Okay, I'll be there.' She slipped the phone back in her jeans. Rakesh came with a towel.

'I need to go now, Rakesh. I'll see you later.' As she got up and left, Rakesh ran after her and into the small corridor out the main door.

'I am sorry, Nishani, if mom did anything wrong.'

'I need to go home, that's all,' she was already midway down the stairs.

An hour later, she was sitting beside Rehan in Bandstand when Rakesh called.

'I was wondering if you have reached home safely.'

'No, I'm still on my way. I'll call later.'

As she cut the line, she noticed Rehan ogling at a couple smooching right next to them. She nudged him.

'The guy is getting his tongue wrong,' Rehan remarked.

'Let the girl decide that.'

It was the third time they were meeting. And each time, Nishani felt he was making a move of sorts. Every time he opened his mouth, it was either to impress her subtly or directly or to tell her how saintly he was and that whatever sins happened in his life happened because of his ex-girlfriend's high horny quotient.

Rehan suddenly looked amused as if remembering something funny and said, 'You know one of my friends recently went for a dirty weekend with his girl in Matheran.'

'Dirty weekend?'

'Just the two of them and lots of uninhibited sex.'

'Why dirty? Why not a sex weekend?'

'What's the difference?'

'Dirty weekend sounds like they have already considered sex as a derogatory concept,' Nishani clarified.

'Wow!' Rehan shrugged in surprise. 'Seems like you worship sex, is it?'

'I don't worship sex. It's not important for me. But why frame something as taboo when everyone does it sometime or the other? I guess something that everyone does remains under cover in a society. It's the things that nobody does that are preached and taught. Like abstaining from sex because you love someone. Few do that.'

'You are so philosophically sexy! I never dated a girl like that.'

'What kind of girls have you had?'

'The whining kinds. They are yours till you are cute. Anytime you are not, they will complain. Or the reverse—blame kinds. They are yours till you, initiate everything. They may want something more than you, but you've got to take the first step. What kind of boys have you had?'

'From when do boys have types? They are all the same, aren't they?'

Rehan responded by slowly placing his hand around her waist. She glanced at him momentarily and then surrendered her head on his shoulder. He planted a soft kiss on her forehead. For a passer-by they looked like a couple in love, deeply committed, but for Nishani her heart, in that moment, resembled a graveyard where the ghosts of ambivalence had just started to party.

While driving back home alone, Nishani's bike broke down. She somehow managed to park it by the road side and called Rehan. After three full rings, the call still wasn't picked up. She called Rakesh. It was picked up on the second ring.

'Rakesh, my bike broke down at Ville Parle. Could you please come here and help me out a bit.'

'It's almost ten thirty, Nishani.'

'Yeah, so?'

'Let me ask my mother.'

'Never mind.'

As Nishani cut the line, wondering why she even called these two people, an autorickshaw slowed down in front of her. The driver told her about the man who sent him and informed her he would even arrange to deliver the bike at her place.

Nishani looked in the direction the auto driver pointed out. A silhouette of a man was visible at a distance. It was her stalker, her secret admirer. She hadn't seen him for the last few weeks, but she felt good to know that he was still following her. She got inside the autorickshaw. When someone is interested in the other, every act of the other is read as a signal by the one interested. How will he interpret this particular signal of hers?

She reached home safely. While moving into her room she picked up the newspaper from the centre table. In her free time, Nishani dutifully cut out news items featuring Shahraan.

Flipping through the newspaper's entertainment supplement, she saw a picture of Shahraan and Reva together. The headline read: *Time to move on from being just good friends.*

Nishani skidded to the kitchen, dumped the whole supplement inside the mixer jar, and switched it on. It relaxed her.

Love was like darkness. The more she got used to certain portions of it, there was a whole lot left to adapt to.

Three months had gone by since Rakesh proposed to her. It happened one day during their lunch break. As a response, she only smiled at him. Rakesh didn't know a woman's smile is a catalogue for the rarest of colours which can never be accurately labelled. Rakesh mistakenly labelled the colour in her smile as love. He opened his bank account to her that very night over phone.

'Listen, baby,' he began.

'Baby?' Nishani intercept.

'People in love call each other silly names. If you are not comfortable, I can call you Nish as well.'

'Nish' brought back memories of Balloo to her—her one friend in school with whom she experienced the first kiss of her life. Did he also love her? She would never know because Balloo had suddenly left. But, did he really love her? Then what about Rakesh? If he too loves her, and so does Rehan, and the man who stalks her harmlessly, then it meant that one person could be loved by many at the same time. So why can't one person love more than one at the same time?

'Anything but Nish,' she clarified.

'Then baby?'

'Hmm.'

'So here's the thing—I have saved four lakh rupees till date. My mother said the engagement expenditure would be from your side.'

'Engagement? I'm not even a graduate.'

'Nobody will stop you from completing it. Anyway, the marriage expenditure will of course be from the girl's side as per tradition. The reception however would be from my side. I shall use two lakhs for that and a lakh for our honeymoon. Mom is already talking to a travel agent for the best deal for three.'

'Three?'

'You, me, and my mom.'

If people's words were medicines, then Rakesh's banter would have had the side effect of her throwing up, Nishani realized and said, 'Don't you think we are going too fast, Rakesh?'

'Call me baby, please.'

'Okay, don't you think so…baby?'

'It's important to plan everything. You know my father isn't alive and I'm the only one.'

Her father was alive, but she still was the only one. She could have died of an emotional choke then and there but she held on somehow.

'What I can't understand is the need to plan everything right now. Why are we deliberately deciding a destination? Can't we just wait and go with the flow instead?' asked Nishani.

'But you love me and I definitely love you, so what's the point in waiting?' Rakesh sounded confused and a tad disappointed. Nishani was about to retort when she heard a beep. It was another call. The name read: Shweta AD.

'Rakesh, I will just call you back.'

Before Rakesh could react, she was on the phone with Shweta.

'Hi, how are you?'

'I'm fine, Nishani. I wanted to inform you that one of the three shortlisted candidates for the sanitary napkin ad is you. Please confirm if you can come to our creative office in Mahim tomorrow around one in the afternoon.'

'Count me in.'

A week before, while traipsing in a mall with Rehan, she passed by an entourage of young people who were calling in youngsters for their portfolio for an advertisement. Stating she had to freshen up in the washroom, she made Rehan wait for half an hour during which she met Shweta who was one of the five youngsters present there.

'But I don't have any portfolio,' said Nishani.

'Never mind. We have an in-house makeup artist who will give you a touch up. Then you need to talk about yourself in front of our camera. And that's it! Simple stuff.'

She was thrilled to know she had already ousted a minimum of one hundred girls who were there to try their luck. Only Nishani was trying her intent. It was her first step towards a life where more and more people will thirst for a miniscule glimpse of her. And of course, it will be a step closer to Shahraan.

Ecstatic, she called up Rehan instead of Rakesh.

'Dude, I made it to the top three.'

'Congrats! Guess it's high time we partied at Matheran. Only you and me; what do you say?'

Nishani went quiet with a sense of repulsion. People have a thing for destination. But, does love alter if destination alters? A thoughtful pause later, Nishani decided to give the guys what they didn't want; a dirty weekend to Rakesh and lots of marriage planning to Rehan.

Two months after Nishani successfully shot for the sanitary napkin, it started regularly featuring across television channels and on billboards at certain traffic signals in the city as well. Every time someone gave a second look at her on the road or elsewhere, Nishani felt fertile from within.

Nishani shared the piece of news with Rakesh only once the ad was out. Rakesh was happy to know about it but when he told his mother, she took offense. 'Sanitary napkin? What nonsense! Are you sure you want to marry her?'

Rakesh suddenly found himself sucking hard on the nipples of shame.

'What are you talking about? It was not a condom or a cheap viagra product that I was featuring in. Not even lingerie,' Nishani chided him while savouring steaming noodles as lunch outside her office.

'We don't talk about sanitary napkins freely in our community.'

'I hope the women of your community use them at least.'

'Please baby, try to understand.'

That's what Nishani's whole agenda was: to try and understand a relationship.

'So what do you want me to do?'

'I don't. My mother wants you to stop all this advertisement business and focus on the job at hand. She has also asked for your kundli.'

'I don't know where my kundli is and I've resigned.'

Rakesh's jaw dropped hearing the latter.

'What? Have you applied somewhere else? You should have told me.'

'I have told you.'

'When?'

'The fact that I've done an advertisement *implies* what my desire is.' It was a taunt.

'I am sorry but I don't get it.'

'I want to be a movie star. You know who my dad was, right?'

Shekhar Rai—he did know. But that was a matter of yore. And she now wants to be a movie star. A movie star! He could feel his mother's hands throttling him to death for choosing Nishani.

'That's a dangerous and cheap line for girls. Forget about mom, I will never allow that to happen.'

Allow! It was Rakesh's good luck she didn't stab the noodle fork into him.

'You know how much I was paid for the advertisement? More than our three months of salary taken together!'

The mention of money silenced his moral tempest like nature silences man's arrogance with a calamity.

'I will talk to mom once, tonight.'

'I had to ask you something,' Nishani wiped her mouth with a paper napkin and then said, 'What do you think about a dirty weekend?'

She didn't notice any budge or twitch in Rakesh. With a mouth full of noodles he mumbled, 'That happens mostly during monsoons when there's mud all over.'

'Idiot! A dirty weekend as in you and me alone and some sexual activity.'

'I will talk to mother... ' He paused with one piece of noodle hanging out from his mouth like a tail.

In the last few months, Rehan was busy touring with his rock band. Unlike Rakesh, who was like a bird who would sit on your balcony and shit loyally, Rehan was a passer-by bird who would shit only when nobody was watching. Whenever Nishani met him, she would sense a detached attitude in him. He would congratulate her if something nice happened but never encouraged or discouraged her to do anything. The only consistent thing in his behavior was a subtle persistence about sleeping together. When alone, Nishani used to wonder why couldn't he tell it to her face. I want to fuck you. Period. Did he want her to say so, instead, in order to share credit of the act?

'What do you want from me?' She put it straight one day they met in Juhu Chowpatty. He wanted to sleep with her alright, but didn't want any associated guilt. Like what he did with the last six girls, he would sleep with Nishani first—few times if luck was with him—and then cite an excuse and move out of the relationship, claiming to love her truly all his life or be a friend if she wanted him to be.

'What do you mean?' Rehan played it safe.

'A long-time relationship or...'

'Or?' He sucked hard onto the straw dipped in the coconut.

'Why do you need any options?' Nishani threw her coconut away.

'I only want to know what's in your mind.'

'Marriage,' Nishani lied.

'But I'm a Muslim and you are a Hindu.'

'Then why are we in a relationship, Rehan, if you are so much into this religion shit?'

Rehan had no answer.

Nishani could have stripped him of his pretence and spit on his pathetic nude self, but she played on because all she was interested in knowing was why they were sharing time if neither wanted to get married. And one of them didn't want the sex part either.

He threw his coconut too and said, 'Nishani, I believe in the physical expression of love. Not the emotional, spiritual, or the committal aspect of it.'

'Hence your intentional mention of the dirty weekend almost every time we have met till now.'

'Yes.'

Now he was being honest, Nishani thought, and said, 'What if I say my kind of love is about getting married first and then getting intimate? Whose kind of love do we as a couple give preference to? Yours or mine?'

They could sniff the scent of a mutual break up in the salt-laden sea wind.

'What do you want, Nishani?'

'What do you have, Rehan, apart from a circumcised dick?'

Rehan dropped his eyes and with a laboured gait, went away. The moving away was symbolic, Nishani realized, for that's what he had in his mind anyway.

As she walked towards her Enfield, she saw a figure at a distance. A gaze later, Nishani waved at him. As a response, the man allowed the darkness to consume him totally.

It was Nishani's flat where they were supposed to have their dirty Saturday night while her mother was gone for work to New Delhi.

From the morning itself, Rakesh felt emotionally constipated. He didn't know whether to feel happy that his girlfriend trusted him so much that she wanted to willfully surrender her virginity to him or should he be disappointed because he himself wanted to have sex for the first time in his life after marriage. He didn't have the courage to tell Nishani, lest she thought he was a coward. It took five calls from her before he picked up.

'Are you coming or not?'

'Baby, I am not feeling well.'

'So, you are not coming.'

'I am sorry.'

'It is okay. I am coming to your place.'

The line was cut. Rakesh went back to sleep—the best temporary escape ever conceived.

Within an hour, Nishani was there. Dressed in a black tight tank top, blue jeans, and aviator glasses, she was looking highly desirable.

'So, you are so sick that you won't even smile seeing me?'

'Sorry, baby. See, I am smiling,' Rakesh beamed.

'Now tell me, what's the matter?' Nishani pushed herself inside. Rakesh first closed the door and then came to kneel down in front of her as if he was her most trustworthy and benign servant.

'I can't do it.'

'Can't or won't? They are two different things.'

'Won't, I mean.'

'Why? Don't I arouse you?'

'Of course you do. I think you have it in you to arouse the whole world.'

This flattered Nishani. To arouse people was a requisite for a movie star.

'So what's the problem?'

Rakesh stood up and sat by a steel trunk-turned-stool.

'I never wanted to tell you this. But now…' He glanced at Nishani once who was awaiting his next words.

'My father never married my mother.'

'What?'

'After impregnating my mother, he promised to marry her, but eloped with a co-worker of his. My mother had to go through a lot of shit to sustain both of us. You know how society treats a young woman who has a child outside wedlock.' Rakesh looked dead serious. He wasn't crying. But Nishani was sure he was within. She also knew his personal wrath hollowing his core would melt because of his uninterrupted stream of words. When he was quiet, she went close to him and held his face. For a moment Nishani's heart sank. As if in that moment two pains coalesced to form one giant pain of which, now she knew, Rakesh too was a part. They craved to do away with the pain, to disown, become amnesiac towards it. But then if they could do so, life would have been stripped of its hallmark. Both Rakesh and Nishani, in that moment, were trying to crawl towards the happiness that succeeds sadness with the baby steps of their tears.

Nishani missed her father and all that which never happened between the two of them but could have. Suddenly the wishes seemed so distant that they were miles away from the harpoon of a memory.

'I am sorry, Rakesh.' She was relieved to know the emotions had not choked her enough. Rakesh looked up at her. His eyes glistened with tears.

'I am sorry too.'

'Why are you sorry, stupid?'

'To make you say sorry, I'm sorry.'

Nishani kissed him on his forehead. The moment had taught her what togetherness was all about; to leave aside the exotic dishes of the world and get lost in each other's emotional cuisine.

'You knew we were never made for the other and that's why you wanted to get me as quickly as possible, isn't it? Marriage was a means to your inner insecurity.'

Rakesh nodded a yes.

'But I can't—' she'd only started.

'You don't have to say it,' he completed. Nishani delicately freed herself of his wrap and looking at him said, 'Goodbye Rakesh. Have a great life.'

Rakesh was too scattered within to respond. Though Nishani knew she was done with both Rakesh and Rehan, she wouldn't forget the two crazy facts about companionship they respectively taught her: one, everyone is not made for everyone no matter how common the voids are. And two: sex, in the end, can neither be a means to a companionship nor an end. At best, it's a part-and-parcel thing.

While riding her Enfield back home, she once again saw an autorickshaw following her. This time, stopping by a traffic signal and looking at the man, she gestured with her hands and mouth.

I want to talk, she meant.

After she made it clear she wanted to talk, her stalker sent her an sms with the exact place, day, and time to confirm the meeting. Nishani wasn't surprised he had her mobile phone number. These days, everyone is only a decision away from everyone. The fact that he had taken the trouble of getting her mobile number made her feel important. And within the core of importance, Nishani realized of late, lay cocooned one of her favourite aphrodisiacs.

Morning was an unusual time to meet a stranger. There was nothing inspiring about the place even. Looking at her watch, Nishani tried hard not to read into the stalker's intention of deciding to meet her here. Reading someone's intention without meeting a person was like trusting a subtitle of a foreign film—you will understand the subtitles but you can never be sure of its accuracy. The next minute she saw her stalker step into the bakery.

'Do you know what's there in a name?' the man said immediately after he told her his name—Vishwas Naik—and sat opposite her. 'Gossip,' he smiled. 'No name, no gossip. No gossip, no name.'

It made Nishani smile. Seconds later, a boy came over and kept two cups of steaming tea and two apple pies in front of them. The apple pie, Vishwas said, was Yazdani's specialty; the place in South Mumbai where they were sitting.

'So, what do you want to talk about?' he asked.

Nishani noticed his one large sip emptied half the cup. Was he in a hurry?

'I don't know. I just wanted to. Tell me, why do you follow me around?'

'I knew you would want to know that. You have the right to.'

'Do I?' Slicing the pie with a fork she realized it was softer than she presumed.

'Yes, since we are in a relationship.'

'A what?' The piece of pie stopped inches before her open mouth.

'Relationship. Didn't you know?' Another large sip and he was done with his tea.

'Excuse me!'

'We are in a relationship whenever we repeat anything willingly or otherwise.'

Looking at her please-clarify stare, he looked at his watch and then continued, 'Like, he glanced outside, 'You see the man running away there.' Nishani followed his gaze. Precisely then, a man indeed ran across the road. Is this guy an illusionist? She wondered.

'Whenever I come here, and I do so often, I see him do that. It was only day before yesterday that I followed him. He runs every day at this time to catch a particular bus. It means he is in a relationship with the bus. If you come here tomorrow to have the tea and the apple pie again, then you will be in a relationship with it and the bakery as well. Doesn't matter whether you approve of it or not.'

There was silence during which Vishwas finished his pie. He ordered another one and looked at Nishani, 'You know why people have one-night stands?' Considering Nishani's vulnerable face he answered, 'Since more than a night will turn it into a relationship.'

'Hmm. So, why did you follow me all these days?' Enough of beating around the bush, she decided.

'Why do you think?'

'To get into a relationship with me?'

'That's eventual.'

'I thought you were obsessed with me and wanted to perhaps sleep with me.'

Vishwas looked at her, held his sight and then burst out laughing. Some portions of his apple pie came spraying out and got stuck around his mouth. He took out a white handkerchief and wiped them off.

'Sorry, I just imagined my wife's face if she'd heard you right now.'

'You have a wife?'

'Parvati. And two kids. Sonal and Suraj. Six and three years old.'

'That's weird.' Nishani quickly gestured to the boy for another pie—was she already in a relationship with the apple pie?—and said, 'Don't mind please, I thought you were some sexually frustrated middle-aged bachelor, but you sound like a content man.'

'You got the middle age and content part right.' His face contorted a smile.

'Nice. If you are happy with your wife and still following a young girl around, what does that make you? A saint?'

Nishani's crisp sense of humour was appealing. 'A saint is one who can sin without feeling guilty about it. So no, I'm no saint.'

Nishani's facial muscle twitched in appreciation.

'That's weirder. You feel guilty and yet you do something that you are not supposed to do. I mean, my sympathy would be with a sexually frustrated person than a happily married man following a girl.'

'To escape. That's exactly why I have been following you around.'

'From what do you want to escape? Your family?'

'Oh no. That's dear to me. It's reality that I want to escape from.'

Vishwas gave her a hope-you-are-done glance and called for the bill.

A minute later, they were out on the streets standing by a cigarette shop. As he lighted his cigarette, Nishani touched its end with hers. As they exhaled, their smoke coalesced and became one.

'Isn't your family your reality?'

A puff of cigarette later, Vishwas spoke.

'I turned thirty five the day before I first saw you at the traffic signal where my auto stood parallel to yours. Nobody really cared to wish me except my two sweet kids and adorable wife. At my age, you don't really need a truck load of people around you. But at night, after my family and friends had wished me all through the day and I'd taken my wife and kids out for a sumptuous dinner, I felt it was time for some introspection.

Sitting under the shower, I thought: I have a well-paying government job, a good wife, two wonderful kids, all my flat's EMI will be over in another five years, and I have already arranged for the money. Plus I have no parents or siblings to take care of; in all a stable life. But when it dawned on me that life has gone the way I prayed and worked for, instead of being happy I turned shaky that night. My guts churned as the cold water rinsed my body. I thought my life, in a passionate attempt to turn it to perfect, lost its essence. Suddenly I craved for it to let me down. Just a bit, if possible. And when I saw you—young and spirited—I realized in this life I won't ever be like you. That sure was a letdown; something that I won't be able to achieve no matter how settled I was. Weird, as you may call it, I loved the feeling. To keep it alive in me, I kept following you. Perfection should always be elusive. The moment you achieve it, you realize that's the most imperfect thing ever.' A pause later he added, 'Does any of this make sense?'

'I don't know. Maybe not or maybe it has and I'll realize it later.'

The steady flow of pedestrians made it difficult for them to walk side by side. Out of nowhere, a harried man approached them.

'Excuse me please. What's the time?' he asked Vishwas.

'Twelve thirty,' Nishani said. The man looked at Nishani as if he didn't expect her to be with him and scooted away. Vishwas looked at his watch. It was five past twelve.

'I wanted him to run to wherever he was going,' she said with a hint of a giggle.

'You like controlling people.'

'I love control.'

'But you don't love either Rakesh or Rehan.'

He moved ahead. Nishani's look held his elusive image as the footpath suddenly turned even busier.

Finally, they boarded a bus together. Nishani had intentionally not brought her bike while Vishwas always travelled via public transport.

'You are right. I loved neither but then I also don't know what love is.'

Vishwas shot an incredulous look at her and then moved a strand of hair from her forehead with his hand.

'But I know what hate is. I hate someone.' She allowed herself a contemplative pause and then said, 'That's also a relationship, isn't it?'

It took a trice for Vishwas to realize her query was drenched in covert worry. 'Yes, it is. Perhaps more intense and self-destructive than love. But whom do you hate? Me?'

'No,' she managed a smile. 'I don't want to name him, but I really loathe him with all my heart and want to take back from him what is rightfully mine in the first place.'

'Which is?'

'Life.' Neither Nishani elaborated on it nor Vishwas poked her to do so.

'Anyway, I broke off with Rakesh and Rehan both.'

'Why?'

'Both had made me the target of their obsession. For Rakesh, it was about marriage and spending a life together till death do us apart; while with Rehan, it was about sleeping together till one of us called it quits. I don't understand why to limit a journey with a destination?' Vishwas bought two tickets from the conductor.

'Look, I am not asking the journey to decide the destination even. All I'm saying is can't a journey be just that—a journey! Who made this stupid one life-one love diktat? I mean if I am committed to one, I might love someone else as well. Why does love have to limit me to one?'

'Love is a choice. You are making it sound like an obligation.'

'Hold on, let me try explaining this. I love a guy. The guy loves me. We get married. But won't that mean we are claiming we wouldn't love anybody else because I love him and he loves me? Won't we constantly remind ourselves, with the unfolding of our marriage, not to even think of falling in love with someone else even if in the veil of our hearts we know reality is or could be the opposite; that people can fall in and out of love all the time. Then, now, and later! That it's okay to have the urge to sleep with someone other than your partner and not think of it as infidelity because it's okay for you. Okay for him.'

'My thing is I don't want to make any such claim. Nor do I want the same claim from my partner. By the way you are married, so you should be able to tell me: what does a marriage mean? I love you? Or I love only you? Or I won't love anyone else? Or is it the worst—I *can't* love anyone else anymore?'

There was silence between the two amidst the chaos of the traffic around them. The conversation had come to a point when neither knew what to say because too much had been said. A few minutes later, Nishani asked, 'Do you too have a destination to whatever relationship we are in?'

'Yes,' he returned her look with the same intensity. 'But the destination that I had in mind was my own internal thing. It didn't concern you or us. I wanted to escape reality just by following you. But tell me, why does it upset you; the destination thing?'

'I don't know. It's not that I am a flirt and I'm piling on excuses just for guy hopping. In fact before Rakesh or Rehan, I never had any guy in my life.' For a second, Kaash's chubby face flashed in front of her. And their first kiss too. She moistened her dry lips and continued, 'I know if someone doesn't want a destination out of a relationship, people say the person is merely passing time. It's the "no strings attached" theory at work. But I don't think the kind of complexity we carry between our ears and legs would ever allow us no strings. There's always a string which eventually becomes a rope and if not catered to, might end up being a chain too.' A pause later, she innocuously added, 'Am I making sense?'

'Perfectly. Perhaps, I followed you to unleash myself from that very chain. But that doesn't answer my question: what's wrong with a destination?'

'I have realized the destination of every relationship—good, bad, ugly—is separation. And I am afraid of separation. Since childhood—' Nishani checked herself. Though she liked Vishwas, she couldn't trust him with the most private secret just yet.

Vishwas shrugged, signalling her to carry on.

'I have been like this since childhood.' Her words changed course.

'They say a person feels ruined if someone leaves him or her. But I believe the ruining process starts with the acceptance of someone in your life, for separation foreshadows acceptance. Like you said you hate someone. That's an acceptance as well. And one day you will be separated from that hatred too.'

Nishani suddenly felt like throwing up. She couldn't foresee a day when she would not hate Shahraan Ali Bakshi. It was impossible. Period. Even after she had destroyed him beyond anything, she would still hate him. Very much!

Vishwas dropped Nishani at her place in an autorickshaw. Initially, he had not taken a day off, but he wanted to hold onto her company for as long as he could. Strangely after their lengthy discourse in the bus, they didn't speak one word to each other for the rest of the day. They went to Marine Drive, Gateway of India, and lastly to Flora fountain. And wherever they went, they took along a silence which seemed not to judge but understand the other.

'Is it always this crowded?' Vishwas said, checking out a heap of cards and a media van.

'No, it's not. There must be a party or something happening at someone's place.'

'Hmm. I don't think we will meet again,' Vishwas sounded curt.

'Never?'

'If we meet again, it would be a relationship totally unlike what I experienced following you around all these days, including today. And I don't think I am in that place in life where I am allowed to desire such a relationship. You asked me about marriage earlier in the day.'

'And the last statement is your answer?'

Vishwas beamed. He had judged her smartness right. Nishani looked at him without blinking. Next, she leaned sideways and kissed him on the cheeks.

'Goodbye,' she said. The autorickshaw driver was ogling through his rear-view mirror, wishing for some further public display of affection.

'Goodbye,' Vishwas tapped on the driver's shoulder and he drove off.

The main door to her flat was slightly ajar and she could hear people in groups inside the flat talking in hushed tones.

Before she could understand what was happening, she saw her grandfather approach her with a solemn look on his face. And then, she stopped dead in her tracks. 'What's happening, dadu?' she enquired, mustering courage. In her head, she already feared the worst.

'You lost your father this evening.'

Only a few loyal old journalists, film producers, and a few industry people who had once stood by Shekhar, though had recently lost touch, were allowed inside the Rai bungalow. There were a few media people waiting outside, but due to lack of anything spicy, they soon dispersed. Shekhar Rai was a forgotten hero.

Inside, Nishani kept on staring at her father's dead body for five hours straight. People around her were crying, sobbing, wailing. But she turned dead quiet from the moment she heard the news. *You lost your father this evening*, she was told. *But when did I ever have him?*

The moments that could have been and the moments that were started a fierce duel within her. A father and daughter relationship is different from a mother and son one. The latter is about an inseparable attraction while the former is about a fervent attachment. *Separation foreshadows acceptance*, Vishwas's words rushed to her mind. There were a thousand and one flaws in her relationship with Shekhar. But never did she doubt that fact, never did she ask 'why him?' to God about it.

When the others took the dead body to the nearby burning ghat, Nishani, for the first time, entered Shekhar's room. There was his wheelchair next to a neatly done up bed. A wardrobe lay adjacent to it. The door of the attached toilet was closed while a series of three windows with pitch black panes on the opposite side of the bed were shut. There were no curtains because the windows were never opened. Nishani felt the room had the same plight which Shekhar existed within all these years. Soon her eyes fell on the wall opposite to the wardrobe. Finally, tears burst out of her eyes like rain from a clouded night sky. On the wall right in front of her were her photographs—all framed to perfection—from the time she was an infant to the time she ate for the first time to when she started walking to her first school dress to her wins in school and lastly a photograph of her college time; all different moods, different point in time, different memories but one life. Nishani cried her heart out as she realized for the only time in her life there was someone else apart from her who had missed out on a whole lot just like her—her father.

It was evening and she was alone. The servants were sorting out the bouquets which had poured in from all over the country. The maid was calling out the name cards on each of them in her attempt to read who the bouquet was from and then handed over the bunch to another servant who sorted out the fresh flowers from the dead ones. One of the names the maid called out was of Shahraan Ali Bakshi. It piqued Nishani's interest.

'Give me that,' she instructed. The maid handed her the elegantly done up bouquet. The flowers were fresh. They smelt like shit to her. She read the tucked message on a small card on it.

RIP. I am sorry.

Nishani locked her jaw till it ached.

'You aren't sorry yet. Not till Nishani Rai makes you sorry.'

Life was going to be a different game from now on. She knew.

Nishani decided to visit those producers who had come to Rai bungalow to pay their homage. They were single producers who were giant names during the 70s and 80s, but most of their cinematic instincts had fizzled out with time. The list named ten of them who had assured her help in the industry if she decided to give it a try. *Try? You are kidding me. I'll rule the industry just like my dad did.* She laughed at their ignorance.

Five out of ten producers in her list, as they confessed to Nishani, were too broke to conceive a large scale Hindi film, never mind make one. Three, who used to go by star power not script power, hadn't had a single release in the last fifteen years. And for the sake of Shekhar Rai who gave pots and pots of currency to them Friday after Friday, they could least be honest with his daughter. Nishani appreciated it. Only two producers were left by the end of a month: Nirupam Agarwal and Jignesh Shah.

Nirupam Agarwal had debuted as a producer with Shekhar. His horror film titled *Janam se Pehle* ran successfully for twenty weeks. Inspired by his first success, he kept his eye on the horror genre only. As Nishani went to his small but busy office, there were numerous posters of some successful horror films and a few upcoming ones framed all over the walls.

'I have an appointment with Mr Agarwal.'

'Nishani Rai?' The receptionist almost had a man's voice and appearance. As if she had walked out of her sex change operation midway. 'He is waiting for you.'

Nishani knocked at Nirupam's cabin door which was covered with the poster of a skull. Between its jaws was written: the Horror King. Nirupam opened the door the next instant.

'Nishani ji! Please come in.'

The outside was only a trailer. The inside was the real film, Nishani realized, looking at the walls which were covered with horror film wallpapers. One side had all the famous Hollywood horror releases from *The Exorcist*, *The Entity*, *Poltergeist*, *The Hills Have Eyes*, *Nightmare at Elm's Street*, and *Evil Dead*. On the other wall were Nirupam's own films. The similarity in the poster designs told her they could all be rip-offs.

'Please sit down, Nishani ji.'

'Call me Nishani, Mr Agarwal.'

'Nirupam.' He smiled in a shy manner and further said, 'What can I do for you?'

'During dad's funeral, you had asked me to meet you for some film.'

'Oh yes! We are starting a film soon. And I am indeed looking for a fresh face.'

'Who is the male lead?'

'Not decided. It's a woman-oriented film. So I won't go for a known male lead. Nobody will agree to play second fiddle to a newcomer. Hope you understand.'

'I do.'

'Honestly, since the corporates have come up along with the multiplexes, the financial structure of the entire moviemaking business has changed. I try to keep it simple these days. Make a movie for one crore, release it in single theatres in selected cities, and make a net profit from a theatrical release of fifty to seventy five lakhs. Of course, there is satellite rights and other means of securing some more funds.'

'What is the character about?'

'As I said, it's a woman-oriented film. The girl, our protagonist, is avenging the death of her mother who was killed heinously by some village people.'

'Why?'

'I don't know. The writer is working on that. We'll cook something up in the flashback scene. Don't worry. There is also a poignant love story between her and a police officer who helps her with the revenge.'

'Interesting. What is the name of the film?'

'*Chudail ki Beti*. The daughter of the witch. You'll do the title role. If it does well, we can make its sequel: *Laut Aayi Chudail ki Beti*. We can take your audition today itself.'

By the time Nishani was out of Agarwal's office, she swore not to meet the man again.

Jignesh Shah had retired from his family business of film exhibition, distribution, and production long ago and his two sons—Himesh and Pravesh—had taken over the mentle quite fruitfully. They turned their company—Shah Brothers Films—into a studio where multiple projects were being green lighted at a time. Also, they were known to flag off new faces, both in television and cinema.

Though Jignesh seldom came to office but for his favourite actor's daughter, he made an exception.

'Jai Shri Krishna, beta.'

The first thing Nishani noticed in the swish office room was a life-size gold-framed poster of the movie *Hawa Ke Saath Saath*. The Shah Brothers Films' biggest money churner in India and abroad which they had made with Shahraan five years back. She averted her eyes towards a smiling Jignesh.

'Hello uncle. How are you?'

'Krishna is kind. Jai Shri Krishna. What will you have?'

'Stardom.'

Jignesh burst out of laughing.

'You have your father's sense of humour. Where were you all these years?'

'Preparing,' Nishani smiled smartly.

'I am impressed. But unfortunately, I don't have much say in the company affairs anymore. I'll introduce you to my son, Pravesh.'

'Okay.'

A boy came and kept a glass of water beside her which she picked up immediately.

'Before that, I would definitely like to tell you something. Stardom is a game of snakes and ladders. You need to be proactive enough to judge whether you are about to land on a ladder's base or a snake's mouth. There'll be people who would seem like ladders at first, but shall eventually turn into snakes. So trust people, but don't have faith in them. Believe what people say but don't rely on it. Life is strange. But in this industry, it is stranger. Being Shekhar's daughter, it was my duty to alert you.'

Being Shekhar's daughter. She liked the sound of it. Nishani smiled. 'Don't worry, uncle. If life is a horny bastard, I'm a bitch in heat.'

Jignesh didn't know how to react.

If faces were placards, then Pravesh Shah's read: *I am shrewd. Fuck you very much*. As he sat down with Nishani, she gave him her pen drive and he checked out her pictures in his Macbook.

'I think you have a saleable face. But film wise, we are booked till the next three years. And the casting has been locked too.'

'Three years is like ages.'

'I'm sorry. Your dad told me about you, but I'm afraid this is what the position is right now with films.' He looked straight at her like a robot. There was nothing in his face to suggest he was something otherwise. She knew Pravesh was waiting for her to leave now.

'Are you interested in television?' the robot spoke out of turn.

'Television?' All the regressive plotlines and characters flashed in front of Nishani in that moment.

'We are about to start a new romantic saga in a month's time. Casting is on for a fresh face opposite Neev.'

'Opposite whom?'

'Neev Dixit. He is—'

'I know.' Reva Gupta's ex. *And Reva is Shahraan's present while Shahraan is her target.* Nishani did some quick math.

'I'm interested.'

Pravesh called someone from his mobile phone and talked in Gujarati.

'My elder brother Himesh will see you in a minute in our board room. He looks after the television part.'

'Thanks.' Nishani got up to leave. The robot didn't smile back.

The first thing Himesh Shah experienced after seeing Nishani sit across him in the boardroom was a full-on erection. Unlike his younger brother, Himesh was an acutely religious guy who was married with two kids.

'Jai Shri Krishna,' he said. One look and Nishani knew he was a younger version of Jignesh Shah. Only he had a constant tinge of nervousness on his face. As if he was afraid someone will unmask his actual face.

'Hello. I'm Nishani Rai.'

'Yes, I know. Pravesh told me about you. So you want to be in television?'

'Yes. My pictures are in this pen drive. Pravesh told me you are starting a new television serial.'

As Himesh quietly perused the photographs, his erection was going northwards. By the last photograph, he knew he couldn't get up without being embarrassed.

'Nice,' he adjusted himself, sinking a bit more into his chair before continuing, 'Yes, we are. Casting is on. By the way, what are you doing tonight?'

For the next fifteen nights, they met over dinner at various restaurants across Mumbai. They talked about films and television industry in general, how he and his brother took the company a step forward from where their father left, and about his future vision for the company; his wife, their love story, his kids, their whims, his tryst with God, and his beliefs. But not a single word was spoken about the upcoming serial for which Nishani decided to tolerate him. Whenever Nishani queried about auditioning for the role, he maneuvered the topic with appreciable dexterity. He wasn't even being flirtatious for her to presume anything. Nor was he imposing himself onto her. It was just a friendly dinner.

On the sixteenth night, sitting inside yet another posh restaurant in Juhu, Nishani's patience finally ran out.

'So, am I doing the serial Himesh?'

She observed his body language. He was touching his own fingers; defensive.

'I don't know.'

'The head of the television department of the Shah Brothers is telling me he doesn't know? Then who knows?'

'I don't know.' Himesh's touching of himself was now a notch furious.

Finally, Nishani got the cue. He wanted to sleep with her. But he wasn't able to tell her. He wanted her to get the cue and take the initiative, so he became the poor. god-fearing man who succumbed to the seductress.

'Okay, if I sleep with you,. will that help your ignorance?' Nishani's eyes meant business.

'What are you saying?' Himesh sounded shellshocked. 'I am a good man. A family man. I don't take advantage of girls. I am also the father of two sweet girls.'

Nishani slammed her fork on the dish hard. 'Then what is it that you want from me, Himesh? I can't fucking dine with you anymore!'

'I—' He felt his dry throat as he swallowed a lump.

'I only want a blowjob. I don't have the courage to sleep with you. My God will never forgive me.'

Bloody-mother-fucking-religious-cribber. Nishani shot a look of disgust at him.

'Is the blowjob the only criteria for me to feature against Neev Dixit?' *And in the end reach Shahraan...*

'Yes.' It was a meek confession.

Himesh, who drove his BMW himself, tried to relax inside as he saw Nishani open her purse.

'What are you doing?' He thought she was going to call someone. Or worse record their act.

'I'll have to disconnect with myself,' she said plugging on the ear plugs of her iPod. One of her favourite Beethoven symphonies started playing, making her mind swim in a different world where there were no tides of morality to disturb her.

'Is your tool clean?'

'I just washed it with Dettol in the toilet.'

Nishani took a deep breath and closed her eyes.

Ten minutes later, she was set to star in the most-awaited television serial—*Acha Jee Main Haari*—paired against the recent heartthrob of the small screen: Neev Dixit.

Their pair was like a rocket embellishing a dark sky with a spectacular expression.

It had taken exactly six months before the television serial aired for the first time. Nishani was on for twelve thousand an episode to start with, whereas Neev—fresh from his last television hit *Hum, Tum Aur Pyar*—was signed on for fifty thousand an episode. With the TRP behaving like the mercury of a thermometer out from a feverish mouth, the producers themselves increased Nishani's take home to twenty an episode while Neev's escalated to sixty five.

Nishani met Neev for the first time during the photo shoot

for the serial. It was Pranav Khatri, whose brainchild the serial was, who introduced them.

'Neev, this is Nishani. And Nishani this is...'

'Neev Dixit,' Nishani completed.

Neev smiled exhibiting his irresistible charm. He loved the way stardom spared his need for introduction.

'Where are you from?'

'Mumbai. I did a few ad films and then got lucky.'

'The best wait, the luckiest sail,' he said and excused himself.

As the photo shoot commenced, Neev's irritation at the photographer's inability to click the perfect photograph at minimum clicks was attaining peak. In the end he called out, 'Make-up dada!' and dashed out. An old man with a make-up kit followed him urgently.

As another make-up man attended to Nishani, she asked him, 'Is he always like this?'

'No. Usually he cooperates well. But—' The make-up man whispered next, 'Reva ma'am left him. Everyone knows.'

Whoever had written her meeting with Neev, she wondered, had got the timing spot on. She intentionally didn't talk or exhibit any concern for his erratic behaviour that day because avoidance was her first step to attract.

The shoot was more like an office job from nine in the morning to ten at night. Since they were the lead pair, Neev and Nishani had to be there on set almost every day for twenty one days of the month. But to Neev's notice, Nishani precluded herself from any kind of friendship on set. She was mild and modest with everyone, but there wasn't one person whom she hung around with. Everybody saw her, nobody knew her. Post shoot, she either disappeared inside her make-up room or simply sat on her chair listening to symphonies on her iPod. Just before a scene, Nishani would listen to the director or his assistants intently and give perfect shots on the first take.

Neev didn't read in her a lust to go to the top like other beginners, yet she seemed to take nothing for granted. The mystery, the edginess, made her such a sexy mix that he suddenly found himself desperate to unravel what Nishani Rai was all about.

On fine day Neev finally asked her, 'How are you unwinding this weekend?'

'My usual, Pilates classes.'

'I have been invited to a Sunday brunch at Waqil's place.'

'Waqil?'

'Shaukat Waqil, the fashion designer and Page 3 rocker.'

'Okay.'

'I told him I'll be there with you.' The second part was a lie.

'Thanks. That's wonderful of you.'

So that's what Nishani Rai is all about. A little bit of fluff and she is all yours. Lame! Neev concluded.

'I would rather catch up on some sleep. See you next week.' She was gone before Neev could surmise the right excuse to stop her.

How could she possibly deny a date with the heartthrob, was Neev's only query. He saw her coming back. Neev relaxed his shoulders, expecting her to pop out an apology.

'Forgot to tell you, please don't take any decisions on my behalf. I'm not a kid.' Nishani knew how to feed the infant of interest so that it grows into a man of obsession.

As Nishani disappeared, Neev hissed under his breath, 'I'll make her my bitch soon.'

What he didn't know was she would make him her pet sooner.

Nishani knew she had scored when Neev joined her Pilates class. They only smiled while changing postures. Till then, he had seen her mostly with make-up and a few times without it. But that was when she hadn't impregnated his mind with any intent. Now things had changed.

Nishani was wearing a black tracksuit that fitted her snugly. As he eyed her succulent-in-parts body dripping with sweat, Neev felt tempted to let go of the restraint which labelled him as a human. He realized there was something primitive and unabashed about her.

He caught up with her as they moved out of the class an hour later.

'Can I drop you somewhere in my Tavera?'

'My Enfield will feel bad if I don't ride it back home.'

'You ride an Enfield? That's so macho!'

'Only a real woman rides a macho,' she winked and drove off.

Every morning, Nishani's door bell rang dot at seven. And a red rose lay at the doorstep with a card that read: *Have a nice start*. It made her smile, but for a reason only she knew. The day went by shooting with Neev, but she made it a point to not talk to him. They seemed like strangers to any prying eyes. But at night when he called her, his talks had a hint of intimacy. Nishani played it safe: neither too much indulgence, nor too little of a tease. A woman, if she is a woman, doesn't need a weapon. Moreover, Neev was already an injured heart. Show an injured heart a spark, she wondered, and he shall lap it up, assuming it to be a light source.

Due to heavy rains, shooting was cancelled for a few days. It was on one of those days that Ashlesha and Nishani were both home. Till Shekhar's death, they were mother and daughter. But afterwards, they had degenerated into roommates, with neither having anything to do with the other. She knew Nishani had become an actor like her dad, but she kept her suggestions to herself. But on that gloomy night, she was angry after learning that Nishani had dropped out of college in her third year a week back.

'You should have completed your graduation at least,' Ashlesha spoke from the kitchen while heating her dinner in the microwave.

'I decide that.' Nishani was lazily surfing channels on television.

'What have I done to deserve your constant wrath?' Ashlesha came out and confronted her daughter.

'What *have you* done?'

'I have done all the duties a mother should do for her child. I have given you proper education, a house to live in, never made you feel what struggle for existence is all about.'

'There's something beyond duty as well which you have always fallen short of. As a mother, as a wife.'

'As a wife? What do you mean?' Ashlesha was waiting for Nishani to look at her which she didn't.

'You could have stayed with dad or brought him here to live with us.'

'You know what his position was.'

'So what were you doing being his wife? Isn't marriage all about an inseparable companionship? But you made it look like it's a companionship of convenience.'

'I did what I could for Shekhar. I had my life too.'

Finally Nishani switched off the television and stood up.

'And now, I have mine.'

Nishani went to her room.

'Then why don't you live in a place which you can claim as yours as well?' she heard her mother scream. It sounded like a proposal.

Once inside, Nishani felt frustrated. *Since my mother had a life, she left my father. Now I have one, so she should be left alone.* When she checked her mobile phone, she found three missed calls from Neev. She called him on a whim and said, 'Do you know any middlemen? I need a flat for myself.'

He kept her on hold. Almost a minute later, he spoke again. 'Would a studio apartment in Khar Road do?'

'Is it secured?'

'Take my word for it. I stay in the adjoining apartment.'

From strangers, to colleagues, and now neighbours—a journey was taking place.

It took a month for Nishani to settle into her new apartment. The day when the last bit of the interior was done, Nishani invited Neev to celebrate with a bottle of scotch. They sat sipping their drink right beside the French window which framed an empty park outside and the loneliness beyond it. It was one in the night. The sky had a few stars and a lot of clouds.

Nishani's mobile phone buzzed with a message. She read it and in an instant gloom took over her face.

'What happened?' Neev said, adding one more ice cube to his drink.

'I'd asked my friend to book the tickets for the Iron Maiden concert next month in Bangalore. She is saying it's sold out.'

Neev picked up his phone, dialled a number, and talked crisply.

'Yes, the one happening the next weekend. Don't disappoint me on this. It's for a special friend.' Neev glanced at Nishani while saying so. 'Thanks.' He cut the line and said, 'What about you, me, and your Enfield to Bangalore?'

Nishani spoke after a thoughtful pause. 'Why are you doing all this for me, Neev?'

'Just like that.'

Nishani looked at him for a moment and said, 'Guess what, I wasn't born yesterday.' She sported a mocking smile.

'Well, you were the damsel in distress and I played the knight in shining armour.' He gave her his best smile. It was a killer, she had to admit.

'To your lie,' an amused Nishani raised her glass. Neev clicked it with his and said, 'The truth is, I like you.'

'Like me? As in?'

'Someone told me she wasn't born yesterday.'

'Uh-huh. That someone likes you too.'

For a moment they kept looking into each other's eyes. She finished her drink in a gulp. He copied. They kept their scotch glasses aside. As a soft breeze invaded the window and caressed their senses, they leaned forward with tilted heads and smooched. Finally, their lips unlocked, and as they sat closer than they were before, Nishani said, 'I don't want a relationship that will demand from me a physical, emotional, or spiritual ownership.'

'Then what is love for you?'

'Love, like everything else, is only a reaction at a particular point in time. That's all. A reaction to someone you see, to something you come across. And I must be free to do whatever my instincts tell me in that instant. It's the same human instinct because of which we are alive tonight, sipping this scotch, and kissing. Everything else apart from that instinct in a human is a faux pas.'

Neev was in a momentary trance.

'I never associated such depth with you.'

'You are not the only one,' Nishani winked, amused.

'I'll try my level best to live up to your kind of love.'

'Don't worry. Even if you don't, I won't demand it of you. In fact, you are even free to commit infidelity being in a relationship with me.'

Neev was stunned.

'That's the only way the infidelity will not be an infidelity, right?' Nishani added.

The very reason, Neev wondered, which took him away so many times from Reva was nothing to Nishani.

'Basically, you want an open relationship with me,' he said.

'No. An open relationship again has a defined boundary of non interference. What I am talking about is a 'no definition' relationship. No emotional narcissism. We'll do what our instincts tell us. We won't do something because of any expectation. We won't mutually decide to act something out in a specific way and then spend our life maintaining that decision even though we both know it doesn't hold. Life's a mini skirt, Neev, and hypocrisy of any kind only makes it look like a bikini.'

A consuming silence ensued. After which two animals unleashed themselves onto each other, initiating a carnal war where losing was winning and winning was about losing it all.

'Maiden! Maiden! Maiden!'

It was a human sea of around twenty to twenty five thousand fans of the iconic heavy metal English band—Iron Maiden.

After cracking her voice to the full in the concert, Nishani thanked Neev by demanding a love-making session. They had intentionally used fake names to register themselves at the small hotel they were in and had come in dressed as vagabond bikers with leather outfits to mow away any weed of recognition.

Though Neev was not into music, he was happy to make the non-stop mini road trip to Bangalore. For some hours, Nishani drove the Enfield, but for most, Neev did. They got down thrice; once to have their lunch which they had packed from their home and twice to answer nature's call. When Neev was away for one such call to the nearby country side fields, Nishani, waiting by the Enfield on the highway, realized he had not taken his phone with him. He seldom cared about it. She picked it and went straight to the message section. One particular message in the sent items caught her eye. It read: So is this what the fucking deal is coming to? You know how much I love you. Nishani kept the phone noticing Neev waving at her from a distance. They hit the highway again.

'When did you lose your virginity?'

'Three-four years back,' said Neev and then corrected, 'No actually five years back. What about you?' They were shouting in each other's ears.

'Last week, with you.'

It made Neev turn once.

'You kidding me?'

Nishani nodded with a mischievous smile.

'Man, for a beginner you had the confidence of a porn star.'

Nishani laughed out loud. Next, she threw at him the real reason why she initiated the conversation.

'You must have lost it with Reva.'

For a split second, Nishani saw the speedometer of the bike slow down and then pick up again.

'What do you know about Reva and me?'

'Pretty much what the world knows; you guys were kind of committed till Shahraan came in.' The last bit was deliberate.

A few seconds passed by in silence after which Neev asked, 'Can you tell me why people need someone?'

'I feel we don't have any internal dump. We have a production unit inside alright, but not a dump. So we need to be with someone for dumping our emotions, whims and, you know, all that shit. A tangible, physical walking-talking dump is all we need alongside all the time till we breathe.'

The quietude that followed stretched till they reached Bangalore.

It was all quiet when an exhausted Nishani woke up in her bed; naked and thirsty. She smiled to herself wondering how would the population, who idolized her because of her immensely popular girl-next-door television avatar with all the qualities a typical Indian male would want in his future wife, react if they knew a couple of hours back she was involved in kinky sex inside a cheap hotel. Idolization is the progeny of illusion and ignorance.

She turned on the bed to realize Neev wasn't there by her side. Nishani quickly put on her undergarments followed by her jeans and a tee. She switched on the light but there was indeed nobody. Not even in the toilet, she checked. Wondering where Neev could be in the dead of the night, she noticed his mobile phone on the table beside the bed. Next, her eyes fell on his shorts which he must have doffed before...she realized his jeans were not there; nor was his leather jacket. His leaving in a hurry was obvious now. Nishani sat on the bed; nonplussed. Her eyes discovered his wallet atop his backpack which he had thrown carelessly after they checked in. He should be somewhere nearby. An impulse made her check her bike's keys in her jean's pocket. They were there. He must be somewhere near.

Moving out of the hotel, she soon discovered a petrol pump which was as deserted as a graveyard. Half a minute of walk later, she reached a roadside motel which had a few bulbs on. There was a truck stationed nearby. Some people were having dinner. Nishani was about to go to the motel when she saw a car parked a little ahead of the truck. And a man's voice hit her ears. She was confident it was Neev. As she increased her pace and reached somewhat near the car, she noticed someone else standing by him. The one with whom he was talking animatedly. For whom Neev had left her alone in the hotel room at this hour.

It was Reva Gupta.

From a slit in her blanket, she noticed Neev unlock the door. He was holding a whiskey bottle and a glass. When he sat down to open the bottle, she further noticed his fingers were trembling. As he gulped the drink neat, his facial redesigning told her about the whiskey's journey down his throat. Once half the bottle was gone and his hands were not able to pour it properly in the glass, Nishani feigned waking up.

'Oh, Neev,' she said in a raspy voice, 'I had a bad dream.' And then she shrieked. 'What on earth are you doing with that bottle?' She sat up holding the bed sheet to her bosom.

'She ditched me.'

'What? Who?'

'The bitch ditched me.'

'Answer me Neev, don't rhyme.'

'Reva.'

'Reva? Reva Gupta?'

'Yes.'

'But you two were done with each other anyway.'

'No, no, no. She has finally ditched me.'

Nishani realized sitting on the bed won't do. She stretched her hands in front. The bed sheet slid down, exposing her soft yet firm breasts.

'Come here, my love. Come to me.'

Like an android, Neev stood up, climbed the bed, and hid his face in her lap.

'Now like a good boy, vent it out. It'll help.' *A woman down with love and a man down with alcohol are at their most vulnerable state*, Nishani knew. *A soothing touch, then, can get you anything reasonable or otherwise.*

'I met her just now.'

'Just now? But you are with me.'

'I know.' His babbles were getting difficult to understand.

'Come on, tell me.' She slapped his cheeks softly.

'I went to meet her. We broke up. She promised me not to—' And Neev was done for the night. Disappointed, Nishani placed his head on the bed; her mind an opera house of thoughts.

She knew a chance was lost as in his senses, Neev would be tight-lipped about Reva's and his encounter. *Why did he say she ditched him? Weren't they separated yet? Then what's Reva doing with Shahraan?* Nishani didn't know when those questions turned from emotional caffeine to a perfect lullaby.

Neev was incorrigibly silent throughout the journey back to Mumbai and in the days that followed. Neev's screen performance abruptly declined, he started coming late on sets, and picked up fights with the crew on the slightest of excuses. Months passed. Soon the serial's TRP dropped from 12.5, the highest across all channels, to 10 to to 8.6 at the last count. The chaos inside him didn't allow him to organize anything outside.

All through these days, Nishani remained a silent observer. She didn't want to impose herself on him, or his privacy. Yes, they were in a relationship, but that didn't mean either owed the other anything. They were individuals and Nishani wanted them to remain that way. It was only after the director requested if she could help sort him out, she decided to intervene.

The after-shoot dance rehearsals were a new addition on their otherwise fixed schedule. It was for a dance-based show on television where they were having a special celebrity episode. When Nishani messaged him saying she would wait for him downstairs around eight, Neev informed her he had withdrawn his name on the pretext of health problems. She reached his flat; enraged.

'What bullshit is this, Neev?'

He was as silent as winter.

'I have been quiet till now doesn't mean I haven't witnessed anything. What and why are you doing all this?'

'You won't understand.'

'If you think I won't, then don't tell me. But you have no right to pull your name out when you know that we were in this dance program as a couple. You should have at least consulted me.'

Neev was still.

'Though I never wanted to ask you, Neev—' she took a moment to frame her words right, 'but what happened that night in Bangalore really?'

Neev looked at her for a moment and then said, 'I can't dance where Reva is one of the judges.'

'But we are not in the competition. It's just one episode special we'll feature in. What's the big deal?'

'The big fucking deal is that I love Reva.'

'You love her? Or you can't see her go to someone else?' A moment later, she added, 'Weren't the newspapers right? Didn't Reva leave you for Shahraan?'

'No. That's not correct.'

'Then what is it?'

'I can't tell you.'

'Alright. Tell me this: whose Neev are you right now? Mine or Reva's?'

For the first time since the night in Bangalore, the face of sanity popped its head up from the mud of confusion for Neev.

'Honestly, I thought I was getting into a relationship with a man, not a kiddo.' She sat down with a thud on the sofa.

'You know how low the TRP's of our serial are going? People are complaining they don't see the spark in us anymore. I told our director I would take care of you. But tomorrow I'll tell him I also failed just like everybody else because I too am nobody for him,' Nishani broke down.

The gravity of it hit Neev hard. Every word Nishani said was true, he knew. He walked up to her, knelt down, and taking her hands into his asked her to open her eyes. She did. Looking deep into them he said, 'I'll be back in a minute.'

'I want my Neev.'

'Your Neev will be back in a minute. Trust me.' He went to the bedroom to change while Nishani rubbed the fake tears.

The dance show episode shot two weeks later was a success and in a way marked the comeback of the Neev his fans were in love with.

'You two look great together.' That was Reva's only comment for them that night.

The producers of *Acha Jee Main Haari* cashed in on the regained popularity and its TRP was on the rise again. Two months later, on the night it attained a steady 12, Neev took Nishani to a corner during the shoot.

'Thank heavens you were there for me, else everything I earned would have gone to the gutters by now.'

She responded with a prolonged kiss.

'By the way,' Neev seemed excited, 'Next year's telly awards co-presenters are our producers—the Shah Brothers.'

Did he just announce the winners, Nishani wondered, and kissed him again.

At the prestigious Indian Television Awards held in Singapore the following year, Nishani and Neev won the Best Jodi award, while Nishani won the Best Newcomer award as well as the award for Best Actress. And it was none other than Shahraan Ali Bakshi who did the honours of presenting her with the last one. *There was something about Shahraan, awards, and me*, she wondered. She thought perhaps she was destined to kill him on stage someday. Walking on the stage in a designer black full-sleeved tight kameez with a lace border and a black churidaar, teamed with six-inch heels, loose hair, and a glowing smile, Nishani redefined elegance. As Shahraan handed her the award statuette to stentorian applause from the spectators, he spoke into her ear.

'Congratulations. You look like the perfect Indian diva.'

'Thanks. This is the second time you are giving me an award.' Their eyes linked. Shahraan's eyebrow contorted. 'Really?'

'St. Jones Senior Secondary 2001, annual sports event.'

Shahraan's face trumpeted his cluelessness.

'Never mind. This may help you. I am Shekhar's daughter.'

'Shekhar who?'

'Superstar Shekhar Rai.'

The award, the accolades were nothing for Nishani compared to the way Shahraan's visage changed. As if she had stripped him naked on a public platform with his hands tied.

'Do meet me backstage,' said Shahraan as they smiled at the flashes of cameras together.

She met Shahraan in the green room right after receiving the award.

'So, you are Shekhar Sir's daughter?'

Shekhar *Sir*? That's a pleasant surprise. 'I am.'

'He will always remain a 'Sir' for me. He was such an inspiration, a benchmark for my generation.'

'For other generations too.'

'Sure.'

Nishani was looking straight at Shahraan while he fidgeted with his Mont Blanc pen. She knew he had the words—whatever they were—ready in his mind. But why was he buying time?

'What are you doing these days?'

'Just this serial.'

His face was a concoction of disturbance and thoughtfulness.

'You like films.'

'It's in my blood.' She was intentionally trying to bring everything back to Shekhar. Back to square one.

'Right. You want to act in one? I am sure it will give your career a big boost.'

'Do I need to give you a blowjob for that?'

It sounded casual, but for some seconds, Shahraan looked as if he didn't get her words right.

'I had to give a blowjob to secure the role that fetched me the award tonight. And I don't know how it works for a movie.'

A faint twinkle appeared in Shahraan's eyes after which he sniggered out loud.

'No, no. You don't have to give me any job for that. I think you fit the kind of face ATM is looking for his next film. It'll start sometime after my Genghis Khan film.'

'ATM?'

'Arunodaye T. Manjrekar'

'The box office king.'

'Same guy.'

'I'll be more than happy.'

'Good. I'll ask my secretary to arrange a meeting with him in my office sometime soon.'

'Great.'

Acha Ji Main Haari's success bash happened in Mumbai, a couple of days after the award show. It was a grandiloquent affair with all the cast and crew present along with other prominent faces from the television and media world. For someone stepping inside the lounge that had been booked for the purpose, it would seem everyone was enjoying. But amid the dance moves, the happy greets, the joyous hugs, and the constant flying kisses, people were ticking off their priority list. A priority of relationships they needed to invest in for future returns. Nobody complained because everybody indulged in it. Nishani was sipping her John Collins, maintaining a plastic smile, and waiting for Neev to come out of the toilet when someone whispered to her, 'Nishani Rai, St. Jones Senior Secondary High school?'

She didn't have to turn for the man was there in front of her now; a tall, fair, and handsome looking man with playful eyes and an innocent smile. For a moment, the rewind button of her life was switched on. And she time travelled, scrutinizing every face she had ever come across; who could this be? The answer blew her mind off.

'Kaash Balloo Sehgal!'

Kaash scratched his forehead playfully and with a broader smile said, 'So, you remember me.'

'Idiot, I never forgot you.' Nishani's happiness glistened with genuineness.

'Thank you.'

'But,' she looked at him bottom up, 'where did all the fat go?' She stared at him in disbelief.

'Where did all the past go?' He could have cried there.

Nishani gave him an appreciative smile which had a spark of nostalgia in it.

'What are you doing here?'

'Your director is a friend of my producer.'

'Your producer?'

'I am doing a small budget, independent film. The shoot is going on.'

'Oh my God! Balloo, you are going to act? I mean, beat that!'

'Not more than our meeting.'

'Damn, yes. I shall prefer the past tonight.'

'Isn't that a sin?'

Nishani frowned for a trice and said, 'Well then, how about a sin tonight?'

THE SENSATION

KAASH SEHGAL

12:30 a.m., 2008

It was nice to meet you. His message read.

She replied: Same here. My friends are jealous because I talked to you.

Tell them I liked you a lot as well.

Haha. Just did that!

Great! BTW, like to do me?

What do you mean???

A favour.

Oh, certainly.

Then do me.

What?

A favour.

What favour?

Doing me.

Are you trying to seduce me?

I'm seducing you to try me, Aravali.

You are fast, Kaash!

Hence guilt doesn't catch up easily. BTW, call me Big D. That's my moan name.

What's a moan name?

The name one's partner screams out during climax. What's your moan name?

I don't have one yet.

Care to gift yourself one tonight?

If you promise not to make me pregnant.

If you promise not to make me your husband.

What am I? Today's special in your favourite restaurant?

Wink!

Next, they left the nightclub together for Kaash's bachelor pad; Cyanide.

In the belly of the night, they satisfied the sexual poet inside the other with rhyming acts of carnal verses. While Kaash did almost everything a man could do to a woman on bed except for a lip to lip kiss. That didn't happen even once. '*But why?*' wondered Aravali.

Two hours later, as they lay naked and sapped atop each other, she somehow managed to say, 'Finally, I get to know my moan name: spice doll. I like it.' They slept inhaling each other's musky odour.

It was around four-thirty in the morning when Aravali felt an urge to pee. She got up and emptied herself in the toilet. When she came back, she noticed Kaash lying naked on his side. She smiled. From the time she saw him at the special screening of his debut film, *Mumbai Dogs,* Aravali wanted to experience this moment, but she never thought it would happen this soon and so easily. It wasn't exactly that she wanted to sleep with him. Easy things never intrigued her. It was something more risky that she had in mind: to get involved.

At twenty-nine, Aravali Pathak was a respected film critic, a newspaper columnist, and a sub editor at one of the largest selling film magazines—*Sinema*.

Kaash's debut film had turned him into an overnight sensation in the industry, more so, after it went onto win the Silver Bear Best Actor award for him at the Berlin Film Festival; an unprecedented feat for any Indian actor. She saw the film for the first time in Cannes where it featured in the *Un Certain Regard* section. Once home, she found herself obsessing about him. Her last break up was two-years-old now and post that, work pressure had disconnected Aravali from normal human needs of companionship within her. Kaash rekindled it. She tried to search the internet, but nothing substantial came out regarding him. She tried to get in touch with him, but he was cold over phone. To extort attention, she wrote a negative review of the film, butchering both the film and his performance. Though this immature behavior surprised her the most, she also knew if someone could force you to exhibit kid-like behaviour, then the person was worth a follow up. The negative review garnered her some brickbats from the producers, the director of *Mumbai Dogs*, and also from a certain section of the industry, but nothing from the man himself. If what she had for him was an ember, from that point onwards, became a mad fire.

One fine night, while attending a friend's birthday party at a nightclub, she chanced upon him. As she introduced herself, Kaash took notice. Neither knew when their discourse took a flirtatious turn. It excited her down-on-slight-alcohol self. Mobile numbers were exchanged, messages happened next, and now he was responsible for her life's first orgasm.

With a halo of curiosity, she got up and perused Cyanide. She went to the modular kitchen at the far left. It was cleaner than hers. She touched the shelf, the sink, the coffee maker, the microwave, the oven…trying to leave an impression. In the middle of the kitchen was a neat and tidy dining table. There was a heap of red shining apples arranged at its centre. She picked up one. The bachelor had so far impressed her with the way he maintained his pad. *What about his women?* On the right corner, she noticed a small bathroom cabinet. She caressed its translucent door, sighing, as if in the empty bathroom she could see certain arousing images. Then her eyes fell on a slightly ajar wardrobe. She felt tempted to open it. She did. Inside were clothes, shoes, travel bags, and other usual stuff. A half open first-aid box peeped out from behind a pile of tees. She thought it was a strange place to keep a thing like that. As she picked it up, intrigued, she could already see its contents: a few sheets of paper. She held one of them. The heading read: Dear Nish. The rest of the papers too started with the same two words. *Love letters? Should I read them?* She threw a furtive glance at Kaash. He was sound asleep. Now that she had seen the letters, Aravali knew she wouldn't rest in peace without knowing their content. She sat down on the furry mat right in front of the wardrobe making herself comfortable, took a bite from the apple, and opened the first letter.

February 6

Dear Nish,

It's important to notice things around you. And what is more important is nobody should notice you noticing things. But like me, if everyone starts noticing while nobody is noticing, won't everyone end up noticing everyone's eagerness to notice while no one's noticing?

Forget it.

God helps those who help themselves. That's what is written on the scenic poster above my roommate's bed. It's funny because every night he masturbates right under it. As I'm writing this, my roommate here is actually masturbating under his blanket. Why else would his blanket rock right at the point of his groin? He is also using a torch inside to see a nude picture of Pamela Anderson. I saw him slip it in. But he didn't notice me noticing it. I hope. Though this is not the first time this 'noticing' lesson has worked for me. You must be thinking where did your Balloo vanish suddenly? No, not yours. Just Balloo. But then why not yours? Yours Balloo. Yeah! Whenever I try to be honest, with you or anybody else, with you especially, I end up thinking what will you think of me if I'm really honest? The thing is everybody wants honesty, but nobody can take it. Perhaps this was one reason why I used to be a lonely soul in St. Jones as well. It has been just over twenty days in this boarding school. Twenty one, I just now counted.

It all happened a month after our annual sports event at St. Jones. Mom told me I'll have to study in a boarding school till my graduation. She gave me a Cadbury's which was a signal for me to not ask questions. Did I ever tell you whenever my parents are in distress and want me to keep my queries to myself they give me Cadbury's instead of a clear answer? And they think I don't notice. What they never notice is that I notice them as well as the fact that they don't notice.

I'm sorry I couldn't even tell you that I was going away. If you are angry, please accept my sincere apologies. At first, even I didn't like the idea. Why this boarding school and why not St. Jones? 'Why': that's the word I guess features in every person's monologues with God. Anyway, after mom gave me the Cadbury's, I didn't ask her or dad about anything. I never ask dad anything anyway; Cadbury's or no Cadbury's.

Hence I'm here: The Shimla School for Boys. It sucks. I read in one of the books you recommended me that school is interesting only if it has someone you look up to in a special way. And for me that's you. You know it, right? Even if you don't, that's besides the point. I know you are special to me; that's the point. After watching a few movies and reading a few love stories, I thought I was in love with you. But then I thought the boys and girls in movies have a few hours to meet, express, and copulate, while in books there are a finite number of pages to do so. But life's finiteness can't be judged. So why should I hurry? If I feel something for you, let that boil inside me, let it toss the lid of my heart out only then I would let you know. I mean, I don't have to get you within the next two or three hours like in a movie or by one hundred and fifty page of a book. We don't necessarily have to date lest the readers think nothing is happening in this book. This is our life. So who gives a damn if our excitement is someone else's boredom? Thus I have decided even if I love you, in the truest sense of the word, I shall not tell you I do. So when you read this don't think I love you just as yet. Though, I like you. I admire you. I can't resist you either.

My roommate just ran into the bathroom. This time, I am sure he noticed me noticing him scampering to the bathroom holding his crotch.

Happy Valentine's Day, Nish.

August 7

Dear Nish,

If I love you and entertain this love, I shall continue to love you. Obviously. But what if I consciously choose to push myself away from you, mow all the grass of feelings that I have grown for you within me? Will the love I have for you still exist? If it doesn't, it doesn't. I too shall hang onto the excuse that there are other needs too a human has to fulfill; social, physical, psychological, psychosexual, psychosocial, and all that behavioral crap. But if... if my love for you still does exist, even after I consciously pull myself out of you, then don't you think in that case no power howsoever powerful will be able to separate the two of us from the core of the other? And that, don't you think, is what love is? I don't think anybody tries it. I mean it's so easy to keep loving someone when you do nothing to not love the person, isn't it?

I don't know how much of it made sense, but this is what was disturbing me since the last few months and I don't have anyone here to talk to. I try to, but they call me an emotional chutiya, and so I curb myself.

I know you have not read the first letter I wrote around six months back. I never posted it. I had written your address, pasted all the necessary stamps on it, and had then gone to the post office to post it as well. There was a surprisingly long queue and standing in it I thought what is more important: my thoughts actually reaching you, or my thoughts surfacing within me with a zealous hunger to reach you? I wasn't sure and so I decided not to post the letter. And now I think I did the right thing. The best way to not complicate a relationship is not letting the other person know that you are already in one with her. Indulge, but never claim. Engage, but never claim. Even involve yourself, but never claim. If I had posted the letter, either you would have replied or you wouldn't have. If you had replied, I would have felt happy, but if you had not, then my ego wouldn't have allowed me to write another letter. And if you had never replied, then this particular letter that I'm writing now wouldn't have happened. Nor the thoughts associated with it. Maybe. Again, if we had indeed exchanged letters, it would have slowly exposed us to each other's strengths and weaknesses. And we would have adjusted our thought process accordingly in lieu of not hurting the other knowingly. As a result of which our honesty towards the other would have corroded with time. And I wouldn't have written this letter, or the subsequent, with the same honesty that I am writing with now. Of course, the taking-for-granted and the expectation factor which I have not taken into consideration also would have played their part. It's not easy to keep them aside if it's a close relationship which ours would have been if I had posted the first letter. Now I thank the devil I didn't!

Instead, I have decided to write a letter to you whenever I'll feel only you would understand the essence of it. As I write this one, it struck me why the sun doesn't come an inch closer to earth? Since it knows, one step forward and it will burn the earth beyond repair and recognition. So sometimes distance is what is necessary to keep a relationship, a relationship.

The rest in life is as usual. And as promised, I won't write to you anything about any as-usual things. But in short, I have settled well in this school simply because I don't give a damn about what would have happened if I hadn't settled. I don't give a damn about the boys who are my batchmates and hence, I'm used to the loneliness here. I think I am happier here than I was in Mumbai. It's an irony, I agree, but then I think irony is the nest where the bird of your heart lays the egg of joy.

By the way, mom and dad have changed. I don't know how exactly, but they have. This time, they were a day late in wishing me on my birthday. I'm feeling too sad to write anymore.

Happy Friendship Day, Nish.

March 13

Dear Nish,

I am not a fear for my fear. For if I was a fear for my fear, than my fear would not be my fear.

Mom was here yesterday. After mom and dad left me in this boarding school last year, this was the first time they came. They called me every weekend alright, but is it too much for a son to ask his parents to visit him regularly? I asked the same thing to mom and she broke down. She was crying like I used to in my junior classes. I remember you had once seen me do so and had called me cute. But mom wasn't looking cute at all. In fact, I loathe thinking about it. Their health has deteriorated a bit. Especially dad. Mom said he has diabetes, so he has lost a bit of weight. I didn't know about this disease or else I would have tried to acquire it for my own weight issues. Dad wasn't looking nice though. It seemed to me they were hiding something from me. They didn't even bring any chocolates.

Anyway, let me come to the point why I decided to write this letter. Something unusual happened. And it reminded me of you. And our first kiss. Remember? I still can taste it in my heart. I wasn't prepared for it. I think the best and the worst things of life happen when you are least prepared. I also remember you said how innocent I am. I was actually. A year in this hostel has changed me. Tell me something, whenever we meet next, if you come to know the one thing you liked about me the most isn't there anymore, will you start hating me? It's such a scary thought. I wish I could hold onto my innocence forever. Why is it that whatever we want to hold onto, flaps its wings the most? I think it's for the best that I'm no longer in touch with you. I can accept my loss of innocence, but I can't tolerate your realization of my loss.

What happened was last weekend my roommate decided to meet his girlfriend in another school here. He bribed the warden with money and me with temptation. He said there will be another girl as well and it could take care of my fledgling love life. He doesn't know about you. Nobody does except me, my pen, and the letters. So, I gave in to the temptation and we went to meet the girls bunking our horse riding class. I don't know what he did with his girlfriend, but I squeezed the other girl's small breasts. She said I could do that and I did. I was happy, but when she tried to kiss me on the lips, I lost my cool. My lips belong only to you, Nish. I slapped her. She called me a dog. I called her a bitch and ran away from there. My roommate thought there was a police raid or something since we were meeting in a park. So he too ran away. Then we had a fight in our room because his girl and he were up to something and he thought I disrupted it. As I write this, I realize why I couldn't allow the other girl to kiss me. If she'd kissed my lips, I felt, she would have snatched you from me. Though pressing her breasts didn't feel much wrong comparatively, I'm still upset about it. What is wrong, Nish? I hear this word 'wrong' a lot among my love-struck classmates. The moment you have someone in your heart, they say everything in life becomes black and white. One tends to categorize things into something specific like 'I should' and 'I shouldn't'. And the ones who don't do so are called ditchers. Did I ditch my feelings for you today, Nish? I thought the deal was I shouldn't allow anybody to creep into the space where you are. But then I think if that's really the deal in love, then it's a kind of cowardice, isn't it? I'm a coward, Nish, because I don't have the guts to test my love for you by allowing a chance to someone else. I think sometimes we are too scared to disappoint ourselves of our own choices. I probably slapped the other girl because I feared if she kissed me, it would taint something I referred to as pure—our first kiss. And why did I assume our kiss was the purest without even caring to kiss all the girls all over world? Love! Thus I believe love really makes you categorize things into black and white.

I know I'm funny. But my feelings for you are funnier.

Happy Holi, Nish.

December 21

Dear Nish,

The usual things are going the usual way. The unusual thing is I now know what I need to do all my life. Act! Yes, I have joined the drama wing of my school. I did it on a whim. But playing one of the three witches in Shakespeare's Macbeth, I realized this is the coolest thing one can do in life: to be someone else! I enjoy it like as much I hate being myself. Do you like to be yourself? I know so much about myself that I get bored to death being myself. I have started reading books on drama and cinema. I remember how you used to tell me about world cinema, underground theatres, and all. Though I understood nothing then—I confess—but I used to listen to you as if my life depended on it. I'm also sure you knew it but you never taunted me. I never even yawned at your face like others did when you talked about things which people ten years older to you should have been talking about. It was so cool, wasn't it? Me not understanding a word and still listening to you; you knowing I am not getting shit and still you continuing. I wanted to listen, you wanted to talk. The perfect couple! Sometimes I crave to look at you. I don't have any photograph of yours except for a sports day group photograph which I look at through a magnifying glass that I stole from the Physics lab.

So why am I writing this letter? To tell you about my dramatics class! But also to tell you something is wrong. The principal has summoned my parents twice since the fee was not paid in time. The fee is paid here at six months interval. But I have learnt that I have been a defaulter for two terms now. It's very unlike my parents. Anyway, mom and dad are coming this Friday. I'm a little scared. What if they rusticate me? It was very difficult for me to adjust here to begin with and now that I somewhat have, there's this danger of another shift. Can you tell me, Nish, why we have to keep changing space and coordinates in life? It often happens the moment we start feeling confident and comfortable in the present coordinate.

Finally, there is this girl who likes me. She is in the drama class with me. She is a year senior to me. I like her too. But I don't like her the way I like you. I imagine her naked and all. I think I shouldn't have written this. But now that I have written it, I have realized honesty is difficult to stick to. But I can lie to myself, not to you. I get a hard on seeing that girl. I jerk too. I'm no longer the Balloo you liked. I have realized this. It's good I came over here. Physical distance from the one you love is a good way to escape one's rottenness. Is this normal, Nish? Does everyone rot after a point of time or is it me alone? I can't see you rot ever. So it has to be me. You can slap me when we meet next. No, I'll never meet you again. What will I do meeting you when I'm not the person I thought I would be all my life for your sake? What will you do meeting me when you'll know the very thing that made me appeal to you is no longer there? And we are not even married! I say that because I think only in a marriage can two individuals feel obligated to find something in their spouse which appeals to them after knowing what they liked the most about the person is gone. Not in our relationship. And if what I just said is true, than I would never like to get married to you. Marriage puts us in a risk of getting used to a person. And I don't know if I'll ever be ready to take this risk. It makes me wonder if incompleteness is the best way to keep something alive. Sometimes I have a feeling whoever designed this earth and its innate laws had a thing for paradoxes.

I am under suspension for two days. My roommate read one of the letters I wrote to you and mocked me. According to him, I'm a freak, because if I don't post the letters, then what the hell am I doing writing them. I beat him up pretty badly.

Merry Christmas, Nish.

January 2

Dear Nish,

Life is about doing what you never wanted to do. Love is about doing what you never thought you could do.

I dropped out of school. I am in Mumbai now. My life has changed, Nish. The last one year has been unbelievably bad. Or should I say educative. If I'd written to you before, I would have only cribbed, abused others, and fetched your sympathy. I'm happy I am writing now because now I'm somewhat used to this new life.

Remember I told you about my fees not being paid in time? It was true. I never knew my dad had a jewellery shop in Zaveri Bazaar here. Dad had three employees under him who steadily cheated him. By the time he realized it, he was under a debt of one and half crore. The shop was on lease so when he couldn't pay the rent, it too was taken away. Now we are living in a chawl. Dad has now set up a small catering business with a friend of his. Our income has come down substantially. Mom wanted to work as a teacher in a school, but I asked her not to. Instead, I work. It's a small hotel, Hotel Sundar, near Mumbai Central where I work as a receptionist. I get four thousand five hundred a month. The owner said when I'll turn eighteen, he will increase it to six. Though I'm underage, the owner, Shubash Sir, was impressed by my English and charm. Oh, I didn't tell you, during all this shit, I lost a lot weight and now weigh only sixty-nine kilos. Funny number, I know.

Day before yesterday, a couple came to our hotel. The girl had hair just like yours and for a moment I thought it was you. I excused myself out. Of course it wasn't you. Or was it? I don't know. I don't know what made me hide like a convict. I smoked an entire box of cigarettes just thinking about it. Yes, I have started to smoke. And drink too. I think I never wanted you to discover me like this, even though this is my resilient side. Weird! It was because this particular side existed in me that I didn't succumb to depression and other shit. I call it the jacket-over-Jack syndrome of mine. I always react to the 'jacket', than care about the Jack wearing it. Ideally, I should be proud of the Jack in me who is helping his family at the age of seventeen, but I am instead ashamed of the jacket that presented me as a small-time receptionist in an unimportant hotel.

Guess where I am right now? As the world celebrates New Year's Eve, I'm inside a police station. Shubash Sir's wife, Vinita, said I tried to rape her. And I was dutifully handed over to the police.

Three months back, I met her for the first time when Shubash sir sent me to his home to fetch a few of his belongings. After that, I'd been summoned there a number of times by her for some errand or the other. It was her chance to talk to me about her life, her sexual life, her emotional life, and every other shit life she led. She always used to be extra appreciative of me. Then yesterday, she said she loves me and asked me to elope with her because Shubash Sir used to beat her. She never showed me any scars. Vinita is twenty five. Shubash sir is forty. I told her I don't love her. She slapped me. I told her I have other responsibilities. She slapped me. I added I have someone in my heart. She slapped me. Then I punched her once. She started bleeding from her nose. She called Shubash Sir and cooked a lie. Nobody believed me. Before calling him, she said if I was sorry and agreed to be her slave forever, only then she would take her statement back.

An hour ago, when dad was here, I finally said I was sorry. He realized I had actually done the dastardly act. He asked me not to see him again. He thinks I have insulted his entire pedigree. He didn't give me a chance to explain what the real issue was. Mom came, cried, and went away. I'm sure I'll be released by tomorrow after which I will not keep my promise of being Vinita's slave. I would have to search for another job and a new place to live.

People around me have been charged for different crimes, but inside all are accountable for the same sin: Life!

Happy New Year, Nish.

September 27

Dear Nish,

Are relationships like toothpaste? Everyday we unknowingly empty them one squeeze at a time and then one day we realize there's no more left. There's the tube, of course, but no more paste. What do you do then?

I changed my job but Vinita didn't leave me. I don't know how she tracked me down. I never asked her. I'm working as a flight steward with a domestic airline. I faked my school passing certificate with the help of a middleman. Thank god ours is a democracy.

Vinita sponsored my three month air-steward training course. At first, it hurt my ego, but then I thought I also have a life to take care of. I'm earning eleven thousand a month. I give four to my mother so that she doesn't have to work. She tells my dad that she is working and that it's her income. I haven't met dad since my release. Mom meets me secretly. She knows where I stay. Whenever she is here, she arranges everything in my small rented place. Vinita comes here during her safe period. We fuck like mad. If I don't fuck her, she bores me with her emotional life, spiritual life, sexual life, and the other lives she lives in this one life. Once I gave her some hints about you. She responded by saying there are two worlds: one within your heart and one outside. And the dissatisfaction we garner from the outside world determines from whom we crave satisfaction within the heart world. And when the real world's and the heart world's intentions synchronize, we call it 'happiness'. I never thought Vinita could think also.

Priyanka is my colleague; an air hostess. She likes me a lot. How do I know? When we have some feelings for someone, our entire look and body language becomes a meaning of our feeling. But she scares me too because being close to her, I feel, disturbs the equilibrium I have with you in me. I think whenever we come in contact with someone, that person starts to translate us. With every translation, we drift away from our original self and become a translated version; for better or for worse.

I fear if Priyanka and I come close, I may invariably be translated further and I don't want that. I am so content with this arrangement: me not having to meet you ever, not having to sleep with you ever, and not having to risk a separation with you ever. It's not that we always get to fly together, but whenever we do, I like her company. We discuss a lot about cinema, authors, books, poetry because she writes as well. I have read some of her work. It's good. It's because I love her company that I avoid her intentionally. It's a tug of war between attraction and attachment. Sometimes, while lying beside Vinita who loves to caress my naked chest, I wonder whom I am kidding? Let me tell you a secret and that will give you a glimpse of my condition: I have fucked Vinita a lot of times but never have I allowed her to kiss my lips. Weirdly unbelievable, isn't it? That's exactly what you have translated me into, Nish.

I still dream of being an actor. I practice late night in front of the mirror. Vinita said she had a cousin in the film industry and shall recommend me if I marry her. I haven't responded to this proposal of hers. Right now, I only want to save some money for my mom. I can't afford to leave this job. Circumstances circumcise the dick of our desires. I think I'm drunk. I better end here.

Happy Diwali, Nish.

July 8

Dear Nish,

Love is only the realized part of a connection.

And I have realized the other portions so organically, unwillingly too, that it has become ineffable for me. The unrealized part are there in me, but my conscious lets that part sleep. When I said love is the realized part, I meant it's only the tip, the good part of a heart to heart connection. And a normal person is happy to realize only the tip. The rest is for people who think a lot, who feel, and whose awareness of self defeats their ignorance hands down.

I have realized there's a spiritual libido in me. Then there is an emotional libido as well. And finally, the libido for the flesh is also there. Vinita satisfies my physical libido. Priyanka satisfies my emotional libido. And you, Nish, you take care of my spiritual libido. I thought about it a lot in the last few months. Vinita for me is only an object. We fuck. We talk. We fuck. She wouldn't have been with me if either of us didn't have hormones. I'm with her because of the same reason she is with me. She claims it, I don't. She is responsible for unlocking a sexual maniac in me. Through her I have realized that in order to satisfy the physical libido, it doesn't matter who you are with.

With Priyanka it's different. I like to be with her even without a hard on. I guess when a man feels so for a woman, he should secure her through marriage. But as much as she satisfies my emotional libido, I feel the hunger of my spiritual libido. It's like you go for a roller-coaster ride, you enjoy whatever number of loops it has, but when you come out you feel a void in you which says another loop would have been just perfect. It's elusive satisfaction that I'm talking about. And I feel it every time Priyanka and I finish our discourse. It makes me crave for another 'loop'. She, with her presence, has connected me to the emotional cribber in me. Now I know why nobody can live a solitary life.

To experience that extra 'loop', I am pushed to you; the one who satiates my spiritual libido. Like there is only one God, there can only be one spiritual satisfier. Here the objectivity I feel toward Vinita doesn't exist. The subjectivity I suffer from with Priyanka doesn't mean anything. That's why, Nish, I won't be able to get over you. The reason is simple: I don't have to. Lucky are those who get to satisfy oneself of all three libidos through one person.

Anyway, Priyanka finally proposed to me. She didn't say so directly, but I understood it was a proposal. Her parents want her to be engaged to an IIT-IIM boy who is here on vacation from the US. They don't know each other. They are supposed to stay together for the rest of their lives. Hail man's lust for domesticity! Anyway, since the proposal I have been thinking about what I should tell her. If I'd never met you, I would have certainly said yes to her. Nish, you are not merely a realization. You are an awareness for me. And I can't explain you to her. I only told her there 'was' someone. Sometimes the present comes out in past tense. She didn't probe much.

This February, Vinita introduced me to the distant cousin she'd told me about before; Ricky. He is a line producer. He said he would see what he can do. But later Vinita discovered about Priyanka. She has always been possessive about me. I have seen her sniffing my clothes in case I am cheating on her. As if my saying yes to Priyanka would qualify as a betrayal for Vinita and my relationship. Anyway, this was how things were two months back: Priyanka thought I *would definitely say yes to her, I wanted an excuse to say no to her because I have you. Vinita said in case I needed any connection in the film industry, then I had to forget Priyanka. And these are how things are right now. Priyanka is engaged, I was part of a film unit for a month, shooting some cheap commercial flick with a big star, while Vinita and I are no longer together. When I told her about my not accepting Priyanka's proposal, she was so ecstatic that she convinced Ricky to make me a part of a film shoot as a prop boy.*

One day, during lunch break I heard Ricky abusing the caterer for not bringing proper non-veg food. I couldn't control myself and beat him up like mad. The caterer was my dad. I was, of course, thrown out of the shoot. I met my mom after the incident who said I did the right thing. I said I did what I did. Adjectives are such a waste of time. Right now, I don't have a job since I'd applied for leave because of the shoot, the airlines officials hadn't accepted and so I'd resigned. I don't have Vinita. The Ricky bash up didn't escape Shubash Sir's ears. And when he came to know Vinita had requested him to take me, he was extra rude to her. I heard she is pregnant. Except for some savings, I have nothing. Tomorrow is a stranger. Yesterday is a stalker. Today is the savior. But when the savior is confused, the stranger begins to stalk and the stalker becomes even scarier.

I miss Priyanka even though I said no to her. Don't you think at times we behave as spineless versions of our desires? Why else am I more committed to the person who happened in my heart but not in reality than to the one who could have happened to me in real?

Happy 'First Kiss', Nish. I suddenly remembered it's this day, a different year, that we'd kissed.

August 13

Dear Nish,

If I can defeat myself every day, then I don't need to give a fuck about any other race!

Every time I sit down to write to you, there's some change in me, my life, and my surroundings. Or maybe it's the other way round. Now I stay with my parents and I work with dad in his catering business. Mom somehow managed to explain to him it wasn't my fault that I landed up in the lock up—just like it wasn't his fault he lost his money. I don't know if dad has really forgiven me. Mom said he blames himself for what happened to me in the last few years. The truth is, I have never blamed him for anything. You can't come between someone and his suffering. It's the strongest of all relationships.

The catering business is going alright. We have shifted from the chawl to a proper one-bedroom flat in Mira Road. We cater to birthday parties, weddings, and film productions as well. I go to talk to clients: what all they would like to order, number of people they are looking at, kind of food they want, and the like. Dad supervises the entire process whereas mom looks after the cooking part. We have four cooks. She doesn't want to compromise on the taste. That, she says, is the soul of the food and food is the heart of our business. Taste is the soul of our food; I like that. If there's no taste, the food is useless; doesn't matter how nice it looks. Nish, have I lost my taste doing what I did in these years?

With no Priyanka or Vinita, I feel very lonely at times. I try to immerse myself in work, read a lot, watch films, try to improvise scenes in front of the mirror, criticize myself, depress myself, hate myself, but when someone praises our catering, life seems good again. There are times when I think I'll be the next Shahraan Ali Bakshi and then sometimes I think I will be lost into oblivion forever. I think I'm sick. Anyway, I still remember how nuts you were about Shahraan. I hope it's not like that anymore. They say adolescent crushes wear off easily. I say a lot of adolescent things wear off easily except their memory of it.

I met a guy during one of my catering stints with a film production. He is a FTII pass out. He is into direction. He was supposed to make a documentary for his college when I met him. I suggested him the subject: our catering business. He stayed with me for a week, followed our business, and was fascinated by the number of lives it touched. Avinash and I are good friends now. After he shot the documentary, he took me to the editing room. We sat together for the background score session as well. It's such a mind-blowing world, Nish! I told him I wanted to be an actor and showed him some of my improvisations. He was impressed. He told me he is writing some kind of a new-age film: shoestring budget, dark story, unknown actors, and gritty storytelling with his FTII friends. He said he would ask me to audition once they finalize the script. The working title is 'Mumbai Dogs'. I'm waiting for him to get back to me on this. It's always good to wait for something in life. I think that increases our gravity towards it. But don't we always end up waiting for something in life? If this guy had not come in contact with me, then I would have waited for a chance to come to me. Now that I have, I'll wait for him to get back. As a kid, I used to wait intensely for so many things. As I grew, my 'waiting for' list suffered because life convinced me some things are not worth waiting for.

By the way congratulations, Nish! I saw you in the advertisement. You looked like a natural. Well, you have it in your genes. I'm happy *we'll be in the same industry, but I don't want to come across you. Guess why?*

It'll take care of the biggest wait of my life.

4:30 a.m., 2008

Kaash showed signs of life on the bed. It made Aravali quickly fold the letter in her hand. There was only one more to be read.

From the time she opened the box to the moment she closed it, she knew a journey had taken place. And she'd learned a lot: about life, about relationships, about how both can merge to form a lethal combination and most importantly, about Kaash. He was a living paradox: a compulsive playboy in his mind and an obsessive true lover in his heart. *How I wished all my life for someone to love me like this*, Aravali wondered, *like an uncouth wild animal loves a manipulative forest with unadulterated admiration*. She believed Nishani was lucky in an unlucky way. Lucky because she'd triggered things in a person that girls can only dream about and unlucky for she never knew about them. Or so she sensed reading the letters.

Aravali cautiously kept the letters back in the first-aid box. The way Kaash was turning in his bed, he could wake up anytime. She stood up and placed the box inside the wardrobe like it was before.

She picked her watch lying lazily on a small chair by the bed. The time triggered urgency in her. She had to catch a flight to Kolkata to attend a short-film festival inauguration at Nandan around noon.

Kaash opened his eyes abruptly. He sat up only to realize Aravali was hurriedly dressing.

'I've got to run!' she said and hoped she wasn't looking as nervous as she was feeling.

Kaash only smiled. Once dressed, Aravali picked her bag from the floor and looked at him.

'Can we meet again?'

Kaash nodded.

'Thanks!'

Till she slept with him, she'd only imagined what he'd be like as a person. But after reading the letters, she'd actually seen his emotional genitals.

'See you later, fornicator.' As she winked at him, she was sure nothing on earth could take him away from her now.

SCENE 34

Location: Mumbai Studios

There was an omnipresent hostile energy in the set and a conscious restraint in everyone's demeanour as if a poltergeist was scheduled to strike anytime. After the media claimed the two actors had some raunchy sex on set and followed the news like hunter dogs, the producers realized of all the surgeries in the world, sealing people's mouth, figuratively, is the costliest.

Inside her sophisticated customized vanity van in the parking lot, Reva's eyes were fixed on one of the city's leading tabloids.

Everyone makes mistakes. The quote was highlighted within a box and written in bold black. It was assigned her name. But she never said it. The entire article was knitted with lies. That was the journalist's ploy: either report what was said or report what's not and squeeze out a reaction. It was true for most of the newspapers and channels reporting the nude-scene fiasco.

The bad thing was she knew Shahraan must have read the stupid media stories circulating like poverty does in an underdeveloped country, but the worse was his silence on the issue. It was more depressing than the entire media hullaballoo. She would have loved it if he had asked for an explanation. That would have given her a chance to sort things out. Frustrated, Reva took out a tiny bottle of sleeping pills from her Gucci and popped one in her mouth. She woke up only when the shot was ready.

The scene: Shahraan's and Reva's characters would be sitting under an umbrella across a table for two in a resort. Kaash, playing a waiter, would come with drinks, and while serving, would accidentally spill some on Reva's dress. Her character would be shocked to see her former lover while Shahraan's character, her present husband, would slap the waiter in response. And it would be a cut.

As the actors assembled on the set, Reva tried not to look at either Kaash or Shahraan. The latter sat across her. No words, no emotions. As Arunodaye said action, everything went smoothly till Kaash spilled the drink on Reva's dress as per the script.

'Oh, shit!' Reva, in character, blurted standing up. Shahraan too stood up, but instead of slapping Kaash, he placed a tight slap on Reva's supple cheek. There was an instant collective sigh from the crew, followed by pin drop silence.

BOOK TWO: 2012

CRIES OF A SIN

In the otherwise quiet and dark room, her abrupt laughter had a satanic echo. Lying beside Neev at five in the morning, Nishani wasn't sure what gave her a better orgasm—Neev or the news Vikrant gave her. The slap, she knew, was only an ember. The real arson was only a matter of time now. From the moment she was given the opportunity to appear in the film by Shahraan himself, she was determined to turn this movie into Shahraan Ali Bakshi's swan song. An ugly, dirty swan song beyond which there would only be doom to sleep with for him. Oh! Was she waiting for this film to start!

'What happened?' Neev woke up with a clouded mind. He thought he'd heard her laugh.

'Vikrant called. Shahraan slapped Reva on set.'

'What the fuck!' Neev sat up rubbing his eyes. He seemed thoughtful for a while and then relaxed saying, 'Finally, she got what she deserved. Only it should have been me slapping her.'

Nishani's face scrunched up as if the genre of her mind had suddenly changed. Neev stepped down from the bed and pulled up his Cocksox briefs.

'Where is my phone?'

'Bathroom. Probably.'

It had been a year and a half since they'd moved in together. But for the media and public, they had two different flats. The producer had requested them to keep their personal life incognito and pretend as if they were a replica of their primetime appearance where they played a traditional Indian couple who preferred heart to hormones, for whom even one kiss before marriage was a cardinal sin. Image management was the name of the game. Unreal reality always hooked the audience.

Neev came out of the bathroom, laughing. He was gawking at his mobile phone. It seemed the ghost of mirth had left Nishani and possessed him. Nishani shrugged.

'Beat this—after avoiding me for several months, Mrs Reva Shahraan Ali Bakshi at this obnoxious hour gives me a total of five missed calls.' He threw the phone on the bed for Nishani to check and added, 'It's my time to bite back.' He went inside the bathroom again.

Nishani saw the missed calls and wondered: Reva, all this while, was perhaps trying to be a perfect wife in front of Shahraan, but to accept him, she had to reject her past and perhaps her true self as well. The same self that made her call Neev after such a long gap. It only meant a part in her still longed for him. That was good news as far as Nishani was concerned. She didn't care about what happened between Kaash and Reva. She was only interested in the perceived truth: that they did each other. She was hoping the fact distanced Shahraan from Reva and going by the missed calls, she could safely conclude that's what has happened.

If right now she was Reva, Nishani further wondered, she would need some serious emotional solace. And what better than to call one person who had always been with her. But for her plan to work, Neev had to be sympathetic.

'Why did Shahraan allow Reva to do the nude scene with Kaash anyway?' Nishani picked herself up, wrapped the bed sheet around her bosom, and went to the refrigerator.

'He was being professional. And who knows, perhaps Reva chose to do it. Do you seriously think Shahraan knew about their past?' Neev was relieving himself in the toilet. 'Or for that matter anybody? Even I came to know about them after Kaash told you they have been fuck buddies or whatever.' A pause later he said, 'To hell with her.'

Nishani grabbed a beer from the refrigerator and ensconced herself on the 'Bombay Fornicator' chair beside the bed.

'I think you should call her back.'

'What the fuck do you mean?'

'I mean she is the reason why you are doing this film.'

'Cut the crap.' As he came out of the toilet, he was surprised to find a beer can thrown at him. He caught it alright.

'Both of us are in that sonofabtich's movie because he is one of the producers and he wanted to cash in on our television popularity. That's all.'

'One word from Reva and you would have still been licking the small screen.' Nishani saw Neev take a large gulp from the can. He knew she had a point.

'Now is the time for you to give her a shoulder. It's always handy if one can have the hen-that-lays-golden-eggs as a pet. You are smart enough to gauge what you are saying.' Nishani said noticing Neev's facial contours. She knew he would say yes. Neev was an emotional fool after all. And Reva Gupta was his greatest foolishness.

Neev leaned against the bathroom door, sipping his beer and trying to understand Reva's predicament. He never accused her of any infidelity when he learnt she was in a sexual relationship with Kaash while they were living together. The reason was simple: he too was guilty of it. And the whole world maybe gender biased when it came to infidelity but Neev wasn't. *But should I really call her back?* he wondered. Reva went to Shahraan for her need and now was hoping to get to him again for her own selfish need, then why couldn't he once again become hers to secure his own tight ass? *Need!* It's not a mere noun in a dictionary. It's a fucking law of nature.

'You're right.'

Nishani looked at him.

'I'll call Reva.'

Like a train approaching a station from afar, a smile finally arrived on her face. Nishani gestured with her finger for him to come near her. He did. She poured the remaining beer on her slender feet and started rubbing it on his face slowly.

Reva was in Mehfil Mansion—the sea-facing bungalow in Bandra where she lived with Shahraan. The slap incident had rocked her to the core. It wasn't the first time she had been hit by a man. She'd had her share of violent relationships, be it with Amjad or Neev, but with Shahraan it was different. She never associated him with violence. The worst was, she knew she deserved it.

She was always the woman the world feared and accused of social blasphemy for the silliest reasons because she was a woman with the instinct of a man—uncontrolled and rudely impulsive. Had Shahraan done the same, he would have had the courage to come up to her and demand forgiveness. She was not even entitled to such audacity. And what was Shahraan doing anyway? The two-year long courtship with him could have been a dream for any average Indian woman, but for her it was an inauspicious premonition.

Instead of respecting her individuality, he used her as an emotional bridge to connect to his feelings for Mehfil and give them a more materialistic vent. That was his sin. Reva never complained. This was her sin. By accepting Shahraan, she had jumped right at the top of the food chain in the industry from where she could swallow whoever she wanted to, but there wasn't anyone to swallow her except for her own incorrigible instincts. One such instinct led her to the momentary loosening of her senses with Kaash. Human beings are dangerous she now knew; one temporary slip, one permanent guilt scar.

It was a pack up right after Shahraan left the shoot without completing the scene. Nobody knew where he went. When he wasn't home after two in the night, she asked Krishna to inform Shahraan if he wasn't home soon, she would pack and move out to a hotel without caring much about any subsequent media hoopla. An hour and half later, Shahraan turned up at Mehfil Mansion.

'Avoiding me won't solve the problem,' she almost screamed.

Shahraan could tell she had been crying all the while.

'I need time.'

'Why do you think I didn't come up to you all this week? I gave you time. And today, in front of everyone you...' Her voice trailed off as she started whimpering.

Shahraan threw an icy glance at her and sauntered across the hall room to the lavish bar at the other end. Reva was expecting an apology, since he came across as a guy who won't like a woman crying.

'Don't worry. No newspaper will carry this news. Krishna has made sure of it.'

'I don't care. I don't smile, cry, or sleep with the world. I want to know what your heart thinks, Shahraan.'

All Reva got was humiliating indifference as Shahraan continued making a drink. Rubbing the tears off her cheeks, she charged towards him and snatched the bottle.

'The doctor has asked you not to drink.' She held on to the bottle while Shahraan, as a reflex, tried to snatch it back and in the process it fell. The sound made her miss a heartbeat.

'I don't give a rat's ass about who you sleep with. I have been in love all my life with someone who did just that as a profession.' Shahraan hollered. 'What really hurt me was that you didn't anticipate what your act would do to me. Just the sound of it makes me feel like a loser from here.' He beat on his chest hard. 'And if you did anticipate it and still went ahead, then I don't know what we are doing living under one roof and eating into each other's life.'

'Kaash and I didn't do anything that day. Believe me!' Reva was surprised at how naturally the lies came out and how genuine she sounded. 'Only the words of the script were followed. And I sincerely don't know how this insane conclusion was drawn by the media.'

'Stop lying. Krishna overheard some spot boys talking about how the fresh paint of the room was blotched after the shot.'

Reva felt choked by her conscience. Even if one lies for the good of a relationship, it's always tough. She managed to stand her ground though, observing Shahraan who agitatedly put his hand in his trouser pocket and took out something. He threw it at Reva and said, 'Try finding an excuse for this as well.' He walked off. As she looked down at the I-pill paper box, she knew it was the same she had asked her girl Friday Geeta to bring on the fateful day. That means Shahraan must have had her bag searched. Her breathing went berserk. A sudden rise of anger took care of her inertia. She took a step and her foot landed on two sharp pieces of glass. She didn't feel anything. With her left foot leaving blood marks on the otherwise crystal clear floor, she arrived at the stairs which took her to the room on the mezzanine floor. It was the smallest room of the house. It had a mirror for a wall on one side and a big coral curtain on the other. There wasn't any furniture at all except for a large-sized canvas stand and the associated paraphernalia for painting. The room catered to Shahraan's emotional rants: he painted there.

He had stripped off his shirt and had his trousers rolled up till his knees. His hands were coloured with paint which, kneeling down, he was smudging rhythmically onto the large empty canvas in front. There was a threatening demeanor about him. Reva still came and stood right in front of him.

'So from now on, I'll have to live with a husband who will frisk me emotionally by going through my stuff secretly.'

Shahraan didn't respond. To secure his attention, Reva kicked the canvas. Shahraan stood up glaring at her. For a second Reva thought she actually kicked her good luck right in the groin.

'I'm sorry for whatever unpleasant things you had to go through for me, but I never thought you could come down to this.' The words came out like water does from a municipality tap; in a series of drops.

Shahraan's piercing eyes were enough to make her body shudder. For some time nothing happened and then he pushed her into the nearby wall. Her back hit the switchboard and the lights in the room went off. In the darkness, she felt his hands on her face. She could smell the paint. She fidgeted, her back hit the switch again, and the lights came on. She could see herself in the opposite mirror. Her face now was dripping with red paint. Reva was too numb to even understand why he did that. She saw his hands grab her gown in the middle, she flinched, and darkness descended once again. The gown was torn. Her breasts suffered a hard squeeze for once. Switch on. The breasts and the now loose bra cupping it, the mirror told her, now donned green paint. Shahraan flipped her with an authority that told her she was his Pygmalion. He tore the remaining dress from behind, pinning her hands to the wall. Retaliation wasn't a friend anymore. A second later, Reva's back was wet with black paint. Before she could utter a word, Shahraan flipped her once again and slapping her butt fiercely, moved his hands down her outer thighs to her feet. She glanced at her reflection—she was blue from waist down. He stood up heaving when he smiled at her in a way a man on his death bed would, realizing life's a joke.

'Doesn't matter how many colours I bathe you in,' he said, 'you can't be Mehfil.' Shahraan left the room. If he had spit on her, she wouldn't have felt as humiliated as those words made her feel. All she could do was drop to the floor and cry her heart out.

'I am Reva Gupta. The icon. I don't want to be anybody else' was all her acutely choked self could come up with.

It took a proper hot water shower to get rid of the colours. Feeling helpless and fighting a desperate urge to connect to someone who would not judge her in any way, she called Neev several times. But nobody answered.

'Oh no, I won't be able to do it. Please let me down. I have vertigo,' Aravali earnestly requested as Kaash made her stand on the cemented barricade fencing the terrace of the twenty-first floor apartment where he lived.

She tried her best not to look down, but her fear was an antagonist. Kaash helped her walk the entire square barricade of the sprawling terrace after which she jumped down and hugged Kaash tight, allowing her heart to calm down.

From the last few days, Aravali was complaining of life being a bore. Tonight, Kaash was free to prove her otherwise.

'Whenever life seems boring, give death a chance,' he had told her and brought her up on the terrace for demonstration.

'I did it!' she said. Her skin was cold. 'Thank you, my thought star!' she added kissing his cheek.

It was supposed to be a one-night stand to start with. But after reading the 'Dear Nish' letters clandestinely, Aravali had viscerally felt compelled to invest her life in a man who had that rare space in his heart intact, where once upon a time men of valour kept their women and men of today keep chauvinism. The impact of those letters was such that she too wanted someone to treasure her the way he had treasured Nishani Rai. Aravali was twenty-nine and he was twenty-three and yet whenever they met, he was twenty-nine and she, perhaps sixteen.

'Let's climb up there.'

She saw the solitary water tank standing at a greater height from the terrace. There was an iron ladder from the terrace to the tank for cleaners to reach.

Kaash climbed first and positioned himself looking down.

'Come on.'

She closed her eyes and climbed those iron steps one by one. The turbulent air that hit her brought back her fear, but she somehow didn't entertain it. Soon she joined him on the tank which had a small iron lid in the centre but sufficient space around for two people to lie down. When they lay down side by side, all they could see was the star-studded sky above and a blinking light of an aeroplane afar. While all they could hear was each other's breathing.

'I love you,' said Aravali gazing at the sky.

Kaash glanced at her once and then at the sky again.

'Though I know you love Nishani,' she now completed.

'Who told you that?' For the first time, Aravali felt a sense of intrigue in Kaash. In the last two years, that night was the first time she mentioned Nishani to him.

'I'll tell you everything, but first tell me did you know Reva would fuck you that day?'

'Reva didn't fuck me. We fucked each other. We always were strangers who met to fuck. And we fucked to meet again.'

'You guys never talked or felt like knowing each other?'

Kaash shook his head.

'Unbelievable!'

'Hence true. The calm that you like about me exists because I have someone to take care of my inner chaos.'

'What do you mean?'

'I was nineteen when I first realized there's an inherent chaos in everyone which becomes an indomitable energy at some point of time. It makes people do things which they wouldn't do otherwise. More often than not this energy takes a sexual expression. And strangely enough, every time Reva and I met and unleashed ourselves, I felt relieved of the energy. Temporarily but certainly.'

'How did you guys meet?'

'In a pub. Sometimes she asked for it. Many a times I did.'

'You could have got a girlfriend for yourself and could do the same thing. Perhaps without any guilt.'

'Who said I'm guilty about it? That's for the emotional jingoists.'

'Still...'

'Are you my girlfriend?'

Aravali was quick to take out her mobile phone and check the calendar in it. She said, 'Two years, three months and nine days have passed since we spent that one night together in Cyanide. After which, neither you found anyone nor did I. So, yeah, I would like to believe I'm your girlfriend.' The last part was said with a sense of amusement.

'Do we always have sex when we meet?'

'No!'

'That's my answer. I can't always have sex with my girlfriend.'

'Do you want to?'

'Again, that's your answer. I neither can nor want to have sex all the time with my girlfriend.'

'Are you suggesting every man needs a whore in order to attain an emotional equilibrium with his wife?'

'I believe in individualism. Hence generalization is a sin for me. All I am saying is I, as an individual, have found a way to lessen the chaos in my life. Doesn't everyone have the fundamental right to find a way to remain at peace with oneself? And isn't life about this relentless struggle to reduce the chaos within? Some do so by chasing the elusive spiritual goals, I do so by living my sexual dreams.'

'When Arunodaye informed you about the nude scene with Reva, did you plan to fuck?'

'No! It just happened.'

'And she didn't stop you.'

'She didn't stop me,' Kaash echoed back.

'You said you don't feel guilty about it at all. But I'm sure Reva at least would.'

'Even if I feel guilty about it then guilt would be a small price for what Reva and I have discovered for each other.'

'It's a problem, right, when in a relationship one wants to derive sex through love and love through sex?'

'At least for me. I believe they are two different things which seem same to begin with. Thus they shouldn't be searched for in the garb of the other. Sex, I feel, eventually destroys the mysteries that love excites within one. It inhibits a couple from connecting beyond the traditional realm of a relationship.'

And hence, many don't experience the incomparable, incomprehensible, everyday kind of absolute bliss that we as a couple enjoy.'

'I think I know what you are talking about,' said Aravali clasping his hands by her side. Bringing them close to her lips, she planted a soft kiss on them. After the first night, Aravali could count the number of days they had made love. Very few. Something which brought them together didn't seem important enough since.

'Now tell me, how do you know I love Nishani?'

'I read your Dear Nish letters the first night.'

For a moment Kaash kept looking at her face which had a soft glow—of the kind that can steal someone's heart forever.

'Were you jealous reading them?'

'I was so excited, praying to God to give me one such lover, that I forgot to be jealous,' she smiled. Kaash remained still.

'And I have a feeling she still doesn't know,' she said next.

Kaash was quiet.

'What if,' he seemed a tad amused, 'she accepts and I have to leave you?'

'Well, you have Reva as your sexual drain. Keep me as your spiritual drain and I'll be happy.'

Kaash couldn't help but laugh. He sat up.

'I think Nishani is in love with Shahraan.'

'What makes you say so?' Aravali sounded surprised.

'A woman's passion is always more intense than a man's obsession.'

It was eleven when Nishani sat up, stretching, when glimpses of the dream flashed in front of her: Shahraan was begging her to give him what she had taken, but she too was her father's daughter. She only smiled at him and said, 'Only if you return what you took from me.' With time, Nishani had come to realize killing Shahraan figuratively by turning him into an emotional orphan like he did to her would be the best. *Nobody-to-go-to* is the worst suffering in life. Blocking a yawn, Nishani smiled. It was a beautiful morning.

Reva was immersed to her neck in a spacious bathtub, with a bluetooth piece clipped on her right ear. She was talking to Neev who, after a strenuous gym session, was driving back to his place. Since he was in a rush, he'd picked up Nishani's car keys instead of his Tavera, and he was driving her newly-purchased Innova. It wasn't for the first time the car swap had happened.

'Wouldn't it be better if we meet today?'

'I think I'm under surveillance.'

'What's that supposed to mean?'

'Shahraan is keeping an eye on me. He searched my bag as well. I don't know what to do, Neev.'

'You chose it for yourself.'

There was a pause. 'Did Kaash tell you anything?'

'I don't know him well. He knows Nishani. Why didn't you tell me before?'

'That's the point. It was never important for me to even share it with you.'

'But it was important enough for you to carry on with it.'

Reva sighed and relaxed her head on the tile behind.

By the time Nishani finished her breakfast, she was already done flipping through five national dailies. She opened the last one and perused it carefully, but still didn't find it anywhere: *Shahraan slapping Reva on set*. Frustration and disgust by now were playing hopscotch on her face. *What is the problem with the media? Why can't they take their job seriously?* She took her mobile phone and dialled all important print media journalists. Everyone had the same thing to tell her that it wasn't interesting enough. Except Gayatri of *The Bharat*. She said, 'We have been told it's not worth it.' The words made her conclude they had been bought.

She held her head tight and tried to analyze things. This particular news was her divine intervention, her shortest path to attain what she had been craving for since a child—drilling an emotional hole in Shahraan Ali Bakshi's life. A hole big enough to make him see the wrong he did to her, but small enough to rectify anything anymore. Had it appeared in the newspapers, it would have heightened the tension between Reva and Shahraan. Vikrant told her it was during the shooting that Reva was slapped. That means there would be the rushes. On an impulse, she called up Vikrant next.

'Hi Vikrant, was wondering if the shoot was complete yesterday?' She needed a trigger point for a conversation.

'Are you kidding? It was stalled midway. We lost eleven lakhs.'

'Actually, I didn't see it in the papers this morning, so I was like did it really happen?' She indeed sounded casual.

'They have been bribed more than adequately. Some people had recorded the incident in their mobile phones, but they were deleted, and that particular film reel destroyed personally by Krishna. Don't know if the film will even be completed or not.'

'Don't worry. We are all professionals.'

Nishani sat still after cutting the line, thinking of all the different possibilities. The mobile phones were searched, but there remained the still photographer, Arijit Banerjee. She knew he was a veteran in the world of film and fashion photography. Was his camera searched too? Would he allow that to happen knowing how those sensational photographs could fetch him a fortune? She had both Arijit's personal as well as office number. She dialled the latter.

'Sir is busy.' It was one of Arijit's assistants talking.

'Who are you?'

'I am Bejoy; his assistant.'

Nishani had seen the guy on the set a few times.

'Perhaps you can help me. I'm calling from a newspaper agency and wanted to know if Arijit has the Shahraan slapping Reva pictures.'

'Yes, Sir has them, but those aren't for sale. Sorry.'

Nishani looked at her reflection on the dining table glass top and pouted her lips to gift herself a sultry 'muah'.

'But you told me you loved Shahraan,' Neev was finding it difficult to talk and manoeuvre the car amid the traffic.

'I love him alright.'

'Then why did you have to do what you did?'

'At least you don't judge me on that. Is it that important? Can't I do something without being judged ever?'

'I am not judging you. I am saying when everything was going fine, what was the need to screw it all up. And look at the time and place you chose.'

'Everyone's life is screwed some way or the other. Do you think people choose it that way? It just happens, Neev. It just happened! That's what I've been trying to tell Shahraan. And I am sorry about it too. Since that incident, I feel so tired all the time. My achievements weigh on me. They limit me. They dictate me a certain set of actions outside which the real me lives. Where are those days, Neev, when all we had to do was struggle to make a mark? We were so ourselves!'

'Both of us have crossed it, Reva. We are the lucky ones. And now that we have crossed that hurdle, we have to struggle for being understood the way we are and not the way the world is.'

'There was a time when I thought when one has power, name, fame—nothing can touch the person, but it's all a sham.'

'To be honest, I didn't want to call you back. I know what all you have done for me, but remember the night we last met near the highway dhaba and you told me you'd seriously fallen for Shahraan and wanted me to forget you?'

Reva's silence acknowledged the fact.

'I was livid that night. I swore not to ever talk to you again.'

'Then why did you call today?'

'Nishani is the reason.'

There was pause from Reva's side. 'How is it going with her?'

'Steady. The good thing is she never tries to own or manipulate me. She lets me be the way I am. I feel free with her.'

'I used to stifle you, didn't I Neev?'

'I didn't mean that.'

'I am sorry, Neev.'

'Stop it. You'll always be what you were to me. Nobody can take that place.'

'Oh, Neev. Thanks for saying that. I was feeling so unwanted since the last few days. Thanks a lot.' Her voice was clogged.

'It's okay. By the way, did you have a talk with your husband?' He intentionally mentioned the word 'husband', Reva mused, perhaps to underline the fact that she was now married and Neev was *another* man. Strangely, it didn't make her feel uncomfortable.

'He is not ready to listen to me. You tell me what should I do?'

'Hmmm. Do you miss me, Reva?'

There was a prolonged silence. She wanted to speak her heart but chose not to.

'Hi, I am Manoj Shreshta calling from *Indian Times*. I want to talk to Arijit Banerjee.'

'Sir is busy. I handle all his business. Myself, Bijoy. What is it about?'

'I wanted to buy some photographs from you for our newspaper.'

'Which photographs?'

'Shahraan and Reva. The slap ones.'

Not again! Bijoy thought. Since morning he had had several calls from reporters for the same thing. 'Sir will never sell those.'

'I want to buy it from you. Fifty thousand cash.'

There was silence.

'You give me the copies of the photographs in a pen drive. That's all. No wounds, no worries.'

Half a minute passed and Bijoy didn't speak a word. He knew the man was waiting and the more time he took to answer, more was the chance of him succumbing.

'Seventy five.'

'Okay, done. Meet me in an hour by the city mall bus stop in Andheri.' The line went dead.

Nishani was ecstatic. The guy couldn't guess it was a female masked as a male. It had taken her a total of two hours to get hold of a man who gave her an already working prepaid sim card belonging to someone with fake papers. Next, she downloaded the trial version of a popular voice morphing software on her mobile. At first, she planned to execute the transaction through the internet, but that would have been traceable. This one: Nishani Rai as Manoj Shreshtha; no one on earth would be able to crack that.

Searching for her keys, she realized Neev had actually taken hers while he left his at her place. A cab or autorickshaw wouldn't do. She took Neev's maroon Tavera instead and drove to the bank first and then to the Oshiwara signal.

As an anxious Bijoy stood by the city mall bus stop looking at every man suspiciously, a street kid came to him and offered him a packet. Bijoy looked around nervously and took the packet. He could almost feel the crispy notes. A quick check told him there were seven bundles of one thousand rupees and a tiny one of five hundred notes. He wasted no time in handing over the pen drive to the kid. Crossing the road, Bijoy turned to see if he could track the kid. He did. She was handing over the pen drive to someone inside a maroon

Tavera. He waited. As the car turned and drove away, all he could see was a big sticker of a middle finger on the back.

When Nishani stopped by the next traffic signal, she quickly inserted the pen drive in her laptop and checked out the pictures. It was a series of stop motion photographs which, if seen non stop, generated a motion feel. If placed in order, the series would play itself almost like a video.

'I do miss you, Neev. But before coming to Shahraan, I never knew a part of me would also want to be enslaved by him forever.'

'Earlier, I was only angry because you left me when I needed you the most. But when I got this role, I was grateful you still cared.'

'Don't say that. You are talented. I only took care of the opportunity.'

'The day you told me you were getting married to Shahraan was the day I felt I lost you forever. I mean, we have had our share of infidelity, lies, fights, and all that, but every time we did come back to the other. And if you think of it, we never even discussed marriage. We could have stayed away since we weren't morally or legally bound in anyway. But we did come back because we were bonded by some law of nature that whatever shit we are involved in, we two shall turn to the other.'

'True. That's why I called you after feeling threatened by Shahraan.'

'Exactly. Whatever has happened, has happened Reva. We had been together during the shitty struggling days, so why not now? I agree to what you'd told me about us destroying ourselves more than anybody, but things are different now. You have Shahraan, I have Nishani. This togetherness which I am asking you to give a chance now won't be the same togetherness we experienced before.'

'I don't know. When I'd accepted Shahraan's proposal, he was this man for whom I had cold sighs all my life. And when he proposed, I accepted. I think any normal girl would do what I did. Initially, it was only the thrill of being Mrs Shahraan Ali Bakshi, but later he won my heart, because a man like him is rare, Neev. I am not comparing. I'm only saying he made me realize two people can be loved at the same time and perhaps to the same extent, but one can't jumble their coordinates up. Like I couldn't love him the way I loved you. Our relationship dynamics were different and hence the realizations too were distinct.'

As she spoke, Neev had slowed down the car and said, 'I guess you are right. Sometimes when we get into any relationship, and I mean any, I think there's some emotional debt meter that starts running somewhere within us, and a time comes when we nullify all the naked truth about that relationship against the reading on the debt meter. Like I hated you till yesterday, but now I want to get back to you because I know you have done good things for me.'

'Wow. Where was this Neev when I was with him?'

'It took Reva's rejection and Nishani's acceptance for this Neev to shape up.'

He glanced at his phone to realize Nishani's call was coming on call waiting.

'Hey Reva, I'll just call you back.' Neev switched to Nishani's call.

'What's up?'

'It's a fucking dinosaur out there!'

'What?'

'Someone has leaked the Shahraan-slapping-Reva-on-set video on the internet and within three hours, it has got two lakh ten thousand views. And, still counting.'

Neev took his time but still couldn't surmise: was it a good or a bad news?

If media was a mixer grinder, then the slap issue was fresh coriander leaves. Though Krishna managed to block the video from most sites, the damage had already been done by then.

The media, whose hunger had been bribed previously on the incident, had a ball when they saw the video had gone viral on a public domain. Hours after the video hit the internet, it was flashing on all the leading news channels. The same happened with the newspapers the next day.

All the money that was given to the agencies to suppress the news was suddenly not enough. And they anyway were not paid to ignore the leak. From early morning to midnight, the issue was regularly discussed, dissected, analyzed, and predictions of the future between Shahraan and Reva were made. Forgotten people from the industry were invited to the news channel studios to discuss how male dominated the Hindi film industry was. The worse happened when an NGO of women rights protection registered a case against Shahraan for alleged domestic violence. It infuriated as well as wounded him so much that he asked Krishna not to update him on anything for some time. On the other hand, Reva wrongly thought it was he who had intentionally leaked the video to emotionally assault her further; all of it for letting Kaash fuck her. Weirdly, nobody cared about Kaash's take on it.

The producers had employed a private security agency to guard the studio where the day's shoot was scheduled to take place. Everyone who entered the set had to deposit their mobile phones and any other objectionable items to the security personnel. Only the still photographer Arijit and his assistant Bijoy were officially allowed to click pictures.

'No. No. No.' The numero uno choreographer and a prominent gay activist, Fanny Da Cunha, bellowed on the loudspeaker. He shot a helpless look at ATM who was sitting in a corner and sucking on a straw that was siphoning freshly made lemonade into him. Going by whatever ATM had read in the newspapers and witnessed between Shahraan and Reva in the last few days, he had acquired diarrhoea. He'd forgotten about completing the film the way he wanted to, with the producers and him ready to give a hefty offering to Vaishno Devi if the Goddess would allow them to at least finish the film on time. The only good thing going his way was that today he wasn't supposed to direct the two. It was the choreographer's duty.

'There's no chemistry between the two, what the hell should I shoot? And then they say Fanny has lost his fucking special touch!' Fanny said softly to ATM who pretended to care about the ongoing proceedings.

'Keep trying,' he suggested to Fanny and laughed like a masochist in his mind.

Amid the hullaballoo of the extras, Shahraan hissed at Reva, 'Why aren't you getting it right?'

'You are not getting it right, Shahraan.'

For a moment he didn't understand what.

'Grow up and focus on the work. Home is where we discuss the personal things.' They were standing beside each other taking a breather and waiting for Fanny's further instructions.

'Home is where we remain quiet these days.'

'So you have been saving all your spite for this day? I slapped you on set, so you want to embarrass me on set?'

'I am not surprised you've interpreted it that way instead of understanding me. And thanks for leaking the video.'

'Shut up. I didn't leak any video.'

'Positions everyone,' they heard Fanny say. 'Shahraan sweetheart, just maintain your intensity and the pelvic thrust should be more fun. Reva darling, sizzle the way you usually do. Muah. Let's rock!'

As the dance started with full gusto, they came close for

once and Shahraan managed to whisper in her ear, 'Half of what you are is because of me. Don't you ever forget that.' As he held onto her shoulder and Fanny shouted 'seven-eight-nine thrust,' Reva shrugged off Shahraan's hand as if it was an unwanted touch. The entire rhythm broke.

'Cut it!' Fanny noticed it first. Everyone gaped at Reva with a collective what's-wrong-with-you look, as she walked off rubbing the clandestine tears off her cheeks. The music came to an abrupt halt.

Fuck you guys, Fanny thought. 'Tea break,' he said aloud.

Inside Shahraan's vanity van, Nitu Sridhar, his publicist met him.

'I think,' Nitu began in her usual confident self, 'It was good we didn't respond for a few days. Now let's click some photos of you and Reva together. Perhaps cuddling or kissing or walking hand in hand. I'll build a counter thesis to what's going on in the media. People always love to move on. Enough of you guys fighting. What's next? Next would be the much talked about couple of the tinsel town realizing their true love. People will forget the slap issue like this.' She snapped her fingers. 'Moreover, we'll also have ATM's interview where he'll state the slap was part of the script. And the leak was sabotage. If Reva can also confirm it, then the domestic violence case against you also gets nullified.'

'I was thinking along the same lines. Perhaps Reva can put up pictures on her social networking account as well,' said Shahraan and looking at an acknowledging expression on Nitu's face added, 'Let's do it.'

'Now?' Vikrant, whom Shahraan had asked to be present, sounded appalled. For him, any publicity was good unless it affected the film schedule.

'The shooting won't be stalled. Take my words for it. A

few casual pictures and we'll be done.'

'Very casual,' Nitu chipped in. Shahraan stretched his hand and Krishna dutifully placed his Blackberry on his palm.

Need to click some pictures. Let's be professional. Shahraan sent the message to Reva who was alone in her van adjacent to his. There was a prompt response.

Professional about our personal life?

Come to my van ASAP.

A couple of minutes later, Reva was sitting beside him. Arijit and Bijoy were also summoned inside the van to capture a few candid moments between the two.

Arijit asked them to come close and look at each other with a normal smile. It was difficult at first, but then they were actors. He smiled. And she desperately wished nothing had gone wrong between the two. When he clasped her hands, she knew this was only a temporary crisis they were in. She clasped his hand tighter. Arijit asked her to kiss him on the cheek. She did so. And it struck her so many days had gone by without intimacy. She felt his stubble with her tongue for no particular reason. As they relaxed, Shahraan rubbed his cheeks. They exchanged a glance. He wanted to forgive her and start afresh. Arijit asked him to take her hand and kiss it looking at her. He did so. The way his lips touched her hand, it seemed like an application for an apology to her. He never wanted to hit her, but he also knew a verbal apology wasn't possible for him; call it male chauvinism or whatever. She looked at him and smiled back; something about the smile brought back memories of him driving his four-wheeler acting school with Mehfil sitting behind. In the last two years, whatever he felt with her, somehow he knew he would have felt the same with Mehfil even though the two women were fundamentally different. Or was it that he was indeed ageing? A lonely life at forty-six can be a good proposition for life to trick someone in ways more than he could anticipate.

'Fantastic,' said Arijit as he clicked them yet again.

'Shahraan,' said Nitu, 'Krishna said later tonight you are scheduled to attend Minister Damodar Shankar's son's wedding.'

Shahraan glanced at Krishna who nodded at Nitu.

'Reva and you should go there together. The more you two are seen together in public, the better.'

Shahraan instinctively glanced at Reva to find her staring at him. Whatever feelings she had on her face seemed enveloped, but he knew those were things which were meant for him and only him.

'We can do that.'

'Hold it,' exclaimed Arijit and framed Shahraan. As the latter remained still for the sake of the photograph, his eyes fell on Bijoy who was looking from behind his back holding onto a few lenses.

'One minute,' Shahraan frowned looking at Bijoy. 'Wasn't he there during the shoot?' Shahraan stood up. The suddenness of it took everyone by surprise. Krishna was the first one to get the cue.

'Arijit sir, you too had those pictures. Right?' Krishna asked.

'Yes, of course,' Arijit responded, 'But nothing has ever leaked from my office. I trust Bijoy completely.'

Everyone looked at Bijoy whose hands holding the camera lens were shaking in a funny manner.

Fifteen minutes later, Bijoy was fired by Arijit. *How would I know those copies would be circulated in the internet like some epidemic and not be posted in newspapers as I inferred from the asshole Manoj Shreshtha's talks? And how would I know the guy didn't exist!* Bijoy thought. Tears were rolling down his cheeks as he started his Activa from the parking lot. Everything looked blurred around him. Then he saw something. He rubbed his eyes and stared at the maroon-coloured Tavera on the other side. It had a 'middle finger' sticker on its back. *It could be a coincidence but...* Bijoy shouted at the car parking staff inquiring about the car's owner.

'It's Neev Sir's car,' said the parking staff.

That took care of the coincidence for Bijoy. He let go of his Activa and ran inside the studio. It was his best chance to save his job.

Neev was shooting on another set in the same studio for the promo of his new television series which was scheduled to go on floor in a week. Krishna waited till the particular shot was over. As the production people scattered setting up the next shot, Krishna approached Neev. His face read only one thing: contempt.

'Shahraan Sir wants to meet you.'

'Why?'

'Now.'

'As you can see, I'm busy right now. I shall be there when I'm done.'

'I've had a talk with the production. It will only take five minutes. Not more.'

Had Krishna not been Shahraan's secretary, Neev would have punched him straight in his vocal cord and taken care of the condescending tone that Krishna could so boisterously afford to come out with before him.

'What is it about?'

'I don't know.'

While walking off the television set, he heard him report to Shahraan over the phone that he was coming. Why was he made to feel like a fugitive all of a sudden?

Only Shahraan and Reva were inside the van apart from Bijoy who was staring at the floor, standing in a corner like a convict. Shahraan gave Reva a curt glance and said, 'I want to talk to him alone.' He said it conclusively.

Reva was too dumbstruck to even consider that Neev went to the disgusting length of first buying the photographs and then turning them into some kind of video and then floating it on the internet. *And what was that bullshit about togetherness he was talking about on the phone the other day?* she wondered.

'I'll stay right here. The video involves me too.' She was surprised she could still speak with confidence. Shahraan's silence confirmed her wish. The next minute, Neev stepped into the van. Krishna preferred to remain outside. That switched on Reva's panic button. When Krishna left Shahraan alone, it usually wasn't a good sign.

'Hey big boss, how are you?' Neev greeted Shahraan exhibiting his fake beaming face to utmost sincerity. Shahraan didn't care to stand up from his chair. It was Neev who took his hands and managed to shake them with his.

'Where were you this Tuesday around three in the afternoon?' Neev heard Shahraan's query.

'What is this about?'

'Just answer him, Neev,' Reva chipped in. 'Please,' she added.

'I was driving back home from the gym. Why?'

'When did you meet him?' Shahraan only glanced at Bijoy once. Though Neev had registered his presence while entering the van, he didn't think he was important.

'Who is this guy?'

Shahraan averted his eyes from Neev to Bijoy and the latter spoke up. 'I was the one by the city mall bus stop.'

Neva looked genuinely confused.

'What's that supposed to mean?'

'I gave the kid the pen drive who went to your car to deliver it.'

'Kid? Car? Are you drunk or something?' Neev almost

barked out at Bijoy. The latter again stared at the floor.

'Someone had bought the slap photographs from Bijoy on Tuesday around the time when you said you were driving back home in your car. He identified the middle-finger sticker on your car by the studio parking.'

'There are so many cars with that sticker. I am sure he is mistaken.'

'Yes, but none of those cars, I am sure, belong to someone who is related to us in some way,' said Reva. Though she appreciated the different Neev the other day on phone, but with him she also knew one thing: you never know!

'What? You too think I pulled off this garbage? C'mon! Why would I do it?'

'I assume—and rightly so—you didn't take your break up with Reva in the right spirit,' Shahraan remarked.

'You knew it would put Shahraan and my relationship under strain.' Reva didn't want to say it,but she did. It turned her husband's accusation against Neev sound all the more true. When it came to the kill, she chose what was best for her.

'Did you see me?' Neev could have killed Bijoy with his stare.

'I didn't.'

'Then? Just because an asshole saw a Tavera and not me means I was in it? Moreover—' Neev paused as if something struck him and then added, 'Alright. You want proof it wasn't me? Here you go.' He took out his HTC and dialled Nishani. He put her on speaker. She picked up after four rings.

'Hey baby.' She sounded groggy.

'Tell me you remember I'd taken your car this Tuesday instead of mine.'

There was a pause as the three pairs of eyes in the van looked at each other with anticipation.

'I was at home all day on Tuesday. If you are saying you

took my car, then you would have. But why do you ask?'

Neev cut the line without another word.

'So you don't have any alibi to where you were during that time. And we have someone who we think saw your car and dealt with you,' said Shahraan as a matter of fact. 'Tomorrow morning,' he continued, 'I'll call a press conference where you'll accept two things: one, the slap was part of the script; and two, you leaked the video on the internet. I don't care what reason you state for the same. And you'll do so if you want to work in the industry. I hope you won't test me on this.'

'Accept what? I have not done anything.' Neev's anger and sheer frustration of not being able to make two adults understand one simple thing made him stand up. It was an aggressive stance. He moistened his lips and turned to Reva. 'Now please don't deny I was talking to you that day while driving precisely during that time. How can I talk to you as well as buy the photographs and do all this shit. I am not a robot.'

That was the real reason why Reva decided to stay in the van. She didn't want the discussion to take the course which would expose her vulnerability towards Neev.

'What are you talking about?' Reva responded, wondering if her lie was convincing enough.

Neev simply stood there, wide mouthed and hands on his hips, with an expression tantamount to the man who worked hard at seducing a girl in the pub only to realize she was a he in the end.

'See Shahraan Sir, Neev sir said he was driving the car.'

Neev gave Bijoy a loathsome glance.

'Bijoy, move out,' said Shahraan. Bijoy scampered out the way school kids empty a classroom after the last period of the day.

'What is he saying?' Shahraan still maintained his poise.

'I don't know.' Fear shook Reva. She had long back promised Shahraan that she'd have no contact with Neev whatsoever.

A man, when he becomes a husband, somehow tends to believe his wife's past is his own even if he wasn't there in her life back then.

'You don't know? Wow! I have a feeling this one is a deliberate attempt by you two to frame me.' Neev faced Shahraan now and said, 'You want to call a press conference? I'm okay with it. I won't apologize there. I shall tell everyone how desperately your legally wedded wife wants to talk to me during the night without your knowledge. Now if you two have played enough of your shit games, then please excuse me.' Neev left in a furious state.

Whatever proximity took place between them during the candid photo shoot had been wasted within a span of a few minutes. Shahraan leaned back on his chair and closed his eyes. In the short silence that followed, Shahraan realized it wasn't Mehfil, it wasn't Reva, and it wasn't him as well. It was love that took advantage of his life; once when he was a simple boy with a big complex dream and later when he was a complex man with a simple, well-defined desire.

'Let's talk, Reva, before we decide not to listen to each other ever.' Shahraan spoke with a sense of profound calmness.

Being dumb about stating the truth in all its nakedness was her favourite sin for which only repentance was possible, not redemption. Reva walked out without saying a word.

Sitting in her van a minute later, she messaged an apology to Neev. That was all a sinner could do. Apologize all her life! To the world, to oneself, till the time when the apology becomes a promise for further apologies.

Nishani was sitting up against the wall on a strawberry-coloured furry floor mat in the flat that she shared with Neev, while he lay stretched in front of her with his head on her lap.

Every time he lifted his head, she helped him drink some of the blended scotch. Her ears were oblivious to the constant abuses Neev was showering on Reva.

'I was there for her even after she'd thrown me away like a paper napkin. And still she lied to my face. She is the queen of all bitches.'

And you are a born fool, Nishani thought. She was neither concerned about Neev's condition nor about Reva's plight. She was running for a bigger mission and that was in danger. Yet again. She had to stop Shahraan from having the press conference he promised Neev, else the whole Shahraan's-emotional-debacle dish would remain half cooked. All she had to do was scratch the wound Shahraan's and Reva's relationship suffered in the evening.

'Neev, was Shahraan really serious about the press conference?'

The bathroom suite attached to the master bedroom at Mehfil Mansion was a sprawling space where relaxation happened naturally. There was a bathtub, a jacuzzi, and a shower cabinet—all at some distance from the other. Reva was inside the bathtub. That was the only place these days where she thought she could let her emotional guard down. She didn't want peace anymore. It was a spiritual justice she was after. She heard the bathroom door open. A turn of head told her Shahraan had come inside dressed in a bathrobe.

'Sorry, I thought it was empty,' he said and half turned to leave. The combination for the number lock of the bathroom was only known to the two of them. Either could come in anytime.

'I don't mind,' Reva clarified. Shahraan's hand played with the knob as his mind toyed with a decision. He locked the door and came inside. Reva watched him take off his bathrobe and enter the shower cabinet. Soon, cold water was cascading down his well-chiselled nude body. Reva thought Shahraan Ali Bakshi showering nude in front of her was definitely a dream. She being his wife was a bigger dream. And she carrying his baby in her womb was the biggest dream of all.

Right after the shoot, she'd gone to Dr Shashtri because she'd missed her period and it was he who gave her the good news. It'd been so long since she had something genuine to smile about that for a moment she didn't know how to react.

Kaash had locked himself in his flat for the last two days. No light, no air, no connection to the outside world. It was his way of preparing himself for an important role. He'd picked up the practice from his first film itself. But every time he thought he got the scene alright, it gave him the creeps. The nude scene with Reva could have been spicy for others, but for him it was just another scene without any emotional connect. He pushed her into committing the real act because he felt like it and he knew she would comply. They always kept it at an animalistic level; from depravity to decadence to delight. But this particular scene was about making love with his wife played by Nishani. The thought of being with her in one bed sheet simply didn't let him stay in the character since it wasn't about sexual attraction anymore. It was about an emotional attachment. He didn't want to flash even a meagre amount of his inner vulnerability to Nishani lest he gets caught red handed. He feared his feelings may be granted a voice in that case. And it's feelings with a voice that never allow anyone to be the way they always were. He believed that as people evolve, their voices only become menacing in nature. He wondered why he couldn't simply go to her and tell her he loved her? It was so damn simple. But he couldn't do it. He picked up his mobile phone from his bed, switched it on, and called Arunodaye. He would request him to chop the scene.

'What else am I telling you?' Neev chided. 'They want me to apologize and announce it was I who'd leaked the video in the internet. I am fucked both ways.'

'But you could have shown Shahraan the missed calls Reva gave you that night. He wouldn't have been sympathetic towards her.'

'What do I care how is he to her? If he kicks her out, I'm not going to shelter her. Not anymore!'

'But don't you want the girl who brought you to such misery get some too?'

Neev tried to make sense out of her words. Alcohol wasn't helping him.

'Damn, I am a fucking fool. I broke my phone out of angst. I only have the sim card now and the call record was in the phone memory.' A pause later he added, 'Nishani, my career is gone.' He suddenly started wailing.

'Let's get some fresh air.' More than him, she needed it.

A few minutes later, Nishani was driving Neev's Kawasaki Ninja, with a sloshed Neev sitting on the pillion, on the lonely Western Express highway. Her mind was cruising faster than the bike. Neev kept murmuring, 'Neev Dixit is Neev big shit!' Nishani paid no heed till she felt his weight on her back. The rear-view mirror told her he was asleep. He never looked more repulsive before. She thought about how he would react if he came to know the video leak was designed by her? Would he leave her or would he empathize and be with her? She realized she didn't care for Neev Dixit enough to wish either. She asked herself whom did she really love: Rakesh? Rehan? Vishwas? Neev? No! There were only two men she was ever doggedly serious about all her life: Shekhar and Shahraan. Nishani turned her bike and drove back to her flat.

'Do you still love Neev?' Shahraan had his eyes closed and face tilted up towards the shower. Though Reva knew they had to talk about a lot of things, she didn't know it would begin this soon. Before she could respond, she heard Shahraan say, 'I may ask you a few things tonight. And I never will do so again. Please make sure whatever you say, you mean it. Ignorance may be bliss, but I am tired of that bliss. So, do you—'

'Do you still love Mehfil?' Reva didn't let Shahraan complete. She thought she saw a slight movement of his head. Nothing more.

'Do you love me, Reva?' he asked.

'Do you trust me, Shahraan?' she replied while staring at his nude back.

It sounded like some stupid teenage game—questions as answers and answers as questions—but Shahraan didn't complain.

'And Kaash? What about him?'

'And the memories of Mehfil? What about them?'

'Did you accept my proposal because you loved me or was it something else?'

'Did you notice me because I was worth it or was it someone else?'

'What do you want from me now, Reva?'

'What did you want from me when you proposed to me, Shahraan?'

'Did you fuck Kaash while we were in a relationship?'

'Do you crave for Mehfil even after we are together?'

'Have you ever thought of Neev when we make love?'

'Have you ever wished for Mehfil after we are done making love?'

'Do you want a new beginning with me, Reva?'

This one made Reva pause. She moistened her dry lips and stood up. Some of the lather slipped down her body. She loosened her still dry hair and stepped out of the tub. As she approached the shower cabinet, she let go of the hair clutch. The next instant, she was inside the cabin where they couldn't move without rubbing onto the other. Shahraan finally turned. The shower water now fell on Reva's face as she closed her eyes. They came closer.

'Hasn't every day between us been a beginning to a new something?' she asked and embraced him tight. She prayed for him to reciprocate. A second later he did; tighter than normal.

Should I give him the good news? Reva thought and decided to wait because she wanted to feel the night in his arms around her for some more time. The last time she did so seemed like light years ago.

'But that's an integral part of the script,' said Arunodaye. He was in the editing room at the time supervising an ad film of his. He got up and started ambling in the spacious room while talking on the phone. 'It's through that scene we are connecting to your character's guilt. I am sorry, but I really can't change it. Why don't Nishani and you prepare for it together? You guys are long time friends, right?'

Kaash would have never done a pathetic thing like changing a scene because he was uncomfortable with it. Such kind of preposterous attitude was never his. And talking to Arunodaye, he realized the best way to escape it was to face it. Perhaps going through the scene with Nishani a few times could numb his jitters. He'd read it somewhere that one of the best way to prepare for a bed scene was to do it with clothes on numerous times over and then once, during the shoot, without them. He was an actor after all and pretence shouldn't be hard. He sat on his bed and thought...immediately he checked himself. If he thought about it, he wouldn't be able to do it. He simply called Nishani. Since she'd given him her number at the party, she'd always been on speed dial though he'd called her—Kaash did a quick math—a total of seven times in two years.

Nishani had thrown herself on the bed after the apartment's watchman placed Neev on the sofa and left. Her mind wouldn't succumb to sleep till she got a plan to strike back. She felt the vibration of her mobile phone in her jeans pocket. She pulled it out to see Kaash's name on it. A genuine smile touched her. She took the call.

'Hey Balloo, what's up boy?'

Every time Kaash heard her voice he tried to, but could never numb his awareness of the motherly affection in her voice for him.

'Nothing much. I was only preparing for my next scene. We are shooting on Sunday. Two days.'

'Hell!' It was then Nishani recollected she had to shoot an intimate scene with him.

'Didn't you know?'

'I knew alright. But with all this happening—'

'What's happening?'

'Nothing.'

Kaash sensed in that nothing, there was a long, untold story.

'Okay. I had a chat with Arunodaye. He suggested we rehearse a bit before Sunday. Will you be game? I can meet you now if you want.'

'Right now? But—' Nishani paused. Something conjured in her mind. A plan! She was sure it would be the final blow for Shahraan. She could already feel her excitement pulsating within her.

'Yeah. Let's sure meet up. Outside Phoenix mall in an hour? I'll pick you up on my bike.'

'I know your place though.'

'I'm outside right now,' Nishani lied for the sake of her plan.

It was nine in the morning. Arunodaye had gone to sleep a couple of hours earlier. It was his wife Sunaina who woke him up stating he was getting innumerable number of calls from the media. For a moment, Arunodaye thought it was what he had dreamt: his film had released and it had been declared the blockbuster of the decade.

When he took the first call from his assistant in real, he had a feeling the film was history. Without caring to relieve himself in the toilet, he ran for the television as suggested by the assistant. He switched on to a leading news channel and opened the newspaper at the same time.

'Reva Gupta clicked with Kaash Sehgal in the middle of the night near a mall: a secret affair or yet another script meeting?' the news capsule said, with the complete story featuring in its entertainment section. The same shots were shown in the news channel as well. Arunodaye could still hear the sound of the slap Shahraan gave to Reva on set a week ago. And now this. His phone buzzed with Vikrant's call. He took it.

'Did you—'

'Yes, just now.'

'What the hell is Reva's problem? She is not the first one to screw around, then why does she want to become the first one not to take care of it? I only hope it doesn't affect the shoot. Rest can go to the gutters!'

'Shoot? Do you think I would be able to strike the kind of chemistry I want between Shahraan and Reva in the film? What is he saying anyway?'

'I can't reach him. Krishna told me he has cancelled all his meetings for the day. He'll get back in some time.'

'What about Reva and Kaash?'

'Miss Headlines is unavailable as well. And I had a talk with Kaash just now. He said it was by chance that he met Reva last night. He was there to meet Nishani for rehearsing their scene.'

'Yeah, I'd asked him to do so. We anyway aren't shooting Reva or Shahraan for the next ten days. Let's focus on Nishani and Kaash then. And Vikrant, let's stay focused. Remember, it took Satyajit Ray almost four years and a helluva problems to complete *Pather Panchali*.'

Of all the people, Nishani didn't expect Neev to be the unhappiest.

'What's all this?' he said reading the morning newspaper.

'Whatever it is, it's there in the open now.' Nishani had come back from the gym minutes back and was having green tea.

She had messaged Kaash to meet her outside a mall. She then messaged Reva using Neev's sim card, pleading to meet up at the same mall, same spot. When both Kaash and Reva were there, she snapped their pictures together. Finding each other there, both talked to the other for less than a minute. When Nishani called Kaash stating her bike had problems, he had to return home while Reva too returned after Neev's mobile kept telling her it was unavailable. Nishani knew the headlines would no way affect Kaash—whose stardom was tiny compared to Reva's—but will break all those fibres that still managed to connect Shahraan and Reva.

'I don't believe this!' Neev said staring at the photographs.

'Why?'

'After whatever happened, I don't think Reva would risk what she has to keep it going with Kaash.'

'And what I can't understand is that a man threatens to

destroy your career because his wife chose to lie to him about you, and still you don't want to believe she may be having a secret dalliance!'

'No! Because this woman you are talking about at some point of time was mine too and I know when she is faking it and when she isn't.'

'Why don't you call her and ask her about it?'

Neev glared at the photographs for some time and then said, 'It's none of my business. In fact, this will only push Shahraan to believe I wasn't actually lying. But the one who leaked the video in the internet... I'll not spare the bastard. I'll...'

Nishani noticed how taut his grasp of the newspaper was. Still, she was okay inside. She knew he would never get to know the truth. And the last thing she wanted was Neev calling Reva and acting like a knight in shining armour once again. Moreover, there was no way Reva would show Neev's message to Shahraan, especially after what happened between them in the vanity van. Even if she chose to tell the truth—she was there to meet Neev and not Kaash—what would she tell him? Why was she going to meet Neev at such an odd hour? Nishani relaxed. Finally all her cards read ace. She did what she wanted to do. Manipulate everything in such a manner that Shahraan remains away from relationships in future like he made her stay away from one important relationship all her life.

Aravali saw the news while coming back from a film festival in Goa. Instead of going to her place, she chose to knock at Kaash's Cyanide. He was having cornflakes for breakfast while listening to a Pandit Ravi Shankar instrumental.

'What's all this?' she said opening the door with duplicate keys.

'What?' Kaash continued to take his cornflakes seriously.

'What, what? What were you doing meeting Reva?' She came and sat beside him in one of the chairs.

Kaash now looked at her and gave her an amusing smile, 'What can I do, dear? You were not here, and I was, so...' He leaned sideways to reach her ear. He tried to lick her lobe.

'I am serious, Kaash. People are saying all sort of bullshit. I want the truth.'

'You can't handle the truth,' Kaash improvised a Jack Nicholson dialogue from *A Few Good Men*.

Aravali pressed his cheeks hard.

'Okay, okay. The truth is, Nishani did it.'

'What the flying fuck? What's her problem?'

'Same as yours and mine. She is in love.'

'But screwing up everyone around her won't solve her problem.'

'Now you know why I love her. Nishani never does a thing to solve or question it. She only does it. Everything else is an eventuality with her.'

'I don't care what happens to Reva or Shahraan, but what about your image?'

'It's a man's world, darling. And in a man's world, when he is photographed with a married woman, she is the centre of attraction and at fault. Go through any newspaper, Reva Gupta is everywhere. Relationships come with an MRP, but when you are Shahraan Ali Bakshi or for that matter Reva Gupta, it comes with a TRP as well.' He was done with the cornflakes.

'I don't know, Kaash. What will Nishani get by doing all this? Shahraan will get to know one day anyway. By the way, did you talk to her about this?'

'No, I didn't. Do I have the right to?'

'Oh yes. You are there in the photograph as well.'

'I am sure she meant no harm to me.'

'But how are you so sure it's she who did this?'

'She called me there last night, then changed the time, and then didn't appear.'

'Which means she would have known you would guess it anyway.'

'That means even without saying it, she has requested me for a specific response; that I should not respond to it. Hence, I'm only obliging her.'

'I have never understood your relationship with her!'

Kaash smiled playfully and kissed her on the cheek.

'Nor have I.'

'Hmmm. But,' said Aravali, 'I really think you should talk to her. If not complain, then at least let her know what she is doing will only destroy her and whatever it is that she is after; Shahraan or whatever really. I mean, look at her. She is a real diva. She has promise; loads of it. But why is she squandering it away like this? It takes people all their life to even reach half of what she has done at this young age.'

'I'll talk to her. I am supposed to meet her tonight at her place for the rehearsal of the scene.'

'The intimate one?'

Kaash nodded.

'I'll be worried tonight.'

Kaash's eyes had a funny twinkle.

'I don't want to lose you, Kaash,' Aravali clasped his hands.

'You know something? I have a gut feeling she knows she is risking her career doing all this. I only hope she wins.' He tightened the clasp. Aravali kissed him on the cheek and placed her head on his shoulder.

'Will you ever love me so much that my weaknesses will arouse you more than my strengths?'

Kaash suddenly got up, picked her up in his arms, and took her to his bed. In that moment, Aravali realized she was in love with the suddenness attached to his personality. The way he made her senses swing between excitement, surprise, and astonishment was nothing less of an addiction.

Kaash threw her on the bed and lay beside her with arms around her and face buried in her bosom. He made her feel like a mother. She kissed his forehead.

'All I can promise is that I'll forever be honest with you, Aravali.'

'That, my dear, is the best gift you can ever give me; an unadulterated honesty. And, by the way, I will not mind even if you sleep with Nishani tonight.'

Kaash glanced at her once and said, 'If I had to sleep with her, I would have done it already.'

She blew some air on his face which fluttered his hair a bit.

Love is only the realized part of a connection...words from one of Kaash's 'Dear Nish' letters ricocheted in her head and now—only now—she understood how true they were.

'Let's end it before I start hating you,' Shahraan said, aware of Reva's presence in his golf simulation room. It was a dark, spacious room, with a giant projection of a gold course on one of the walls. The way Shahraan was scoring told her he was very focused. By now she knew well he was most focussed when he was enraged.

'I want to show you something, Shahraan,' said Reva. She had waited for Neev to turn up for an hour. When his mobile phone was unreachable, she decided enough was enough. She went back but couldn't sleep well, wondering why Neev summoned her like that? His messages sounded emotional and yet he didn't turn up. Shahraan and she had made love after a long time. She didn't want to leave him alone in bed and go to meet Neev. She wondered if she should have done that? Especially after Shahraan and Reva dug hard, hoping there still could be more treasure left in the pit of their relationship. Neev's message said they owed each other one last meeting. *It was true*, she thought during her post-coital bliss lying beside a sleep-arrested Shahraan. She was ashamed of the lie she came out with against Neev in the van. Probably that's why she agreed to meet up. She was sure the meeting would sever her from Neev once and for all and bring forth a refreshingly different chapter in her life. While reading the morning newspaper, she realized she'd underestimated life yet again.

'Neev had messaged me last night to meet up for one last time,' she told Shahraan, who for a few seconds ignored her like one ignores one's own flaws. Then realized avoiding her wouldn't help much.

'And you went ahead even when he lied about you to me.'

'Lied?'

'In the van he said it was you who had called him several times at night. Remember?'

'Oh yes.' Reva, the real liar, felt a knot in her stomach.

'But—' she began and knew her throat was dry. She swallowed and said, 'I thought he would apologize and I could amicably end whatever was left between us.'

'And to meet Neev, you went to Kaash? Is that the best you could think up to fool me?'

I'm only fooling myself. She didn't dare to speak up.

'Last night, I thought we'd made a new beginning. But this morning—' He hit a furious shot. *Bam!* He waited till the projection showed he had pocketed the ball. She heard him say, 'I realized you are incapable of understanding anyone's love for you. I am sorry to say this, Reva, but you are one insensitive bitch.'

The name didn't hurt her as much as the fact he didn't abuse her eye to eye. If he thought she deserved a filthy name, she would have accepted it, but not looking at her was like treating her as filth itself. That, she knew, she didn't deserve. Not just as yet.

'Believe me. I met Kaash quite by accident last night.'

'I don't believe you anymore, so don't insist on it.'

Reva felt a strong urge to laugh out since all her lies till now had been accepted as the truth, but for the only time when she was honest, she was tagged as a liar.

'I'm pregnant, Shahraan,' she spoke out loud and proud. She'd whispered it to him after their love-making session. She was disappointed when she realized he was already asleep, but then she thought there were other naughty ways to relay the best news of their life together. Perhaps in the morning she would write with ketchup on a bread piece: I am pregnant. But she never thought it would come out this way; as a defensive reflex.

The words made Shahraan miss his shot for the first time. He couldn't care less. A sudden glimpse of happiness concocted his face into something that relieved Reva. He let go of his golf club and hugged her tight. She reciprocated. He loosened and held her face next and kissed all over it.

'I am...I am so happy Reva. This is like...like the first achievement of my life...it's like...' Reva looked at him as his initial excitement slowly wore off.

'Is it Kaash's child?'

It sounded like a joke. She was even prepared to laugh if he joined her. But he didn't.

'What are you saying, Shahraan?'

'Okay. So now I get it. You went to Kaash with this news last night. He disowned it, so I'm the obvious father now.'

'What the—' Reva wanted to scream, but she checked herself and said with her jaw clenched, 'Have you gone mad? This is our baby I am talking about. I have been to the doctor. He has confirmed it.'

'Confirmed what?'

'That I am pregnant.'

'But did he confirm I'm the father?'

A few silent seconds later, he answered, 'No!'

Reva tried to hold Shahraan by his shoulder and link her eyes to his, 'You are the father, Shahraan. Don't accuse me of this at least. Please!'

He released himself from her grip and ambled to gold-course projection. His face had all sorts of colours reflecting from the projection.

'Didn't you guys fuck on set?'

That was the cheapest he had ever sounded to her. He was talking like one of those imbecile husbands who never could understand his wife had a heart too like he did. The same heart which was capable of reserving a corner for him, come what may. A corner that, over the years, steadily formed the whole of her.

'Yes, we did fuck on set.' Now was the time to contradict her lie with the truth. Shahraan, in a flash, came to her and raised his hand to slap out what he just heard. He paused and controlled himself. Reva didn't move an inch.

'But this is your baby,' she said softly.

Slapping his hands on his hips instead, Shahraan paced in front of her.

'Okay. Let's do a test. If it's mine, I'll never question you about anything ever.'

'That would be an insult to the trust we have between us. A mother knows, Shahraan. I would have never asked you to father anyone else's child.'

'I have had enough of that trust bullshit. Let's keep it simple and more scientific now.'

Reva's tears had started to drench her cheeks. Not fighting her weak knees, she collapsed on the floor and sobbed copiously.

'Either we are testing it out, or we are getting divorced.

Your call.' Shahraan went out of the room.

For several minutes, she only sobbed as if it was the only solution and option she had, and she was doing so with all her sincerity. She was finding it tumultuous to swim amid the vehement currents of purity present in the sea of her feelings. Reva felt like throwing up. She got up and scooted out of the room, climbed up the stairs quickly, and went to the attached toilet on the floor for guests. Standing in front of the basin, she felt like she had thrown her guts out. Nothing was left. She felt weak. One look at the mirror and she wondered how a youth icon could look like that? The image pushed her to wail again sitting on the bathroom floor itself. Almost an hour later, when she felt dead inside, she stood up and looked at herself in the mirror again.

'Enough of lies and servility, Reva Gupta,' she told herself. 'You got only one bit of clothing left in your emotional self. Self esteem.' The claws of shyness and embarrassment scratched her instantly. 'If you agree for the test, you shall have to live stark naked henceforth. You shall be a lump with all the affluences of life, but none enough to buy you enough self esteem to cover up your bare emotional essentials. You know it's Shahraan's baby. *You know it*. And that's your strength. Hold onto it. If you want to continue to live like the Reva Gupta people know, then just hold on to your residual strength.' Usually mothers siphon nutrition to their babies in the womb, but she felt her newfound sense was borrowed from her foetus. Why else was it alien to her all these years? she asked herself.

A rise in confidence and a touch of conviction made her stomp out of the bathroom. Within a minute, she located him on the terrace.

'Shahraan Ali Bakshi.' She knew what she would say could burn everything she had built till now in one instant, but it was important she did it. Finally, Reva Gupta had learnt that when it comes to your core, one has to surface, not succumb. One has to choose soul over stomach.

'Either you accept what I'm telling you as the truth,' she hollered out, 'because it is indeed one, or...we divorce. Your call!'

Jagdish Dwivedi was an iconic theatre personality. Every major actor of today was a product of his tutelage in the past. Arunodaye himself was one of his students who'd personally requested him to help Kaash and Nishani with the scene in contention. Dwivedi happily obliged. He first gave them a few trust-building exercises, followed by some emotional-availability exercises. After which he preferred to talk.

'Sit in Padma asana. Take deep breaths. And each time you inhale, tell yourself you are dead, and as you exhale, remind yourself you are the characters—Simran and Siddharth—respectively.'

They did what they were told. When they opened their eyes, they saw Jagdish was done lighting the last love candle in the room.

'While acting we are, at times, what our surrounding is. And for the scene we are going to rehearse today, it's important to have the ambience just as written in the script. Love candles all over and right in the middle of the room, a thick mattress.'

As Kaash and Nishani stood up, Jagdish folded the mat they were all sitting on before and kept it at a corner.

'Have you guys learnt the lines?'

'Yes.'

Next, Jagdish dimmed the light and made himself comfortable in a corner.

'Alright kids, if you two can, with your passion, make this sixty-four-year-old hag crave for his fifty-nine-year-old wife, only then I'll okay the scene.'

Both laughed.

They were in casual attire, but the scene required them to be naked. So they thought they were. It was a dialogue-heavy scene. The discourse was supposed to happen post coitus.

Nishani's character, Simran, was in love with Shahraan's character, Aryan, but since he was married to Reva's character, Manvi, she never confessed her feelings to him. This scene happens right after Manvi and Kaash's character, Siddharth, have had an illicit night together. Simran being in an open relationship with Siddharth wonders if it's the right time to approach Aryan.

Initially, they lie down side by side.

'On his arm.' Jagdish directed.

Kaash stretched his hand and Nishani made herself comfortable on his arm. As she kept her hand on his chest, she could feel his heart thumping. *Was that too part of the script?* she wondered.

'Do you love Aryan?' Siddharth asked gazing at the ceiling.

'I do. And will do so forever.'

'What about me?'

'I think—' Jagdish chipped in, 'It'll be better if you glance at Simran once while saying this. And Simran, you don't look at him when he glances, but do so immediately when he again looks at the ceiling. It would be an interesting emotional hide-n-seek on screen.'

And so it went on till Jagdish called it a tea break after an hour. By then, they hadn't been able to do the scene right even once. As Jagdish excused himself out, Nishani quickly checked her mobile phone; no missed calls, no messages. Kaash lay still for some time as if he was still in the scene.

'You are damn nervous, aren't you?' Nishani was still looking at her phone.

Kaash only nodded with a caught-red-handed smile.

'Aren't you nervous?'

'A bit.' Nishani kept her phone away. 'My mind kept going back to our first kiss. Remember?' She had amusement dabbed on her face now.

Remember? She doesn't even know how many lives I have lived only thinking about it, Kaash wondered. 'Yes, I remember, and also the way you bit my lips.'

Nishani giggled.

'Who was in your mind that day, Nish?'

It was so sudden that Nishani didn't have the time to even pretend.

'Nobody, why?'

'They say you can't lie well to the one with whom you have shared your first kiss.'

Nishani smiled compulsively. She could have said any name; Tom, Dick, or Harry. But she knew even though Kaash said it in a lighter vein, he would anyway castrate her lies. There are people in this world with whom even if you don't talk regularly, or probably have had years of separation, the moment they come in front of you, nothing seems to have changed. Kaash was one such man in Nishani's life. Perhaps the only one.

'Shahraan. But don't tell me you didn't already know.'

'I do. I knew it then, I know it now. You love Shahraan like you love nobody else.'

For a moment, Nishani thought it was someone else who said it. She'd never attached such stupidity with the Kaash Sehgal she met after an era of a gap. *I love Shahraan? That could qualify as the joke of the century.*

'No, I don't love him.'

'I have seen your madness for him. The sketches of the eye, his interviews, newspaper cut-outs, the incident in the school where you wanted to spray water on him to get his attention. You always wanted him to notice you amid the crowd of his admirers.'

For a moment, she kept staring at Kaash as a gun does toward its target waiting for its owner to pull the trigger. *He was right*. She then asked herself if she'd actually decided to spray the acid, not water, not to kill him as she thought previously, but to announce her existence? Could it be she didn't kill Shahraan just then because she never wanted to do so? Did she only want to draw attention to herself and to all those mental and emotional sufferings she went through because of him? For what? Did she want him to sympathize with her? Nishani hated herself in that moment more than she'd ever hated Shahraan. She heard Kaash next.

'And to this day, you do everything to gain his attention. Subtly, but surely. All your actions—be it calling me last night to exactly where you asked Reva to turn up or prior to it, leaking the Shahraan slapping Reva video on the internet and now the leaking of Reva and my pictures in the newspaper—every act of yours has been to create a painful corner in Shahraan, whereby you would introduce yourself to him and take it from there probably by being beside him.' It was said in a casual tone; no hint of any confrontation or accusation. As if he was saying yeah-I-know-you-tried-to-screw-me-but-I-don't-have-a-problem-because-I-appreciate-your-reason-for-it.

'I hate Shahraan. I hate him from the time I learnt he snatched my father from me. That day I swore to snatch from him what he craved for the most—a companionship.'

'And what do you think, Nishani? Will you really be able to bereave yourself of him after you destroy him?'

'Yes!'

'No!'

'Okay guys, let's nail it now.' Jagdish entered the room rubbing his palms together and looking excited.

The attempt fell short of Jagdish's expectation. He gave

them another date before the shoot and gave certain pointers to work on. It was when Nishani rode Neev's Ninja bike and Kaash his i20 that she asked him riding parallel, 'Why did you say I won't be able to get over him even if I destroy him?'

'It's a paradox,' Kaash had to raise his voice since a mini school bus had come in between them. When it passed, they were driving parallel again.

'Have you heard the ones we love the most, we hurt the most? Likewise, your hatred is potent with a similar paradox. Your obsession for Shahraan isn't actually hatred as you make yourself believe.'

Nishani was still not getting it. What he was telling her was that we hurt the people we love the most because the proximity makes us blind towards their limitations, and hence the expectation increases manifold which the other, being human in the end, isn't able to fullfil, thus churning out erratic behaviour from us. But falling for the one you have hated all your life, desired so doggedly to punish...loving him? Nishani could not understand that part at all.

'Then what is my obsession with Shahraan all about?'

'You are actually not interested in snatching from him what you have lost. That's what you have been forcing yourself to believe. Trust me, you really want him to *give* you what you have lost. I am sure even you would agree that the ultimate punishment for him would not be begging you for mercy, but giving you the love the way your father would have loved you. You know it because that's what you really want—someone to love you like your father, but you haven't yet acknowledged it because the paradox comes with an unfathomable realization—how can the one person supposedly responsible for your father's decline love you like him? I personally think if there's someone who can connect to those unrealized emotional pleasures you missed out as a kid, it has to be Shahraan.'

They reached a signal from which she had to make a diversion.

'I'll call you tonight,' said Nishani and took a right turn.

It was ten at night when she called Kaash.

'How do you know so much about me, Balloo?'

There was no reply. Nishani rephrased the question.

'How do you claim to know so much? I mean, we haven't been in touch for ages. We rarely talked even after we met at that party, except for those my-life's-great and your-life's-cool kind of pretentious things.'

'Who has said that to know so much about someone, one has to be in touch, one has to talk a lot, or exchange pretentious obscenities like we did that night?'

Nishani was waiting for Neev to come back from his new reality show shoot which he was hosting, while Kaash was awaiting Aravali's return from Pune where she had some film analysis program to attend in FTII. Nishani was sitting beside her French window with her ear piece tugged in and looking aimlessly at a part of the city which had gone to sleep already.

'Do you love me, Balloo?' She said next.

Kaash was lying above the water tank atop the terrace of his apartment which he frequented with Aravali. He'd messaged her to meet him there after she was back. Nishani's query didn't affect him. Ten years ago, the same query would have made him chew all his nails out. Now, he was so used to the impossibility of their togetherness that he wasn't susceptible anymore to his reaction to her questions and to her reaction to his answers.

'No.' He managed a compulsive laughter. 'Of course not!' The last thing he wanted was to tell the truth and drop her an unwanted quandary. So what if he indeed loved her? Why is it always necessary to tell the person you love him or her? Why can't we simply focus on our love for that person?

'Funny,' he heard her say, 'I'm twenty-three now. And for my age, I have achieved a lot. Just like my dad. But while coming home today, I was thinking how many people have I really touched? My mother has no clue what I do or have ever done. My grandparents are too old to matter to me. I have no friends as such. I stay with Neev, we make love, but I don't love him. He doesn't love me. What's this stupid arrangement that I have landed myself in? I don't know how many years I'll live, perhaps many, but right now I have lost so much time already going after someone because I thought by destroying him, I'll get back what I lost. I think you were right, Kaash. Hating someone in order to secure some amount of love for oneself is, in the end, love only. Though I am still not sure, neither convinced, if I really love Shahraan the way a normal woman loves a man.' A pause later, she added, 'How is it going with Aravali?'

'She is a great woman. I mean, any woman who has the wicked sense of loving a man forever has to be a great woman.'

Nishani smiled, though she would have laughed had it been some other day. Today she was feeling sapped of happiness.

'Will you forgive me if I say I'm feeling jealous of you right now?'

'Me? Why?'

'I too want to say there's someone in my life and he's great because he chose me.'

'You may, Nish. You very well may if you accept things. I feel you never accepted anything till now.'

The ruining process starts with the acceptance of someone in your life for separation foreshadows acceptance. Like you said you hate someone. That's an acceptance as well. And one day, you will be separated from that hatred too. Nishani recollected Vishwas's words. *Where would he be right now? Happy once again? He must have kept an eye on my success.* She felt pushed to look over her window if any autorickshaw was standing near her apartment. A silly smile escaped her as she realized that life had finally made her consider a U-turn. Go back to where she started and begin a new journey, accepting things in her heart and finally come back to where she was right now...and life would seem different. Her priorities would seem different. She sighed. It all sounded too magical to be true.

'You know by accepting things, who will you do a big favour to?'

'Myself.'

'That's my Nish.'

For a moment, those words sounded so nice. She wouldn't have minded if Kaash were single. They understood each other the way an indefinite article understands a vowel sound before a word. Nishani felt like asking if he was game about her, but then he said he was happy with Aravali. Happy with someone... she knew how rare a phenomenon that was. Why upset it.

'So?' asked Kaash.

'Just wondering what I should do next?' she said and heard the door bell.

'That would be Neev. Can we continue this some other time?' she said getting up.

'Sure.'

'Kaash Balloo Sehgal; why didn't you come back to my life sooner?'

Kaash had at least ten answers to that, but he chose to say, 'I don't know. But listen...' The voice first broke and then trailed off. Nishani glanced at her phone. The network always played games in the front portion of her apartment. She cut the line and opened the door simultaneously.

'Super screwed-up shoot, but a super sexy mobile phone.'

Neev dangled a packet in front of her and stepped in. Her phone buzzed again. She picked it up closing the door. It was Kaash, but his voice was still broken.

Nishani quickly typed: network problem, shall call later. And sent it to him.

'HTC latest! Good I stomped on the last one.' Neev was the only one to smile. 'Give me your phone, my back-up buddy. I need to transfer the music.'

'Sure. I'll take a quick shower.'

'Okay.'

Neev followed Nishani inside the bedroom. As she locked herself in the bathroom, he sat down on the bed ripping the phone box. Soon he had activated his phone and was transferring the songs from Nishani's phone to his via Bluetooth when a message popped up in Nishani's phone. On a whim, he pressed it open. It read:

Yeah, okay. I was only saying I think you should tell Shahraan the truth. ASAP.

Neev frowned and read the message again. His frown deepened. He looked towards the bathroom. Nishani was taking a shower. What is Kaash talking about? His hands slowly pressed the reply button on the phone and he typed:

What's the truth?

The reply was instant.

That you wanted his love from the day you knew he existed.

The one he was staying and sleeping with was the one who was screwing him, his former love, and her love as well. A fucking soap opera it was!

It was easy math considering the message. And an unimaginable, unacceptable one as well. If there were different categories of bitches, Neev wondered as his body shuddered subtly with anger, Nishani was a category in herself. The last month and a half were rigorous for Shahraan and Reva, for the producer as well as the director. How could she be so heartless? And the last few days had been hell for him...how could she indulge in something like this with a sane mind? Neev looked at his reflection in the mirror right opposite him on the wall. He saw a fool in it who thought he was staying with someone who understood him in difficult times. Little did he know the difficult times were a result of the same person's twisted mind who wanted to break a married man's household and force fit herself there.

He heard the bathroom door unlock. The anger inside him had initiated a demonic hunger which he knew would only be satisfied if he confronted Nishani the way she deserved. Neev got up with a locked jaw and approached her. She paused, looked at him curiously, and shrugged. The next instant, her cheeks registered a tight slap which turned her head sideways.

'You house breaking, betraying piece of bitch shit. I can't believe I never got your real motives.'

It was the first time a man had hit her. *And it better be the last time*, she thought, and in a flash held Neev's shoulder and kneed him in the balls.

'Oh my dear God.' Neev cupped his groin and pressing his legs together, moved away with his eyes almost popping out.

'If you are talking about the video leak, then yes, I did it. Use words with me and I shall answer you. Now when you can feel your balls again, get lost from my place.' She walked off to the other room.

For some time, Neev remained still, absorbing his pain. After a few minutes, he went to the other room. Nishani was blow drying her hair. He dashed to her, held her robe, and slapped her a couple of times. Then pulling her by the hair, he dragged her to the main room. Logical thinking was a far cry for him. Nishani screamed abuses at him which only fuelled his desire to hurt her even more.

'You asked for it. You'll get it.' He kicked her stomach a few times with all his force. Nishani whimpered, spat out blood, and then went superlative on her abuses. One kick hit her face and she started bleeding from her nose and lips. As Neev paused, trying to catch his breath, Nishani grabbed his legs and bit him on his calf. He screamed, releasing himself as a reflex. Nishani stood up. Her resilience surprised Neev.

'I am not Reva Gupta, you dick head. I will tear you into two halves before I apologize to you.' She limped, but reached him quicker than expected and punched him in the eyes.

For a moment, Neev thought she had blinded him. He shrieked and ran to the bathroom, but in between came Nishani's foot and he fell on the floor. For a spectator, it resembled a dog fight—two beings with no brains, no emotions.

Even before Neev could get up, Nishani got hold of a nearby glass flower vase and threw it right at him.

'You'll rot. I'll make you pay, Nishani Rai,' said Neev looking at his blood smeared palms. His whole face was bleeding. Finally, Neev panicked. He couldn't afford to get his face bandaged. It was his bread and butter. Unlike Nishani, he was a sane guy who had higher laurels to achieve in the industry, Neev thought, and crawled to the bathroom. Seeing his damaged face in the mirror, he wanted to cry.

'What the fuck is this?' The pain which had taken care of his incorrigible anger for some time gave up. The anger was back, and with a vengeance this time. He ran out of the bathroom. Nishani was on the hall floor, rubbing away blood and tears together from her cheeks. Her flesh was burning in places.

'Listen Neev, let's not...' She couldn't control as he once again dragged her by her hair and took her to the bathroom.

'Let's see what you did to me?' He made her stand up right next to him and made her see his cut-up face.

'You turned me into shit. And now it's your turn.' He crashed her face on the mirror. It developed cracks, but not more than what she had in her face now.

'Tell me you are sorry, I'll spare you. Tell me!' Neev held her by her hair. She was on the verge of a total collapse. But somehow she managed to whisper, 'Suck. My. Dick. A-hole.'

That was it. What happened next happened so quick that Neev thought it almost never happened. But for Nishani, it happened so slowly that she thought that's what has been happening all her life. Neev had grabbed her robe by her chest, picked her inches from the ground, and pushed her onto the bathroom walls.

'You'll have to say you are sorry. There's. No. Respite.'

The cloth hook on the wall pierced her neck and back deep. She immediately spurted out blood onto his face. Neev held her in that pose and pressed her hard against the wall. The sharp hook cracked into some of the bones and made way into her spine. Neev relaxed only when he realized Nishani wasn't reacting anymore. As he let go of her, she remained hooked on the wall for a few seconds and then collapsed on the floor.

Lifeless.

It was an unprecedented mental zone for Arunodaye. The news made him lock himself in a room without food or light for twenty hours straight. For someone who always believed in one's will and determination, for the first time he'd willingly resigned to fate: this film won't happen anymore. Period. Not in the next few years. Period. His hard work, time, and creativity all would go to the gutters because of some imbecile, love-sick people. He had been working on the script for half a decade now. And now it won't happen. Just like that! He knew he was being selfish thinking about his own work at this point of time instead of inquiring what happened to Nishani and Neev, but wasn't this entire fiasco a result of someone's selfishness?

The financers were already clawing the producers' back to recover the signing amount from the lead actors and director, knowing even after securing the signing amount, they would still supper a net loss of eleven crores, minimum.

Almost overnight, some of the billboards across the city where Neev was seen recommending a tea brand twenty-four hours back was either taken off, scratched, or painted black. The producers of the reality show featuring Neev as the host decided to push the launch date by a month and numb the promotions. The ones who were desirous of taking Nishani in their next television venture were already on the lookout for someone else, but the magazines zeroed in on Nishani. Sympathy has the same sale quotient as sex.

The incident forced the media, on the other hand, to salivate like Pavlov's dog. Nishani Rai's hospitalization wasn't that big a deal, but coupled with it her love for Shahraan Ali Bakshi, as disclosed by Neev, and the violence to which both Nishani and Neev succumbed, was what sensational primetime news items were made of. Out of the two top news channels, one was busy telling its audience, in the presence of one of the country's top psychologist, the psychological aspects that could have pushed Neev Dixit to commit such a heinous act. After all, it was a love quadrangle for the media: Shahraan was married to Reva, Nishani was in love with Shahraan and jealous of Reva, while Neev was in love with Nishani, though both Reva and Neev were once passionately in love. No one cared for the absolute truth, but they were bull headed about their own versions of the truth, as if witnessing the incident with their personal prejudice was eligibility enough for them to make a sport out of it.

The second news channel had set up a large panel of people from across the industry, relationship counsellors, and human rights people, and was trying to give a little bit of everything to its viewers. None of the channels had been able to hammer, or even get close to, the core of the matter, for whatever they knew came from the police and the latter knew what Kaash had told them.

When Nishani didn't reply to his calls or messages, out of an inauspicious hunch, Kaash landed up at her place. He had to break himself in. Inside, he saw an injured Neev sitting up against the bathroom wall—stone cold—his entire body shuddering as he chanted 'I didn't do it' to himself, while Nishani was lying in a pool of blood; unfazed. The ambulance was called first and then the police.

Neev, in a state of mental shock, initially told the police he'd killed Nishani out of rage for no fault of hers. Then, post twenty-four hours, he turned hostile in a lawyer's presence, stating it was Nishani who had tried to screw Shahraan and Reva's relationship since she loved the former quite possessively and in the process, risked his own position in the industry which had enraged him to the hilt. This was how the love quadrangle leaked out to the media. He told them how a heated argument, followed by a bout of violence, resulted in Nishani's comatose state. The problem was that the accused—Neev—was the only eyewitness while the victim was in coma since her arrival in the hospital. On the third day, Neev once again retracted, this time admitting whatever happened, happened in cold blood.

The police were confused. The media was aroused. The public was interested. And more importantly, everybody who forever craved for their superstars' one glimpse, didn't really care about how the unannounced crisis was going to affect them; the ones who were in the epicentre of it all, right from the beginning of this end.

BOOK THREE: 2013

WHISPERS OF A SIN

While doing her make-up for a public appearance later in the evening...

REVA SPEAKS.

A driver is judged by his affinity for accidents. Sure, I have been involved in accidents. So what? Why do I have to live within the limitation of the adjective others choose for me?

When I lived with Neev, I was only aware of the miniscule emotional windows in me. Being with Neev, I thought I would be able to peep out of those windows, but it didn't happen. On the contrary, Shahraan's presence so easily made me look out through those unframed windows of feelings and onto such titanic vistas of personal choices that I finally realized it's possible to be in love with two people at one time: the one who makes you aware of yourself and the one who takes you beyond that awareness into something that's indescribable. Maybe some people have only one person doing that for them, but in my case, my love for Shahraan starts where my longing for Neev ends. And where my obsession with Shahraan ceases, my possessiveness for Neev begins. I never understood true love. Is it snatching away one's own life from oneself? If a lifelong emotional monogamy towards someone is the only criteria for judging true love, then I'll never understand it.

Morality is not the moral of my story. I'll rather be honest than be morally correct. I can't be both. Maybe the world shall judge my honest choices as selfish. But if it's a choice, it's always selfish.

I don't know what to say about the disturbance Nishani created between Shahraan and me. All I know is that it's because of those disturbances I could iron out the wrinkled relationship between Shahraan and me. Sometimes, a war is necessary to sustain peace. Likewise, sometimes love needs to be questioned to make it look neat. As for me, I'll go on like I always have. There are things which destroy us, and yet we find ourselves drawn to them. Life is one such self-destructive addiction for me. And you know why I've decided to deliver my baby? It's because...

I love Shahraan.

While doing Pranayam in a prison cell alone...

NEEV THINKS

Anger makes me act on the worst solution before I realize the best one. I could have simply let Shahraan know about Nishani's intentions. But my anger thought otherwise. It's high time I stop being its bitch.

I have come to understand that a relationship is like a relentless fuck after which the semen of experience stays with us, resulting in the baby of prejudice. And if you analyze it, we only create prejudices for ourselves through someone else. A relationship is an excuse. Good, bad; it depends. In fact, love is a progressive way to realize how regressive it is. When I was with Nishani, I was what she wanted me to be. But with Reva, I was what I always wanted to be. If you get someone with whom you are yourself, you should stick with that person. If I had not strayed, Reva wouldn't have accepted Shahraan's proposal. Guilt would have stopped her. I know Reva. Only guilt can stop her. I don't know if she ever loved me. What is love anyway? A grown up's indifference and a child's ignorance. Being with Nishani, my negativities instigated by Reva's closeness with Shahraan were getting negated, hence I thought I loved Nishani. Even though she didn't love me. We were each other's best arrangement. Arrangements are always temporary; love isn't.

I'll have to work on myself since it's me who is the root cause of all the shit in my life. If not Nishani, then my anger would have made me do something heinous to someone at some point of time.

I'm not only guilty of killing Nishani, but also for Reva and my relationship. If she left me for Shahraan, it was because I prepared her for it. And for this emotional homicide, my only deserving punishment will be...

I'll always love Reva.

Atop the water tank of his apartment, sitting alongside Aravali, burning all the 'Dear Nish' letters one by one in the fire...

KAASH WONDERS

When all your life you claim something as yours, and then something as stupid as death challenges the claim, what do you do? Cry? Smile? Ignore? Shrug? Go mad? Complain? Avenge? She was lying brain dead. I only kissed her lips and moved out. She'd initiated our first kiss, I did the last one. Chapter closed, not the story.

Aravali takes the last letter from me and reads it aloud while I time travel.

Dear Nish

I saw a nightmare. I saw you were floating in the air by a sea shore. I was trying to wake you up, but in vain. I even tried to bring you down to the earth, but again in vain. I screamed for help, and all I saw was different avatars of me—from age seven to ten to fourteen to eighteen—come running towards me. All of us sobbed as you kept floating in the air. Dead. It disturbed me so much that I'm now afraid of death, Nish. A relationship goes deeper within us than we can ever judge, feel, and perceive. And love is only the tip of that depth. Last night's nightmare made me aware of the rest of it. And I inferred if I lose you some day, then I better have an option else I'll lose myself forever. I'll need the option for my own selfish reason of existence. I am not an emotional altruist, Nish. Probably that's why I would be able to love you forever only if there's someone else by my side. That's the way it has been. If you can't forgive me, then please do punish me by forgetting me. I sometimes wonder what would have happened if that first kiss of ours had not defined me. If I ever lose you, I'll be scared all my life...of life.

I snatch the letter and burn it. Aravali turns my face towards her. In her eyes, I see an option. *The* option. I hope she doesn't see any obligation in my eyes. I embrace her and digging my face deep in her bosom, I start sobbing. Probably she will understand I'm only trying to empty my core, and what better place than a woman's bosom. After a while I look up at her. And kiss her on the lips. It's finally time to let go. She breaks the kiss for a moment and looks at me. Her tears never felt so special.

I love you, Aravali.

Sitting inside one of the private suits of a flight to Paris, he remembers he had given Nishani an opportunity so that he could wash his soul off the accident but...

SHAHRAAN CONFESSES

Absence. Our whole life is about absence of something or someone in some degree or form. So much so that it makes you die every day.

In a way, Nishani and I have gone through the same things. The difference being she had me in person to aim all her angst against and I didn't have that luxury. Life took away her father. Death took away Mehfil. Nishani should have told me about her intentions. I would have allowed her to kill me. No qualms. And that too would have been for my own selfish reason. Now, I only have one question for her: was I worth it? We all should ask this when we confront something which we think has the ability to affect us in an irreversible way: *is it worth it?*

I didn't move on after Mehfil. *Was it worth it?* I eventually decided to give love a try, accepted Reva. *Was it worth it?* Now, I am again staring at something which may affect me: should I share the rest of my life with Reva, forgetting whatever happened, or should I move on the way I did after Mehfil went away and before Reva came into my life? *Is it worth it?* Or should I simply pretend nothing—absolutely nothing—happened? Perhaps, pretense is the best emotional underwear.

Love is always worth it. By choosing someone over the other, we are trying to answer for ourselves throughout life. Of course we commit mistakes too, but what's the use in repenting? If it was not because of my sin of trying to live with Mehfil by being with Reva, then how would I have defined myself? Wrong people happen to us so that we can define ourselves. Right people happen when someone else needs to be defined by us.

I have booked connecting flights for the next three months. I don't want to touch earth before my baby is born. I want to fly constantly, even if it makes me sick. I want to stay among the clouds, the sun, the stars, and the moon. I can't feel my stardom here. I don't want to. I can see only one person among these celestial creations...

I love you, Mehfil.

She is not sure of the place, but she likes it. There's no sky, since everything beyond a point looks pearly white. She can hear a running stream of water, birds chirping, someone worshipping somewhere, but she doesn't see them. She can only see her papa on whose lap she has her head. As he caresses her head...

NISHANI FEELS

The most important thing which life didn't allow me to have; death did. I'm thankful to Shahraan for that.

Funny, I tell papa, we remain so much committed to the memory of certain relationships that happens only in our heart, that we forget the ones which happen for real. By hating Shahraan, I had not allowed myself those relationships which would have altered this end of mine. But for you, papa, I don't mind it, for otherwise, I would have craved for you like repentance craves for redemption; here, there, and everywhere. But tell me, papa, was I a bad person when I had life in me?

If you are dressed, people judge you on the basis of your dress. If you are naked, people judge you on the basis of your genitals. Bottom line: people will judge you no matter what you do; good, bad, or ugly, he tells me.

Before, it was only amid the silence between two heartbeats that I used to hear the sound of your presence, I tell papa, but now that death has taken care of those silly heartbeats, it's you for real.

Forget life, now that you are in a better place, he says. *And the best lap*, I add. He is right though. I forgive Shahraan. I forgive Neev. I even forgive myself.

I don't care what others think, but for me, there couldn't have been a happier ending: me looking into my papa's eyes and saying...

I love you.

The End

'Then leaf subsides to leaf.
So Eden sank to grief,
So dawn goes down to day.
Nothing gold can stay.'

—*Nothing Gold Can Stay,* Robert Frost

ACKNOWLEDGEMENTS

A lot has happened in my life since my last novel came out. And I'm sure I wouldn't have finished this particular book had it not been for the unconditional support of certain people and their unwavering presence in my life.

A warm heartfelt THANK YOU to:

My late grandfather—wherever you are, I hope I'm living up to your expectation with my storytelling.

My parents—for strengthening my soul by having faith in my faith and never, even for once, questioning it.

My sister, brother-in-law, and her in-laws—for being a constant source of inspiration.

Mr Arvind K. Rastogi and Mrs Anjana Rastogi—for your love and understanding.

Rajendra A. Pimple, Sanjeevni R. Pimple, and Alesha R. Pimpale—for your invaluable love, care, and support.

Arindam Dey and Rahul Saini—for just being there. At times, that's all one needs.

My readers and friends from the real and virtual world—for appreciating my work and encouraging me all the time. I have learnt so much from each one of you.

Milee Ashwarya, Gurveen Chadha, and the team at Random House, India—for their indispensable support in shaping up the book in the best possible way.

Lastly, the city of Mumbai—for instigating dreams in ordinary hearts and thereby making them extraordinary.

A NOTE ON THE AUTHOR

Novoneel Chakraborty is the bestselling author of ten romantic thrillers and a short story collection. The Forever series was listed among *Times of India*'s most stunning books of 2017. It was also featured among Amazon's memorable books for the same year. The two books remained on the bestseller list for ten weeks straight; *Forever Is a Lie* was one of the highest selling books of 2017 on Flipkart. While the third book in the Stranger trilogy, *Forget Me Not, Stranger*, debuted as the No. 1 bestseller across India, the second, *All Yours, Stranger*, ranked among the top five thrillers on Amazon India. The Stranger trilogy has been translated into six languages.

Known for his dark plots and strong female protagonists, Novoneel Chakraborty is called the Sidney Sheldon of India. Apart from novels, he has also written for and developed several TV shows, including *Savdhaan India* and *Yeh Hai Aashiqui*. He lives in Mumbai.